TALES OF
SILVER DOWNS

FEY

BOOK 2

KYLIE QUILLINAN

First published in Australia in 2016.

ABN 34 112 708 734

kyliequillinan.com

Copyright © 2016 Kylie Quillinan

A catalogue record for this book is available from the National Library of Australia.

Ebook ISBN: 9780994331533

Paperback ISBN: 9780994331519

Large print ISBN: 9780994331588

Hardback ISBN: 9780648903925

This is a work of fiction. Any similarity between the characters and situations within its pages and places or persons, living or dead, is unintentional and coincidental.

Cover art by Deranged Doctor Design.

This work uses Australian spelling and grammar.

LP 10082021

*This book is dedicated
to all those who have endured slavery.*

EITHNE

When I am ill, my dreams are filled with things that aren't really there. Some of these things I have really seen, like the power of a fire as it rages out of control and the might of a winter storm that strips branches from beech trees and thatching from houses. Others I have never viewed with my own eyes. They probably came from the tales my bard brother told. Titania, queen of the fey, glowering at me. Tiny beings no larger than my thumbnail, human-shaped but with wings. A creature, in appearance nothing more than a rock, but clearly sentient. I longed to see these beings but I could never hope to live a normal life, let alone one in which I might actually meet such creatures.

The images repeated one after another but eventually they returned to the boy. Always the boy. He appeared to be around my own age, although the fey can seem any age they choose. His milky skin and crimson lips shouted his fey heritage, and his dark hair was roughly cut as if he cared little about the result. Blue eyes stared at me, never blinking or looking away, just watching, considering. Unusual eyes, for a fey. He stood silently in the corner of my bedchamber and watched as I drowned in fevered dreams. Sweat soaked my linen nightdress and my damp hair stuck to my cheeks.

As the fevers subsided, the dreams disappeared and the boy with them, and I once again became aware of my surroundings. It was always startling to emerge from the dreams and discover that time still had meaning.

I lay in my bed, staring up at the knotted ceiling. I turned my head to see sturdy wooden furniture now coated with a thin layer of dust. Thick green drapes shielded the window. A hand-knotted rug lay in front of the fireplace. The air smelled stale and old. Mother sat beside my bed, her eyes shadowed and her face pale.

"Welcome back, Eithne," she said.

I struggled to sit up but my limbs were weak and I collapsed back down onto the bed.

"How long?" I asked. My voice was hoarse and my mouth tasted dry and bitter. Mother hesitated but I knew she wouldn't lie to me.

"Nine days," she said.

Her words chilled me and eventually I realised I was clutching my woollen blanket so hard that my knuckles had gone white. I forced my fingers to relax and straighten the blanket. Its wool was coarse and prickly.

"It's never been that long before," I said.

Mother nodded.

"It's getting worse, isn't it?"

I needed to hear it, to know that it wasn't all in my head. Like the dreams, no matter how real they seemed.

Mother sucked in a breath. She looked away, towards the window where the drapes were tightly drawn, hands smoothing the skirt of her work dress.

"You can say it," I said.

She looked back at me and her dark eyes glistened. "Yes, Eithne, it's getting worse. We always knew the illness might progress but I had hoped you would have a little more time."

I inhaled deeply, steadying myself. I knew what was ahead of me, had known since I was old enough to understand the truth. She had never tried to shield me from it. Death was the end of the journey for each of us. It just came sooner for some.

"There's never enough time though, is there?" I said, too fatigued to hide the bitterness in my voice. "We are always too young to die."

Mother swallowed hard. "Always too young, my darling." She avoided my eyes as she gathered up the pitcher and mug sitting on the small white table beside my bed. "I'll take these to the kitchen. I'll be back in a little while, to sit with you."

"I would like that."

I knew she was leaving because she needed to compose herself, not because the pitcher needed to be returned to the kitchen immediately. We had servants who could undertake such a task.

I stared up at the ceiling as Mother closed the door. I traced a crooked crack with my gaze and tried to pretend I couldn't hear her crying. Death had ever loomed present for me, from the day I first struggled out of my mother's womb, eager to be born and far too early with the birth cord wrapped tightly around my neck.

A sickness of the blood, the wise woman said when I told her about the recurrent fevers and chills. The days where I couldn't keep down even the thinnest of broths. Nights where my blood boiled within my veins. No cure, she said. Even the druid could only shake his head and say he was sorry. When one lives with the idea of death every day, one becomes somewhat used to it. At least I saw fabulous things in my dreams. They let me feel like I had lived just a little.

EITHNE

*I*n the days following my illness, strength slowly returned to my body. On my better days, I would often sit on a stool in the kitchen and help Cook with small tasks until I grew too tired. But when I was recovering, I didn't have even the strength for that. Instead I passed my days alone, sitting beside the fireplace in the family room.

This was my favourite room in the whole house. On winter nights, we would gather here to share tales or commentary about the day and drink warm spiced wine. The sweet scent of pinecones on the fire would mingle with the spices from the wine and make my nose tingle. I usually sat beside Mother near the fire where the heat from its bright embers could warm my always-cold body. But during the day, only I ever sat here. Mother was occupied with running the house, and Papa and my brothers were busy with their various chores. The large room around me was empty and lonely as I sat and waited for night to fall.

A thick blanket and the dancing fire cloaked me with their warmth, although even the two combined couldn't shield me from the cold nearness of death. Wondering how much longer I might live was pointless, for my time would come, and likely soon. In the meantime, I watched my brothers grow up and lived through them as much as I could.

Eremon, my oldest brother, would run our estate, Silver Downs,

4

once Papa was gone. I had been ill the day he handfasted with Niamh but my brothers carried me outside to watch the ceremony. I had sat in a chair, huddled under blankets while the mid-summer sun shone down on my face. Niamh bore Eremon twin sons, sturdy boys who were now two summers old.

My next brother, Caedmon, left home in his sixteenth summer to become a soldier. He returned every year or so, always looking a little more haggard, a little more battle-scarred. He showed me a wound once, where a sword had pierced his side. The skin was red and puckered, still healing, and the scar large enough for me to place my fisted hand inside. He didn't show anyone else for he said Mother would worry if she heard whisper of it. If he walked a little slower on that visit, and hesitated before he lifted anything, it seemed nobody other than I noticed.

I had no memory of Fiachra, my druid brother, apart from what I had heard from my other brothers. He left with the druids when I was a babe of but two or three summers.

Sitric was the fourth brother. He worked as a scribe in Maker's Well, the town nearest to Silver Downs and a little more than a half day's walk away.

Marrec and Conn were next, two bodies sharing one soul. They would work the estate with Eremon for it seemed they desired no other occupation. I could never think of them in isolation as they were always together. Marrec was the eldest by minutes and they were always Marrec and Conn, never Conn and Marrec.

And then there was Diarmuid, the bard. The youngest of my seven brothers and barely a couple of summers older than me. Sometimes when I was ill, he would sit beside my bed and tell me tales — long complicated things where heroes went on grand journeys and encountered all sorts of magical beings. They lingered in my memory and I would repeat them to myself over and over but with myself in the hero's role.

I took long, dangerous journeys, crossing mountains and rivers and deserts. I faced down evil creatures or deciphered Titania's riddles. Only, unlike in Diarmuid's tales, I would return triumphant, the evil defeated, the monster killed, the fey banished to their own realm. I lived many adventures through my brother's tales and sometimes I even created my own. They were poor compared with Diarmuid's but they amused me well enough when I had no other entertainment.

The fey boy began to feature in the tales I told myself. He walked beside me as I trod across endless fields and climbed vast mountains and battled a dragon. I swooped in to rescue him at the last moment as he teetered on a precipice, his balance lost, or as a sword came crushingly near his neck. And sometimes he saved me.

Seven brothers and a sister. If we were in a tale, it would be a magical combination, for seven is a powerful number. Seven brothers united could withstand almost anything. And the sister to seven brothers would be special indeed and — if my life was a tale — in possession of some magical ability.

In truth, the life I led lacked the excitement and fervour of my tales and I had no magical ability. I sat beside the fire with only my tales for company and let the noise of the household drift over me. Mother directing a servant. Papa and Eremon discussing something, their voices serious. From outside came the shouts and whoops of Marrec and Conn playing with Eremon's young sons. Papa would order them back to work if he noticed. A dog barked, a rooster crowed. People passed by without noticing me. I was the invisible girl huddled by the fire. Perhaps nobody saw me because I was already dead. A spirit lost or maybe trapped. I cleared my throat, coughed. Nobody noticed.

"Hello?" I said. My voice was weak and barely penetrated the emptiness of the room.

The household continued around me. If I really was dead, there was nothing I could do about it. I might as well sit here and enjoy the warmth from the fire while it lasted.

EITHNE

*O*nly a handful of days passed before I again slid into the fever
dreams. Dank caverns and mist-shrouded mountains. A river
so vast it could only be the Great Sea, many days' journey from Silver
Downs. Titania, always with a scowl on her beautiful face and an
expression that said I was worth less than the dirt under her feet. And
the fey boy, standing in the corner of my small bedchamber. He wore
forest green today. For the first time, he crept closer, bit by bit, until he
stood right beside my bed.

"Why?" The words stuck in my dry mouth and it was some time
before I could continue. "Why do you watch me?"

"Curiosity." His voice was smooth and melodious. He sounded
exactly the way I expected, which was only right since he was a product
of my own fever dream.

"Of what?"

"Of why you cling so fiercely to life. Mortal lives are fleeting. Why
do you try so hard to hold onto them?"

"It is what we do. We fight."

"Why? Your life is not worth fighting for. You are either ill in bed or
huddled by the fire. You watch other mortals live and know you can
never join them."

"I conserve my strength. It's how I stay alive."

He raised his lip in something that might have been a sneer. His blue eyes were bright and hostile. "Mortal girls your age dream of betrothals and children and running their own home. Of what do you dream? Rivers and mountains, wind and fire."

"Titania," I gasped, struggling for breath now, for even so few words exhausted me. "I dream of Titania. And you."

He stretched out one slender hand towards me. His fingers were cool and smooth as they traced a fiery path along my skin. "Yes, you dream of me."

He left then, although I could not have said exactly how. With great effort, I managed to raise my arm in front of my face. My skin burned where he had touched me but looked just the same as always. Pale and sweaty, but otherwise unremarkable.

The fey boy had touched me. He was real. I was lost to the fever dreams then and by the time I surfaced again, I was no longer quite so certain that I hadn't imagined him.

The light coming in through the window held the shadows of early evening. My limbs were weak as Mother helped me to sit up and set a tray with a small bowl of broth on my lap. The tray shook as I tried to spoon the broth into my mouth. I spilled almost as much as I managed to eat. The savoury scent of beef made my stomach roll uncomfortably but I forced down a few mouthfuls. Mother sat on a chair drawn up to the bed, her hands clasped in her lap.

"Four days," she said in response to my unasked question.

I hadn't been sure I wanted to know this time. I set down the spoon. I needed to rest before I could eat more.

"Does anyone visit me while I am sick?" I asked.

"I do, of course," Mother said. "And your brothers sometimes."

"Nobody else?"

"I don't understand, Eithne. Who else would come?"

"I don't know. I'm confused." I felt bad about lying to Mother but how could I tell her the truth?

Several days passed before I had the strength to even stand without aid. Sometimes one of my brothers would carry me outside to sit in the sun for a while, but otherwise I could do nothing other than lie in bed and stare at the ceiling. I knew every crack in its timbers.

Now that the rivers and woods and winds were gone, my thoughts were my own once more and they lingered on the fey boy. Was he real or another product of my imagination? For I was not so silly as to think the images of Titania and oceans and mountains were anything but dreams. A reaction caused as my body tried to cool my fevered blood. A healer had explained it to me once.

But the boy, he was different. In my dreams I was always somewhere else: standing in the leaf litter of an ancient wood, or in an underground cavern, or trembling as I knelt on cold grass before Titania. But when I dreamed of the boy, I was always lying in my bed and he stood in my bedchamber. Never before had I wondered whether he was anything but a dream. Until he touched me.

My health slowly improved over the next sevennight. No fevers, no sweating, no sudden weakness or dizziness. I experienced neither vomiting nor lack of appetite, although my hunger had never been strong even when I was well.

The boy consumed my every thought. I had to see him again, had to seek further proof that he was real. Every morning, I stared into my hand mirror, hopeful for some indication of the imminent return of illness. The hand mirror was elegant, an unfair contrast to my thin and ever-pale face. The reflective glass was surrounded by wood carved with swirls of oak leaves and acorns. But my face was no paler than usual and the dark circles under my eyes were no more prominent. If anything, they seemed to fade a little as the days passed.

I slowly made my way downstairs for breakfast, clutching the smooth wooden bannister. The stairs were made for folk taller than I, so traversing them was awkward and slow, especially when I was still so weak. The other reason I walked slowly was because of my left foot, which twisted in on an awkward angle. I always tried to keep it straight and to not limp. My parents and brothers knew, of course, for a young child does not know to hide such a thing. But from the day I had under-stood my defect, I had tried to conceal it, and by now it was mostly forgotten. If I walked haltingly, an observer would likely attribute it to a lingering weakness.

The house was silent as I walked slowly through, the rest of my family already having gone off to start their day. The dining room table bore the remains of breakfast: scattered plates and crumbs, the lingering scent of porridge and herbal tea. The porridge kettle was empty so I made a meal of a slice of bread with honey. I sipped at some tea but it was cold and too bitter for my taste.

I went to sit by the fireplace in the family room. Somebody had thought to start the fire for me — Eremon, most likely — and it had already burned down to embers. I sank into my favourite chair and tucked my feet up under my long woollen skirt. There was no need for a blanket today for even though it was early winter, the day was mild and the fire hot enough to keep me pleasantly warm.

I had never before longed for the illness to strike. Never hoped that by evening I would once again be confined to bed, to sweat and writhe and groan with pain. But if the fey boy was real — and I was not entirely convinced that he was — he would only come to me if I was ill. This time I would be prepared. I would seek a way to confirm whether he was real or just another fever dream. If I could obtain a token from him: a rock, a leaf, a hair, something I could see and touch once I had recovered, that would be proof enough.

EITHNE

*T*en days had passed and rarely was I well for so long. The return of illness wouldn't be far off, but with yet another afternoon drawing to a close and my health still holding, I couldn't wait any longer.

Alone in the family room, I wrapped myself in woollen blankets and drew my chair up close to the fireplace. I loaded kindling onto the dying embers and the fire roared to life. I added a small log and the flames soon settled to a steady burn. Heat bathed my face and hands, and already I sweated within the blankets. I sat as close as I dared, roasting myself like a rabbit over a traveller's fire.

After some time I began to feel faint. My hand shook as I wiped sweat from my face. The back of my dress was damp and my mouth was dry. The heat had become almost unbearable but I wasn't sure my legs would hold me if I tried to stand, so I sat and prayed I was forcing the illness upon myself, until Mother found me.

"Eithne, are you unwell?" She immediately pressed a cool hand against my forehead and brushed sweaty hair back from my face. She frowned. "Goodness child, your skin burns. Move away from the fire."

"I'm cold," I said, hoping my voice was strong and convincing. I had never been a good liar.

"You have a fever." Mother's tone was the one that said she would tolerate no dissent. "You can hardly know how you feel if you sit so close to the fireplace with sweat pouring from your skin."

She pulled my chair back away from the fire. At this distance I could barely feel its warmth.

"No, I need to be closer." I tried to get up but her firm hand on my shoulder stopped me.

"Eithne, you will stay exactly where you are. As soon as one of your brothers returns, I will have them carry you upstairs. I'm sorry, child." Mother's voice was gentler now. "You were doing so well. I can't remember the last time you managed to fight off the illness for so long. But you know you need to rest now. The fever has started."

Shame washed over me. What right had I to cause Mother such worry? And all because I had some silly notion that an image from my fever dreams might be real. I was a foolish girl and if the illness returned tonight, it would be no more than I deserved.

So I waited patiently, ignoring the itch of sweat dripping down my neck, until Marrec and Conn came. They made a chair with their arms and lifted me into the air. They joked as they carried me upstairs and swung me a little too high. I tried to join in the game but in truth I was feeling quite dizzy so my laughter was weak.

They deposited me onto my bed, somewhat roughly, and left. I supposed they thought they had been gentle for they had never experienced a day of illness and had no understanding of how such treatment might jar my bones or make my head pound. I pulled back the covers and crawled under. The linen sheets scraped against my sensitive skin.

For the hundredth time, I examined the place where the fey boy's fingers had grazed my arm. It was unblemished. Nothing to indicate that possibly the most significant event of my life had occurred the day he touched me. For the fey despise mortals. They do not watch us unless they have reason to.

So many of the folk in my family had a purpose. Eremon was the heir. Caedmon the soldier son. Fiachra the druid. The three sons every family desired to produce. More sons, and perhaps a daughter or two, were a blessing. But if a man had three sons, he could die satisfied. My father had seven, plus a daughter, and it wasn't just the first three born who had destinies. My brother Diarmuid was the seventh son of a seventh son and destined to be a bard, even if nobody had told him so.

There was a secret held tightly within our family. Nobody ever spoke of it and it was the reason Diarmuid did not know what it meant to be the seventh son of a seventh son of Silver Downs. The one in that position had the ability to bring his tales to life, although nobody had ever been able to determine exactly how the power worked. Perhaps Diarmuid would be the one to figure it out. Or perhaps the ability had passed him by, for he was nineteen summers old and had never brought a tale to life. Or so everyone thought. I was not so sure. I watched Diarmuid, like I watched everyone, and there was something odd about him. Something *more*.

Our father was also the seventh son of a seventh son. He too was a bard once, but no longer. He told a tale which came true, that much I know. Something to do with his brothers, for they all died in some mysterious circumstances that were never discussed. Six brothers, all dead at the same time, and the youngest to inherit. That must be the result of a tale gone wrong. But now it seemed that I too had a destiny, just like Eremon, Fiachra, Caedmon and Diarmuid.

GRAINNE

"*G*rainne, Caedmon is here!"

I shuddered as my youngest sister's words echoed down the hallway. If I could hear her from the work room at the back of the house, where I was on my knees cleaning the hearth, Caedmon undoubtedly heard also.

"Grainne? Grainne, did you hear me?"

A thundering that sounded much like a herd of cows preceded Jenifry into the room. I sat back on my heels and brushed a strand of hair from my face with coal-dusted fingers.

"There you are, Grainne. Caedmon is here."

I took a deep breath and restrained my impulse to snap at her. "Thank you, I heard you the first time. As likely did the neighbours."

Jenifry pouted at me, all rosy-cheeked and flyaway hair. "But I thought you would want to know. Because, you know..." She dropped her voice to a conspiratorial whisper. "Because you love him."

"And I would much prefer that he didn't know," I said. "Remember how that was supposed to be a secret?"

"I haven't told your secret." Jenifry's voice rose rapidly in both volume and pitch. "I *promised* I wouldn't tell."

I sighed and swiftly brushed the last of the ash into a pan. Caedmon, one of the sons of Silver Downs, was hardly likely to be here to visit with me but I wasn't about to miss the chance to see him, even if I was covered with ash.

"I appreciate you keeping my secret, Jenifry. Do you happen to know why Caedmon is here?"

"He's talking to Father. They wouldn't let me listen."

"I hope everything is all right." Was there an illness in the family? A fire? Some mysterious death of livestock? No, the folk at Silver Downs would have no reason to come so far if they needed aid. There were closer neighbours.

"Aren't you going to go out and talk to him?" Jenifry asked, her voice as loud as ever.

"Will you shut your mouth if I do?" I swept out of the room before she could respond. Of course I would go talk with Caedmon. I had been in love with him since I was seven summers old.

I didn't see him often for Caedmon was a soldier and rarely at home. His last visit had worried me, for he was thinner than usual and paler. He was broad-shouldered, like most of the Silver Downs menfolk, and well-muscled from his occupation. Hefting swords all day was excellent for the physique. But the last time I saw him, he had lost muscle tone and walked slower than usual and with a slight hitch to his gait. I didn't have a chance to speak with him before he returned to the campaign front and I never heard the details of what injury he was recovering from on that visit.

Every time Caedmon left, I felt like I held my breath until he returned again. And every time I wished I had the courage to tell him how I felt. He had not yet taken a wife, although it would be a rare woman who wouldn't fall over her own feet to accept him. There were occasional rumours of dalliances but nothing that lasted more than a night or two and I tried not to envy their intimacy with him. The day he took a wife I would stop yearning after him, but until then I was thankful that Father hadn't insisted I myself handfast. There were several eligible young men within a half day's walk and even one heir who had made it clear he was interested. But none of them compared to Caedmon.

I dashed into the kitchen to wash my hands in a bucket of water. Ash was smeared down the front of my dress and I had knelt it in also but experience told me that trying to brush it away would only make it worse. It was probably on my face but there was no time to find a hand mirror.

I wore a sensible woollen work dress, my hair fastened back tidily into a plait that fell halfway down my back. My skirt was a little too short, showing my leather shoes and stocking-clad ankles. It was not what I would have worn had I expected to see Caedmon today. But he had never noticed me so it hardly mattered. His visit might be brief and I wasn't about to miss the opportunity to see him by being vain about my appearance.

With a deep breath, I pushed open the front door. The chill hit my face and I would have paused to grab my coat except that Caedmon had already seen me. He and Father stood together only a dozen paces away, in a spot where neither lodge nor trees impeded the sunlight. A sturdy black mare behind him nosed at the snow in search of grass.

Caedmon looked more like his usual self than when I last saw him almost a year ago. Gone was the paleness and the slight stoop to his shoulders. His dark hair was shorn somewhat shorter than he usually wore it but I was much relieved to see him looking hale and hearty. He smiled as his gaze met mine and the early winter's day suddenly seemed much warmer.

"Grainne," Father said. "I was just about to send someone to find you."

"Did you need something?" With difficulty, I dragged my gaze away from Caedmon. My mouth was dry and tasted like ash. Surely Father wasn't about to send me on some errand. Whatever moments I snatched with Caedmon now might well have to last me a year or more.

"Caedmon wishes to speak with you," Father said, to my very great surprise. He shook Caedmon's hand and departed swiftly.

I hardly knew what to say. I had never before been alone with him. Why would he seek me out now? Something to do with his sister, perhaps. I knew little of Eithne, just that she was often too ill to attend festivities through the year. But she was the only daughter in the family, whereas I was the eldest of four girls, although younger than our two brothers. It must be something to do with Eithne unless, oh gods, had he fallen in love with one of my sisters? Was he here to ask for my advice in wooing her?

Caedmon cleared his throat and shifted from one foot to the other. He fiddled with his woollen scarf, unwrapping and then rewrapping it around his neck. I had never before seen him look ill at ease.

"You are well, Grainne?" he asked at length.

I opened my mouth to reply but choked on the words. My face burned as I coughed and spluttered. Caedmon helpfully thumped me on the back, which only made me choke more. By the time I got myself under control, I had forgotten his question until he repeated it.

"Oh, yes, I am fine. And you? You look..." *Wonderful.* "Better than when I last saw you. You were recovering from an injury then, if I recall correctly."

Of course I did. I never forgot anything when it came to Caedmon. I could probably remember every time I had ever spoken to him, not that it would amount to more than a handful.

"Oh, the wound in my side. It is a solid scar now. The healer said the skin might not mend evenly and could be uncomfortable, even once it was healed, but it feels good now."

I bet it feels good. I'd like to try feeling it myself. For one awful moment, I thought I had spoken my thoughts aloud. But the expression on his face didn't change. We stood in awkward silence for a few moments before Caedmon cleared his throat again.

"I have decided it is time I was handfasted," he said abruptly.

It was as if the world had fallen out from beneath my feet. How many times had I promised myself I would stop being in love with him once he claimed some other woman as his own?

"I am unconcerned if we do not love each other," he continued. "Perhaps, given enough time, we might learn to, but my priority is to choose a woman who will make a good wife, and someone who can give me a son." Caedmon paused and looked at me intently.

Please gods, let my emotions not be written on my face. If he didn't already know I was in love with him, he must never find out now.

"I see," I said finally, because it seemed he waited for my response. Why was he telling me this? He didn't expect me to help find him a wife, did he? I wouldn't do it. I couldn't. It was one thing to vow to never again think about how I had loved him for almost as long as I could remember. It was another thing entirely to find him a bride. I would refuse. This was something I couldn't do, even for Caedmon.

"Grainne, will you handfast with me?"

Long moments passed before I finally grasped the meaning of his words.

"I... what?" My voice was uneven. Gods help me, I sounded like I was about to faint.

"Are you really going to make me say it again? Once was bad enough." Caedmon's lips curled up into the faintest hint of a grin.

Once again my voice failed. At least this time I didn't cough and choke like a fool but merely stood there with my mouth open and nothing coming out.

"Grainne." Caedmon reached out and took my hand. Good gods, he was holding my hand. Had I cleaned off the ash properly? His fingers were warm and calloused. "I have come home for the sole purpose of taking a wife. I have leave to remain only until the rivers start to thaw and then I must return to the campaign. I don't know when I will come home again. With the knowledge of all of that, will you be betrothed with me?"

There was only one answer any sane woman could give. "Of course."

Caedmon smiled properly now and squeezed my hand very gently. "I'll send a message to the druid community tonight. We will be hand-fasted as soon as a druid can get here. If that is acceptable to you."

"Yes, of course." Husband. In just a few sevennights, Caedmon would be my husband.

He leaned in and swiftly kissed my cheek. "I shall go home then and send the message. I will see you soon." He swung himself up onto the horse.

I watched him leave, hoping he might look back at me, perhaps give some sign that his decision had been influenced by even the tiniest feeling for me. I stayed standing in the yard long after he had gone.

Snow crunched under my feet as I shifted from foot to foot in a futile attempt to keep warm. While Caedmon had been there, I hadn't even noticed how much I shivered. Foolish girl for not wearing a coat. Chill tendrils of air wafted up under my skirt and my teeth began to chatter.

In all my fantasies, I had never once let myself pretend Caedmon might one day ask for my hand. But he just had. So why did my heart feel like it had broken in two?

GRAINNE

*I*t was six days before I saw Caedmon again. Messages had passed between Silver Downs and Misty Valley with arrangements for a betrothal party. Yesterday's message had also advised that Caedmon would visit this afternoon. I immediately decided I would not dress up for him, although I did braid my hair a little more carefully than usual. He would see me in plenty of work dresses after our handfasting so I saw no need to set any higher expectation during our betrothal.

I was still trying to figure out how I felt about the situation. Had Caedmon said he was in love with me — had he even hinted he might be — I would have been delighted. But he had made it clear that his choice was purely practical. I dwelled on his words for far longer than I should have. They were factual and honest. If Caedmon had ever been taught that sometimes one should not say exactly what one thought, the lesson had not stuck. He needed a wife and, for whatever reason, had decided it should be me. Love, or indeed any emotion, did not factor into his decision.

But perhaps it didn't matter whether he loved me. He had chosen me after all. I would live with him, get to know him, and gods willing, I would bear the son he wanted. With time perhaps whatever it was he felt for me would turn into something more. Most women handfasted with men their fathers chose for them and I was fortunate that mine had done no more than hint he would be pleased to see me betrothed. Handfasting for love only happened in the old tales.

My resolve to wear my work dress lasted until I heard the clatter of hooves on the stone path in front of our lodge. I rushed back up to my bedchamber to exchange my woollen work wear for a high-waisted linen dress that skimmed my toes and had delicate yellow day's eyes embroidered around the neckline and wrists.

Should I greet him at the door or wait for someone to summon me? I was paralysed with indecision.

Jenifry solved the problem by screeching through the house. "Grainne, Caedmon is here."

I waited at the front door, holding it open despite the freezing breeze that gusted in and whipped around my skirt. Caedmon wore a woollen tunic with long pants, a dark blue coat, gloves and a hat. Even with the bulky winter garments, I would have recognised him anywhere. The way he stood with his back straight but his shoulders just a little slouched, as if entirely comfortable within his own skin. The tilt of his head when he listened to something and the way he lifted his chin before he spoke. I had watched him, studied every gesture, memorised every movement for years.

Sweat trickled between my shoulder blades and my stomach rolled uncomfortably. Usually when I saw Caedmon, I was filled with excitement, an intent to memorise every word and gesture, and a tiny hope that perhaps he might notice me this time. But now nerves made it impossible to think clearly and I hardly knew how to act.

Caedmon looped his horse's reins around a post and then headed towards the lodge, rubbing his hands on his pants as if to dry them through his gloves. My heart sank. He had changed his mind. Why else would he be nervous?

"Grainne." Caedmon smiled as he met my eyes and, as he reached me, leaned down to kiss my cheek. He was a head taller than me and my startled jerk meant he almost missed. But at last his lips made contact with my skin and I froze.

21

Breathe, I reminded myself. *If you faint because you stopped breathing, he'll think you a fool.*

"Caedmon." My voice sounded oddly breathy.

"Aren't you going to invite him in?" Jenifry hissed from behind me.

"Go away," I hissed back without turning around. At least it was only Jenifry who had taken it on herself to embarrass me. I didn't know where Paili and Vanora were, but at least they weren't hovering behind me. The three girls together could be utterly humiliating when they wanted to be.

Caedmon stifled a smile and pretended he didn't see Jenifry lurking. "I thought we might take a walk."

"I'd love to."

When I reached for my winter coat, Caedmon's hand was there before mine. He lifted it off the hook and held it out for me. This close, he smelled of woodsmoke and the crispness of fresh snow. I again reminded myself to breathe. I pulled my knitted gloves from their hook, hoping he didn't notice the way my fingers trembled.

The winter sky was clear blue from horizon to horizon, with a lone bird circling up high. Snow crunched under my boots. My mouth was dry and inside my gloves, my fingers tingled. Caedmon would think me boring and dim-witted if I didn't think of something to say soon.

"Cold today," I muttered.

Caedmon shot me a brief smile. "I'm nervous too. My sister is too young to be of any help so I'm not sure I really know what you expect of me. If I'm getting it all wrong, tell me. Please. I don't want you to be unhappy because I didn't know what I was supposed to do."

Tears sprang to my eyes and I turned my face into the breeze to dry them before he saw. He wanted to make me happy. And he chose me out of all of the women who would have gladly had him. Perhaps his reasons were irrelevant.

"I don't know what is expected either," I said when I trusted my voice enough to speak. "My sisters are also too young to be useful."

Caedmon took my hand and held it firmly. At least he wouldn't be able to feel my sweaty palms through my gloves.

"Then we will figure it out together," he said.

We walked in silence for a while. I felt like I was not quite grounded in my body, for surely this was not real, the two of us walking hand in hand. The naked branches of birch and beech swayed in the breeze, sending little flutters of snow drifting down to the ground. A pair of wrens balanced on a branch high above my head, their feathers fluffed out for warmth. They twittered together and their conversation sounded small in the openness of the fields.

Our estate was not as big as some, and certainly far smaller than Silver Downs, but most of what I could see belonged to Misty Valley. The snow-covered fields, the barn where the cows and sheep sheltered on winter nights, the stands of birch and ash and beech. Even with my eyes closed, I knew the smell of Misty Valley. In summer, it was grass-covered hills and mist-soaked valleys. In winter, it was the tang of frost and the sharpness of winds from the north slicing in from the Great Sea.

"I've sent for a druid," Caedmon said, darting a sideways glance at me. "I'm hopeful my brother Fiachra might come."

"Do you see him often?"

"Never. He is not allowed to return until he has reached a certain stage in his training. We receive messages from him sometimes though. He enjoys his studies and works hard to excel."

"When will he come?"

"Two sevennights, perhaps." Caedmon's face tightened. "Hopefully no longer."

"That will be just after midwinter."

"Yes, that still gives us a few weeks to..."

"Get to know each other?" I suggested, but the way his face reddened told me that wasn't what he meant. "Oh."

I didn't quite know where to look. The hand that still grasped mine felt warm, even through our gloves.

"I know most hope for three sons," he said. "But give me one and I'll be satisfied."

"I'll try." My face was far too hot.

"The handfasting ceremony. Do you have any requirements?"

For a moment I felt recklessly brave. "I'd really like you to be there."

He laughed and squeezed my hand. "I'd like the ceremony to be held at Silver Downs, if you don't mind. Many generations of my family have handfasted there and it wouldn't seem right to do it anywhere else."

I agreed and we talked of inconsequential things after that until a chill breeze forced us to turn back towards home. Not that Misty Valley would be home for much longer. Although we hadn't discussed it yet, it would be expected that I would move to Silver Downs. We would probably build our own lodge there. At least my family would be only a few hours' horse or cart ride away. As the wife of a soldier, I would be alone much of the year and it would be nice to be able to visit my family often. Caedmon's family would be even closer, probably just a short walk, and perhaps with time I would think of them as my own. I barely knew his sister, Eithne, but she would be my sister soon.

"Should we hold the betrothal party here?" Caedmon asked.

"Oh." I was oddly touched. "I would like that."

A lump in my throat choked off anything further I might have said and suddenly tears rolled down my cheeks. Their warm path swiftly turned cold.

"Grainne." Caedmon looked startled. He stopped walking and turned me to face him, holding my hand tightly so I couldn't pull away. "I... What does this mean? If you don't want me, say it. I would never force you if you were unwilling."

"It's not that." I pulled my hand from his and fumbled with my gloves. I managed to get one off and wiped my cheeks with my fingers.

Caedmon placed his hand under my chin and tilted my head up.

"Why do you cry? Tell me. I can't fix it if I don't know the problem."

"I'm just overwhelmed. It's all so sudden. And this is my home. I didn't expect to be leaving so soon. I haven't really had time to think about it."

"I don't know what to say to make you feel better." Caedmon spoke slowly, as if choosing his words with care. "I wish I did. But we don't have time for a long betrothal. I need to leave with the first thaw. I'm sorry if this is too rushed for you."

His kind words made me cry in earnest this time. Caedmon wrapped his arms around me and pulled me against him. His body was lean and firm and the arms around me were gentle. I rested my face against his chest and breathed in his smoky scent.

I pulled away as soon as I was composed enough to avoid embarrassing myself again. "I'm sorry. I promise I won't cry on you next time you come to visit."

"I hope that next time I will be bringing news of when to expect the druids."

"I'll look forward to that."

I went to put my glove back on but he stopped me, taking the glove and tucking it away in his pocket. Then he pulled off one of his own gloves and held my hand all the way back to the lodge. My hand felt tiny encased in his and no matter how cold my fingers were, I wasn't going to pull away. When we reached the lodge, Caedmon returned my glove.

"I'll see you soon." He leaned down and this time I was more prepared and didn't pull away. His lips brushed mine ever so softly. "Farewell, Grainne."

GRAINNE

On the day of our betrothal feast, I woke with my stomach feeling like it was filled with pebbles. I barely made it to the wash basin on the dresser before my belly contracted painfully and then emptied. The bitterness of my vomit coated my tongue.

My whole world was about to change. In just a few hours, my betrothal with Caedmon would become official. Everyone would know. What if he changed his mind before the druids arrived? What if he noticed some other girl for the first time and wished he had asked her instead?

I had loved Caedmon since I tripped on a rocky path when I was seven summers old. I landed on my hands and knees. My knee started bleeding and I sat on the stones and howled. Caedmon was twelve summers old and already broad shouldered with a physique that promised future muscles. He used his shirt to wipe the blood that dripped down my leg and made a silly comment to make me laugh. And my heart became his.

In all practicality, my only aim should have been to find a good husband. But like all children of our people I was raised on a diet of old tales and they taught that love was to be desired, searched for, and treasured. And I loved Caedmon. It was hard not to wish he loved me back.

But tonight I would sit at his side. Mine would be the hand he held, mine the lips he kissed before he left. My stomach heaved again and once more the contents sloshed into the wash basin. I dipped a cloth in the water jug and wiped my face.

Be calm, Grainne. Otherwise you're going to fall apart before tonight.

I put on a woollen work dress and pulled my hair back into a rough braid. Squeals from the hallway indicated Jenifry, Paili and Vanora were out of bed. A body thudded against my door. Time to face the world or it would likely come bursting in anyway.

I took the vomit-filled basin downstairs and emptied it. After that, the day quickly became a blur. It seemed everyone wanted me to approve one thing or make a decision on something else. I was required to decide exactly where the evening's celebrations would be held. I opted for the spacious living area. There was a fireplace at each end and plenty of room for chairs and long tables for food. I pointed to the corner where I wanted the fiddler and whistler to play, and consulted with the women who had come to prepare the food. A servant woman began to hang festive red ribbons from the rafters. My stomach rolled and I wanted nothing more than to crawl back into bed and pull the covers over my head. What if Caedmon didn't even turn up?

As the sun started to set, my sisters bustled me upstairs. While I washed with a cloth dipped in the bowl of water on the dresser, they lounged on my bed and argued over which of my two good dresses I should wear. I chose the yellow, for its summery shade, the colour of dandelions, reminded me of summer's warmth even in the middle of winter.

Vanora undid my braid and wove my hair into rows on each side of my head, merging them into one thick plait at the base of my skull. Paili had selected a gold ribbon which Vanora fastened around the bottom of my plait. Jenifry produced a small posy of dried flowers, the remnants of some summer expedition: blue cornflower, white honeysuckle and fire-edged sundew. Although they would probably crumble to dust in minutes, I allowed Vanora to carefully weave them through the length of my braid.

The clatter of hooves and wheels outside heralded the first guests. It was time to go down and greet them. And pray Caedmon actually came.

I needn't have worried, for the family from Silver Downs were the very first to arrive. My stomach clenched as Caedmon's eyes met mine and for a moment I feared I would vomit all over him. He strode up to me and kissed my cheek, taking my hand as he did so.

"You look lovely, Grainne."

My cheeks heated and I knew they would be bright red. He would think me a foolish girl for blushing every time he spoke to me.

"Thank you," I murmured, staring at his shoulder to avoid looking him in the eye. I wanted to say how handsome he looked but the words wouldn't come out of my mouth.

"Are you ready to celebrate?" he asked.

"I was afraid you wouldn't come." I regretted the words the moment they left my mouth.

"Why would you think that?"

I shrugged and tried to pull my hand away but he clutched it firmly and drew me closer.

"Grainne, talk to me. Why would you think I wouldn't come? This is our betrothal party. It's a time to celebrate. You and me. Us."

"You don't love me. There isn't really an us." *Damn it, Grainne, stop talking.*

Caedmon's lips straightened. Despite the many years I had studied him, I wasn't sure whether this expression meant disappointment or anger.

"I hardly know you, Grainne, or you me," he said. "But I think you will make a fine wife. Gods willing, there will be time for us to get to know each other."

I nodded, swallowing down the words I wanted to say. Perhaps, with time, he would learn to love me. If I was a good wife to him. If I gave him the son he wanted and stayed faithful when he was gone. *One day,* I vowed, *you will love me. And you'll say it first.*

"I'm sorry." I forced a smile that almost felt genuine. "I feel a little strange today. Overwhelmed. Forgive me."

His easy smile melted my insides until I thought they might ooze out through my skin.

As people poured into the house, I gave up trying to remember who they all were. It seemed that for every friend or relative of my family, there were two of Caedmon's. He introduced me to some but there were too many to remember. His sister Eithne squealed with delight and hugged me. I hugged her back very gently, for she felt fragile in my arms.

"I am so pleased we are to be sisters," she whispered in my ear. "I've always wanted a sister."

Caedmon's mother, Agata, embraced me more firmly. His father, Fionn, looked like he didn't quite know whether to hug me or slap me on the back. He settled for patting my shoulder. The brothers all offered congratulations: Eremon and his wife Niamh, Sitric, twins Marrec and Conn. Diarmuid was the last to greet me. He hung back and didn't look at me, even as I leaned in to hug him.

"Brother," I said. He stiffened in my arms, rearing back as if I had bitten him, and I released him quickly. Tears stung my eyes. He didn't need to be so horrid. What did I do to make him hate me so?

Servant women brought around platters of roasted red deer and freshly baked bread. The fiddler and whistler kept up a constant jingle of merry tunes, some familiar and well loved, and others new to my ears. I tapped my toe to the beat as I watched old folk and young, in pairs or groups or even alone, dancing. They spun and skipped and whirled around the room. A sudden surge of impulsiveness gripped me.

"Dance with me, Caedmon," I said, and grabbed his hand.

He didn't say a word but wrapped his arm around my waist and spun me into the middle of the room. Only when I was gasping for breath did we stop. Caedmon barely breathed any harder than usual but his eyes sparkled. We gulped down mugs of ale and once I had caught my breath, we dived back into the dancers.

As folk tired, they collapsed onto the rows of chairs lining the walls. Every chair we owned had been brought into the room as well as a cart-load of long benches from our nearest neighbour. When Caedmon and I finally fell onto a bench, he draped an arm casually over my shoulders and a thrill danced through me. Finally, I was starting to believe this was real.

My father stood by one of the fireplaces. I had spied him dancing earlier, much to my surprise, and his cheeks were still ruddy.

"Friends." Father's booming voice reached to the back of the room with ease. "Family. Strangers." A titter arose from the crowd and he beamed at them. "Misty Valley extends a warm welcome to you all. Tonight we celebrate the betrothal of my oldest daughter, Grainne, to Caedmon, son of Silver Downs."

Caedmon squeezed my shoulders and smiled down at me. Sometimes the way he acted made it hard to remember he didn't love me.

"We have feasted and imbibed good ale and danced until we are breathless. Now is the time for reflection and contemplation. This seems a fine time for a tale. Caedmon, my boy, I believe you have a bard in the family. Is he here tonight?"

Beside me, Caedmon stiffened but his voice was as relaxed as ever. "Yes, my lord. My youngest brother, Diarmuid, over there, is the bard." He indicated Diarmuid's location with a tilt of his head.

Father turned in the direction Caedmon had indicated. "Well then, young Diarmuid, will you favour us with a tale?"

Diarmuid slunk up to the fireplace where Father stood. He was as different from Caedmon as summer was from winter. Where Caedmon's walk was easy, Diarmuid's footsteps were short and tense. Where Caedmon was broad-shouldered, Diarmuid was slender and he held his shoulders slightly hunched as if he wished he were invisible. Caedmon's smile was free and his dark eyes showed no hint of the horrors he had seen in battle. Diarmuid looked hunted, chased, haunted. I had only spoken to Diarmuid twice, at most before tonight. He would always turn in a different direction and scurry away if he saw me walking towards him. I had never been sure whether he hated me or feared me. But perhaps now I was to be his sister, that would change. After all, we would soon be living together.

Diarmuid stood in front of the fireplace, hands clasped awkwardly in front of him. He held his head high and for the first time I saw a hint of the man he might grow into. He cleared his throat, an oddly presumptuous sound.

"This is a new tale." He projected his voice well. "There was once a woman who had a young child, a babe not yet four summers old."

He spoke well and at first I found myself entranced by his words. A good bard can cast a spell over his audience and make them forget where they are. Even in so few words, it was clear Diarmuid had the makings of a great bard. There was a magical, hypnotic quality to his words and I almost started to believe the mother in his tale was myself. But if I listened carefully, ignored the sweet pull urging me to sink deeper and deeper into his tale, there was something wrong about it. Titania, queen of the fey, charmed both mother and child and sent them off into the woods. Instead of the tale ending with the mother saving her child, she watched wild animals rip her to pieces.

My heart stopped for a moment then stuttered wildly. The image was so strong, it was as if I was there. I heard the cries of the woodlarks, smelled the moss and damp and decay of the woods. The child cries, begs her mother to save her. The mother, also in tears, falls to her knees, but Titania's magic prevents her from moving. Wild boars circle the child, sniffing. One darts in to sample the flesh on her leg. The child cries out, her wordless scream filled with horror. Then the boars attack. The child is quickly brought down into the leaf litter. Her blood stains the leaves. The last sounds she hears are her mother's screams. Caedmon's arm around me brought me back to Misty Valley.

"Grainne." He shook me gently. "Grainne, are you all right?"

"The tale," I whispered. It was all I could say.

Caedmon's face was grim. "I know. His tales are always strange. He wants to please, but..."

"There is something wrong with him."

"Not wrong, just... different. Special. He has a unique ability but has not yet mastered it."

"I never want to hear him tell another tale."

"You will though, I'm afraid. Bards hold a very special place in our family."

Caedmon's arm around me tightened and I leaned against him, soaking up the warmth from his body and trying to shake the awful images from my mind.

GRAINNE

$\mathcal{T}$he day of our handfasting arrived too soon. I was still getting used to the idea of being betrothed, but I understood Caedmon's urgency. He would not be home for long.

When I woke that morning, the sky was filled with thick clouds that obscured the sun. The air was tinged with ice and the snow was thick and fresh, blanketing the earth all the way to the horizon. I had already packed, not that I had much, just my clothes, a hairbrush and hand mirror, a few trinkets, a thick quilt I myself had stitched. Soon it would cover the bed I would share with my husband. I didn't let myself think of that. My bedchamber felt empty and somehow lonely as I dressed. No longer would this place be mine. When I next returned, it would be as a visitor.

I wore a simple grey gown, sewn by the womenfolk of my family, every stitch made with love and care. Each of my sisters had contributed to the design. Vanora threaded bands of silver around the hem and wrists. Paili stitched a honeysuckle blossom and Jenifry a dove, symbols of love and peace. Mother added an elaborate spiral pattern around the throat. As I dressed, my family's wishes of happiness and harmony cocooned me. So it was with a full heart that I departed Misty Valley, leaving for the final time as a daughter of that household.

The ride to Silver Downs passed swiftly. I was snug within thick blankets, the warmth in my chest a sharp contrast with the wind stinging my face. My brief calmness evaporated as we drew up in front of the Silver Downs lodge and nausea again stirred in my belly. This was it. The last moments during which I was considered a girl. I would soon be a wife.

Why choose me? There were prettier girls, kinder girls, and surely others better suited to the role of soldier's wife. Others would be more sympathetic to his career and the long absences from home. Others more patient with his children and better at managing the household alone. But for some unknowable reason, Caedmon chose me. And perhaps, with enough time, he might learn to love me. But even if he didn't, I would love him, and not from afar. Instead of watching him with some other woman, it would be me beside him, holding his hand, perhaps with his son clinging to my hip. Our future dawned ahead of me, bright and sparkling and filled with opportunity. We would be happy. Caedmon would be happy. I would make sure of it.

When we arrived at Silver Downs, Father helped me down from the cart, his beaming face red from the cold air. "You will make a fine wife, Grainne," he said.

Mother embraced me, her arms around me thinner than I remembered. She took a step back and placed one hand on my cheek. "He is a good man and will be kind to you. I couldn't have chosen better for you myself."

Of my two brothers, only Piran was present. He embraced me firmly but said nothing. My other brother, Wynne was a soldier and likely didn't even know I was handfasting today. I had often wondered whether he ever saw Caedmon when they were both at the campaign front but had never asked for fear of betraying my interest.

My sisters hugged me in turn from oldest to youngest. Vanora, then Paili, then Jenifry. A stranger would recognise the four of us as sisters, with our rosy cheeks and dark hair.

Jenifry's chin wobbled and her eyes shone. "I'll miss you," she said.

"I won't be far away. You can come and visit me."

"But it won't be the same. Nothing will ever be the same again."

Her words echoed in my ears as I approached the lodge, flanked by my family. Its grey stones loomed over me, far bigger than our lodge at Misty Valley. It had to be, with seven sons.

Caedmon opened the front door just as I reached it. His dark hair was soldier-short and still damp from bathing. He greeted me with a wide smile and a brief kiss on my lips, then led me through the lodge. My family followed, my sisters unusually quiet. Perhaps they were intimidated by the fineness of Silver Downs. I knew just how they felt. It was hard to believe that this was about to become my home.

Everywhere I looked the wooden furniture was carefully polished to a gleam. Thick tapestries lined the walls and heavy embroidered curtains covered the windows. The colours were dark and sombre: forest green, earthy brown, a deep scarlet. This house spoke of tradition and inheritance, of ancestors and history. The house in which I grew up had been built when my parents handfasted. It was light and airy and decorated in yellows and oranges and bright blues, for my mother was fond of cheery colours.

Caedmon's parents, Fionn and Agata, embraced me. Eithne's hug was enthusiastic, if not particularly strong. The shadows on her face suggested a recent illness and her dress hung loosely as if she had lost weight too recently for the seams to be taken in.

Diarmuid hung back as the brothers greeted me and at length I forced myself to approach him, trying to hide my unease as I did so. Images from his tale still lingered in my mind. The mother on her knees in the forest. The child, broken and bloody, limbs torn off. I shook my head and forced the dark images from my mind. Today was for happy thoughts. I would not dwell on Diarmuid's awful tale.

Amongst the brothers was one I had not met before. I would have known him as a son of Silver Downs even if I had first glimpsed him elsewhere, for he was broad of shoulder and dark-haired and looked much like Caedmon. The druids had sent one of Silver Downs' own.

"Well met, Grainne," Fiachra said as he embraced me with strong arms.

I hugged him back, feeling absurdly shy. He was just another who would shortly become my brother, but there was something about him that was different from his siblings. Some sense of Other, of depth and mystery. Inwardly, I shivered. This was a powerful man. Powerful and, perhaps, dangerous. Fiachra released me and Caedmon took my hand.

"Come, Grainne," he said. "Everyone is waiting outside."

As we exited through the back door into the crisp sunshine, calmness washed over me. Gone were my nerves. Gone was the fear that Caedmon might change his mind before we could be handfasted. Gone was my niggling doubt that perhaps his message to the druids would never arrive and nobody would come. Of course, I could have simply moved into the lodge at Silver Downs, but any child I bore would not be legally recognised unless we were handfasted by a druid.

We gathered beneath a mighty oak, its naked branches providing no obstacle to the weak sun. Fresh snow crunched under my boots. Caedmon and I stood together in front of the druid who would perform the handfasting ritual. It wasn't Fiachra but one of his elders. He was several decades older than Fiachra with a full beard tinged with grey.

"Beings of air and water, fire and earth, bear witness to this event." The druid's voice was strong and compelling. "This man and this woman pledge themselves to each other."

I wondered whether the elementals heard him and came. Perhaps even now they watched. The words of the ceremony flowed past me. I tried to concentrate on them, to linger over the significance of the event, but my mind kept urging the druid to hurry, to speak the words that would bind us. Eventually he wrapped a scarlet ribbon around our wrists, tying us together.

Caedmon's face was grave as he stared down at me and I tried to ignore a sudden sense of doom. Death was an ever-present risk for a soldier. He might die in his next battle, or if not then, the one after. My hands were cold as Caedmon reached for them. He kissed me soundly to the cheers and shouts of those assembled. His lips were warm against mine and the knot in my belly began to unwind just a little. Caedmon looked more relaxed now, almost carefree. Perhaps he too had been nervous.

With the ceremony concluded, long tables draped with red cloths were piled high with platters of steaming food. Meats and roasted root vegetables, various breads and cheeses. The red linen was stark as blood against the snowy background. The distant sound of a raven cawing reached my ears although I saw no sign of the bird.

My stomach growled, for I had been too nervous to eat that morning. I managed no more than a few bites between constant congratulations from well-wishers. Folk were loud and cheerful, hastening to eat before the food cooled. They stood in small groups, eating with a bread trencher in one hand and a mug of ale in the other. A group of laughing children darted in and out of the crowd, ignoring the food in favour of games.

The sun began to sink towards the horizon and the frigid air was thick with the promise of snow. I had thought folk might start heading home as evening fell but instead they moved inside. The family room was warm, with the lamps lit and the fires already burnt down to embers. I accepted a mug of spiced wine from a serving woman. It slid down my throat easily, warming my insides. Somebody pressed a chunk of bread filled with roasted pig into my hands and I ate quickly while I could.

Hours passed and still folk drank and danced and talked. I grew tired of making small talk with strangers. Fatigue began to gnaw at me and my head grew light from tiredness and spiced wine. Caedmon saw me stifle a yawn and then another. He leaned close to whisper in my ear.

"Time for bed perhaps?"

My face grew hot. I had not let myself think of how the evening would end. I didn't know whether to look forward to it or fear it. Mother had pulled me aside a few days ago to ensure I knew what would be expected. I had some idea already, of course. One does not grow up surrounded by horses and cows and dogs without having at least some knowledge of such a thing.

We slipped away quietly without any goodbyes. My legs were heavy and it almost seemed like too much effort to lift them.

"We can choose a site for our home in the next couple of days," Caedmon said as he led me up the stairs. "The lodge here might feel a bit crowded but it's only for a few months until our own is built. I've already hired some men. You can choose where you want our home to be. There's a place down by the river you might like."

He paused outside a closed door, halfway down the passage. "Just a warning, I think some of the women may have been in here. I was told to keep out."

He pushed open the door and we left the chilly passage for the warmth of Caedmon's bedchamber. Our bedchamber. He stirred the embers in the fireplace and they quickly blazed back into fiery life.

I stared around the bedchamber we were to share. Someone had spread candles along the dresser and the mantelpiece. Their tiny fires glimmered, making the room sparkle. Dried purple petals were sprinkled over the bed's snowy white cover. The scent of rosemary and pinecones filled my nose.

Caedmon finished stoking the fire and closed the door. He stepped close to me and slid his arms around me from behind. I leaned back against him, still getting used to the feel of his body against mine. He gently guided me towards the bed, then turned me around to face him, his hands soft on my shoulders. My heart thudded and my hands trembled.

"I'm not sure I know what to do," I said and to my embarrassment, my voice wavered a little.

"I want you to enjoy this, Grainne. All you have to do is tell me what you like and what you don't."

"I think I can do that."

His hands were gentle as he unfastened the ties of my grey gown and pushed it back over my shoulders. It slid to the floor with a whisper. Caedmon lifted me and placed me in the centre of the bed. He lay beside me and leaned in to kiss me firmly and his hands began to roam over my body.

"Oh," I whispered. "I like that."

EITHNE

*A*s I finally sank into the fever dreams, the fey boy had come to stand beside my bed as I had known he would. When I asked for some token to prove he was real, he frowned. I feared scaring him away and didn't ask again. But I hugged my secret knowledge to myself: the fey had reason to watch me. I had a purpose, even if I didn't know what.

It had been more than a sevennight since I started to recover and it was so rare to feel any strength in my limbs that I couldn't bear to linger inside. A glance out of the window showed me a sunny day. The sky was clear and the snow on the ground was thin.

"I think I'll go for a walk today," I said to Mother a little later as we broke our fast with new bread and honey. The honey was a gift from a neighbouring estate and was sweeter than that from our own bees. It lingered on my tongue, sticky-sweet.

Mother and I were the only ones at the table, for Papa and my brothers were all up early to start the work day. Mother too had likely been up for hours already, but she usually waited to eat with me. It was only I who had the luxury of sleeping as late as I pleased.

A crease wrinkled Mother's forehead. "I'm not sure that is a good idea, Eithne."

"I feel good. Strong."

"Don't go far. Stay within sight of the lodge. And dress warmly."

"I will," I said, although I had already determined to walk as far as I could.

Winter was drawing to a close and soon the rivers would begin to thaw and the trees would grow their summer coating of leaves. A lone thrush trilled from bare branches and a patch of melting snow displayed glimpses of the sleeping earth beneath. Already the land stirred and summer felt close. I looked forward to working in my garden again, for Mother forbade me to touch it during the winter months. But when the weather was warm and I was well, I delighted in spending some time each morning pulling weeds or trimming herbs. Servant women would do the heavier work, planting bulbs and turning soil, while I sat on my wooden bench and directed them. When in full bloom, my little garden was a riot of colour with purple bluebells and white wood anemones and yellow tulips.

My heart felt light as snow crunched beneath my boots and the sun warmed my face. It was almost warm enough that I didn't need my heavy coat or my scarf and gloves, but I didn't dare remove them in case Mother watched from a window. I took off my hat though, to feel the breeze in my hair.

I walked slowly and it was some time before the lodge was out of sight. It was not far away though, just hidden behind the small hill I ambled up and then down. Ahead stood a stand of slender beech. In summer their dense canopy provided shade and a cool retreat for birds and bugs, but now their branches were bare, waiting for the new buds of spring. This was my favourite place to linger when I had the strength to walk this far. It was my private place, where nobody else ever came. A large rock, transported by my brothers to a sunny spot beside the trees, provided a convenient resting spot.

As I approached, something was different. It took me some time though — not until I was closer — to see what it was. A figure stood amongst the beeches; not one of my brothers, for his profile was taller and more slender.

My breath caught in my throat. Should I turn back now? I wouldn't be able to run far, but perhaps I could make it to within sight of the fields. My brothers would be working out there. They would certainly come if they saw me running.

The figure was perfectly still, standing a few paces from my rock. A silent, watching presence in a place that had always previously been my own. I still couldn't decide whether to flee, but my feet continued to carry me forward, never hesitating. Finally I drew close enough to make out the boy's features. Snow white skin, black hair cut without care for fashion. Blood red lips. He said nothing as I approached but watched me intently. I felt clumsy beneath his stare. I straightened my back and took extra care not to limp.

"You," I said when I came close enough to speak without shouting. I stopped mere paces away from my private sanctuary, longing to rest on my rock but not wanting to enter while the intruder was there. My legs trembled from the walk, although it wasn't all that far. He didn't acknowledge my words but continued to stare at me.

"I thought you were a dream."

Finally, he cocked an eyebrow at me but I couldn't tell whether he was amused or offended. "As you can see, I am not."

"Why are you here? This is my place."

"You claim this land? We were here long before your type came."

"Not the whole land, just this bit." I gestured at beech and rock. "This is my private place. Nobody but me ever comes here."

"I come here all the time."

"But you can't. This is my place." I was irrationally annoyed. He had already intruded on my bedchamber. How dare he also invade this sanctuary?

"You have no way of stopping me. I shall come here if I please. And when the day arrives that I no longer wish to come here, I will stop."

"That's not fair."

"I didn't say it was." He was calm, unperturbed by my anger.

"But it's not your decision."

"Then whose is it? Yours?"

"This is my place."

"So you said." Dark eyes watched my reaction, noting my increasing irritation.

I stamped my foot, which had little effect on the snowy ground, and wished I could be more eloquent in my speech. "You are infuriating."

"Why does your foot twist?"

A hot flush darkened my cheeks. "How rude."

"I'm not rude. I'm curious."

"It's none of your business."

"Why do you hide it?"

"How do you know about it if I hide it?"

"I am accustomed to perfection. The way your foot twists is obvious, even when you try to hide it."

"I hide it because I don't like being stared at. Not that it's any of your business."

"Why would you tell me if you didn't want me to know?"

"Because you asked." I restrained from stamping my foot again, although only barely. "Why were you spying on me?"

"It's not spying if the other party knows you are there."

"I had no choice in whether you were there or not. You just showed up. In my bedchamber. It's highly inappropriate."

"It's only inappropriate if somebody else knows."

"What if I told someone?"

"Have you?"

My legs were trembling even harder now and refusing to sit was no longer an option. I strode forward, trying to walk evenly, but tiredness always exacerbated my limp. I brushed snow from the rock with my gloved hand. I didn't answer until I had settled onto it, its solid form cold beneath my thick skirt.

"I might have."

"Nobody would believe you."

"You can't just come into a woman's bedchamber without her permission." I looked out towards the mountainous horizon and willed myself to be calm. I had never met someone who could raise my temper with so little effort.

"Would it make a difference if I asked?"

"No. I still wouldn't allow you."

"Then there's no point in asking. I'm going to continue coming to you anyway."

A delicious thrill went down my spine but I pretended it was just a shiver. "Why?"

"Because you intrigue me."

I didn't know how to respond to that. "What is your name?"

"Kalen. And you are Eithne."

He was probably waiting for me to ask how he knew but I refused to play his game. "Where do you live?"

Kalen waived a hand to indicate somewhere behind himself. "There is a portal to our realm in the woods."

"Are you permitted to come here whenever you want?"

"Not exactly."

I glanced at him, wondering at his answer. "Who would stop you?"

"My queen."

"Is that Titania?"

"You know of her?" A flicker of surprise crossed his face.

"Our tales tell of her."

"What do they tell?"

"That she is beautiful. And cruel."

He smiled slightly, amused, although I didn't know why. "She is both of those things."

"Why would she stop you from coming here?"

He hesitated and his gaze flicked away briefly. "I can't tell you."

"Why not?"

He shrugged and looked away.

"How old are you?" I asked. I wiggled into a more comfortable position on the rock. It was starting to warm beneath me but when I moved, I shifted onto a cold spot. I edged back onto the warmth.

"My kind don't measure age the way you do. We live a very long time. Your world will crumble to dust before I die."

"That's sad," I said. "To see everything you know die."

He shrugged again. "It's the way things are. It is neither sad nor not."

"Do you know what sadness is?"

"I know it makes mortals cry."

"Happiness makes us cry sometimes too."

His gaze sharpened with interest. "How peculiar."

"Why do you watch me?"

Again, Kalen looked away.

The sun was starting to sink towards the horizon. Fingers of purple spanned the breadth of the sky. A flock of birds — too far away to tell what — flew in an arrow formation. I wondered whether they would reach their destination before night fell. I clambered off the rock, my limbs sore and stiff. "I have to go."

"Farewell."

"Will you walk with me? Just until the house is within sight."

Kalen eyed me for a long moment and I shifted uncomfortably. Why did I ask such a thing? I barely knew him and he had already been spying on me from within my own bedchamber. My invitation sounded like encouragement. But the words were already said.

"Yes," he said finally and my heart did a strange little leap.

We walked slowly, for I was tired and my foot ached. I couldn't help but limp, but Kalen didn't ask about it again. He didn't seem to mind my silence either, which was a relief for I didn't have enough energy left to talk. As the lodge came into view, Kalen stopped.

"Goodbye, Eithne," he said. "Will you meet me tomorrow?"

My heart beat so loudly that he could probably hear it. "Yes."

I was determined not to watch him leave, but when I finally gave in and looked back, he was gone. I limped towards the lodge, my gait slow and awkward. Smoke streamed from the chimneys and lantern light shone around the drapes. The lodge was bedding down for the night. The animals would all be shut away in the barn, fed and watered. The house would be filled with noise and love and the good smells of dinner cooking. Sometimes I wondered whether I was the only one who ever felt lonely there.

EITHNE

*M*y dreams that night were filled with Kalen. I returned to every word he had said, over and over. Every raise of his eyebrows, every quirk of his lips. As dawn broke I was ready to leap out of bed and rush out to the stand of beech, but rain greeted me when I parted the curtains. It wasn't much more than a fine mist but certainly enough that I knew Mother would not let me leave the lodge. Hopefulness dissipated into disappointment and I returned to bed.

By the time I emerged again several hours later, drizzling rain had become a storm. The air was thick with moisture. Thunder boomed and my room brightened with each crackle of lightening. Disappointment became frustration and crankiness. With the sun hidden it was hard to tell the hour, but the rumble in my belly suggested it must be almost noon. I dragged myself out of bed and washed halfheartedly.

The house smelled of wet floors and smoky fires. It was cleaning day and Mother never let something as minor as the weather interfere with that. The servant women would have arrived at dawn, regardless of the rain. They were four widowed women who were permitted to live on Silver Downs land in exchange for their labour. Four servants was probably more than we needed but Mother wouldn't turn away a woman in need of employment. They were allowed to live in the cluster of small houses that lay a few minutes' walk from the main lodge and when Mother didn't need them, they helped in the fields, thus securing a portion of the crops for themselves. It was a hard way to make a living but Mother said there were worse fates that could befall a woman than honest labour.

The remnants of breakfast had been cleared away and there was no fresh bread left. I found an end of a loaf from yesterday and pulled up a low stool to the kitchen fireplace. Despite my rumbling stomach, the bread stuck in my throat and most of it ended up in a pile of crumbs that I tossed into the fire.

I tried to sit in my usual spot in the family room but my feet wouldn't stay still. I paced the house, getting in the way of the servant women, until Mother flapped her hands at me and shooed me away. I had thought that Papa and my brothers might be here somewhere, since they couldn't work outside in this weather, but perhaps they were occupied with chores in the barn.

I sat on a window seat, staring out at the fields. Everything was grey. The clouds, the rain, the snow on the ground. I couldn't see my little stand of beech trees from here. Did Kalen wait there for me? Did the fey notice weather? Perhaps the rain was of no account to him. He might be there even now, wondering why I didn't come. I pictured him standing in the shelter of a tree, water dripping from his ill-fitting clothes as the branches above him swayed in the wind.

I contemplated slipping out the back door. Mother would be horrified, but perhaps I could do it and be back before she realised. But I would be sopping wet and would have to make my way up to my bedchamber without being seen, likely leaving a trail of puddles on the clean floors.

And what if I injured myself? I might slip in the mud, for the ankle that bore my twisted foot had never been strong. If I fell heavily enough, I might not be able to get up without help. Nobody would look for me outside. If anyone even noted my absence, they would assume I was elsewhere in the lodge. I would have to wait, lying in the mud with the rain beating down on me, surrounded by thunder and lightening, until the storm passed and somebody ventured outside again. The picture in my mind was so vivid, I almost shed a tear for poor Eithne who lay in the mud, cold and injured and alone.

So I didn't creep out to look for Kalen but roamed the lodge until I rounded a corner and crashed into Fiachra's chest. He was solid for a druid, with the broad shoulders and dark hair that is common to the menfolk in our family. I had thought he would be thinner, frailer, but his form was much like that of Papa and Eremon.

Fiachra steadied me by grasping my upper arms. His warmth seeped through the sleeves of my woollen dress. I smiled up at him, somewhat tentatively, for this brother was mostly a stranger to me. He had arrived on the morn of Caedmon's handfasting but I had hardly seen him in the sevennight since.

"Good morning, Fiachra. Are you well?"

He quirked an eyebrow at me. "Is that really what you want to ask, Eithne?"

My mouth opened but nothing came out. I finally realised how close we still stood, barely more than a hand's width apart, and stepped back. His hands released me.

"I was merely being polite," I said.

"I care little for social niceties. Not in private, at any rate."

I had never before been alone with Fiachra, or any druid for that matter.

"If there is something you wish to ask, this would be a good moment in which to do so," he said.

"How do you know I want to ask you something?"

"Because you found me."

"But I wasn't looking for you."

"And yet you found me anyway. Does that not tell you something?"

"Is it not possible I found you inadvertently? That it just so happens we ended up wandering in the same part of the house?"

"I am not easy to find. If you found me, you were meant to. Now, what do you wish to ask?"

I bit my lower lip as I considered my options. Who better than a druid to ask about the nature of the fey? But when I opened my mouth, a different question came out.

"Why did you not want to be found?"

"I don't care much for the company of people."

"That sounds…" My voice trailed off for I didn't want to seem rude.

"I spend much time alone. My brethren and I pass many hours every day in solitude, practicing our training, learning the teachings. I am not accustomed to spending so much time with other folk."

"Why are you still here? Why do you not return to the druids?"

"Things are stirring here. Old power is rising. I am needed."

"What does that mean?"

"Tell me, sister, what is it you really want to ask?"

"What do you know of the fey?" Once I made up my mind, the words came out in a rush.

"Logic, reason, emotion. The fey see these things differently to how mortals do. Things that are important to us, are negligible to them."

"Are the old tales true?"

"Some are, and many more contain elements of truth."

I hesitated. My heart seemed to beat very loudly. "What of the tales of women who fall in love with the fey? Is it true they are never loved in return?"

Fiachra regarded me, his face giving no hint of his thoughts. "Perhaps somewhere, in the history of our people, there has been a mortal woman who fell for one of the fey and whose feelings were reciprocated. Perhaps they are always reciprocated, for a time at least."

I longed to ask more but was hesitant to reveal too much to this brother I barely knew. "Thank you," I said. "Your words… they give me much to think about."

I stepped back and turned to leave.

"Eithne."

I paused but did not turn to face him.

"Time is another thing the fey view differently. Because they live for eons, our lives are but a brief shift in the wind, a momentary flicker of candlelight. Understanding this gives much insight into the mindset of the fey."

I thought I understood what he was trying to say. I nodded and fled.

EITHNE

*T*he wet weather lingered for two days and I was almost out of my mind with frustration by the time it cleared. As soon as the rain stopped, I pulled on my coat and boots and slipped outside. I didn't tell Mother because she would worry about the wet and the cold, and would keep me inside until the ground was dry. How could I sit in the house and do nothing, when Kalen might even now be waiting?

The air was cold and so was the water that clung to everything: the grass, the trees, the hem of my dress. The breeze smelled crisp and fresh and tore right through my coat. I meandered along, trying to appear as if I had no particular destination in mind. My twisted foot always ached in wet weather, so hiding my limp was a little harder than usual. The sun seemed overly bright today, as if to make up for the days of grey, and as the clouds receded they revealed a brilliant blue sky.

As I rounded the rise that hid the trees from the lodge, my heart beat faster and it became even harder to maintain my sedate pace. I wrapped my coat tighter around me and pretended it was the cold breeze that made me shiver. If Kalen was indeed waiting for me, I did not want to look too eager. So I continued to make my way slowly to the trees although try as I might, I couldn't stop myself from walking just a little faster.

As I drew closer, my breath caught in my throat. Just a little farther and I would know whether he was there. With eager eyes I examined the beeches, tracing each silhouette, every familiar trunk and shrub. There, in the dark depths, was that a shadow that did not belong? But as I came closer, the shadow resolved into just another beech.

I walked faster but my foot slid in a patch of mud and I almost landed on my backside. Heart racing, I slowed and paid more attention to where I placed my feet.

"Kalen?" I called when I was close enough. "Kalen, are you there?"

The trees were silent and my heart stuttered. He wasn't there. But as I approached my rock, a shadow separated from the trees and moved towards me. He came out into the open and my heart began a crazy dance.

"You came," I said.

Kalen tilted his head to one side and eyed me curiously. "You did not think I would?"

"It's rained for the last two days. I thought... I didn't know whether you would have wondered why I didn't come. I can't go out if it's raining. Mother worries for me. She thinks I will fall ill." I was rambling. I shut my mouth with a snap.

"You said you would be here. I waited."

"I'm sorry. I couldn't."

He nodded. "I understand. You will not come to meet me if it rains, even if you said you would."

I took a deep breath, inhaling the scents of rain and mud, and willed myself to find the right words. "It's not that I didn't want to."

Perhaps things were different within fey families. Perhaps the younger fey did not have to seek permission to do things. Maybe that's why he didn't understand when I said I wasn't allowed.

"I can't stay long. It's too cold today and Mother will be worried if she realises I am gone. I just came..."

He waited and I tried to find words that were not quite as revealing as what I had almost said.

"I came to explain why I didn't come yesterday."

Still he showed no emotion. Had I upset him? Angered him? How could I make this right? I was growing too cold to stand here for much longer. Goosebumps prickled my skin and I wrapped my arms around my body, trying not to shiver.

"It is Imbolc tomorrow." My words came out in a rush. I had not planned this, had not even considered asking. "There will be a celebration here at Silver Downs."

I paused for breath and Kalen cocked his head at me, as if unsure what reaction I sought. I ploughed on before I lost my nerve.

"Will you come? To the feast? There will be dancing and a big fire."

"There will be many people."

"Of course. Everyone will be here."

"Your family would see us."

Excitement dimmed. "Yes, they might. But there will be lots of folk here. They won't know that you don't belong. You might be... I don't know... a worker from another estate. Or a visiting relative."

"What would we do there?"

"The same as everyone else. We could eat and talk and watch folk dance."

Kalen lifted an eyebrow at me and his face finally showed a spark of emotion. "I enjoy dancing."

"I've never tried. I have not the strength for it. But I like watching the dancers."

The wind changed direction and an icy gust dove under my coat. I could no longer hide my shivers. The sun wasn't shining quite as brightly anymore and a few grey clouds were scattered over the previously clear sky.

"You are cold," Kalen said and his voice was more curious than anything else.

"The wind..." My teeth chattered. "I should go back."

Kalen nodded and stepped back into the trees. "Goodbye."

"Wait, will you meet me tomorrow night?"

But he was already gone. I clutched my coat tighter around me and set off for home. He hadn't said yes but he also hadn't said no. That meant I could hope.

EITHNE

*M*y fingers fumbled with the red ribbon as I attempted to tie it around my braid. It took three attempts before I managed to fasten it neatly. The face that stared at me from my hand mirror wore flushed cheeks and bright eyes. I wrapped another ribbon around my wrist, just beneath the bottom of my sleeve, and admired the glimpse of red fabric as I lifted my arm.

"Eithne, are you ready?" Mother's voice drifted up the stairs.

"I'm coming," I called. I swiftly set the hand mirror down on the dresser and straightened my gown one last time. I had always liked the way this gown skimmed my hips and then flared out slightly before finishing just short of the ground. It made me look not quite as skinny. I envied Mother's broad hips and ample breasts, while knowing I would never have such a figure. My gown hung a little looser than usual but I had not thought to try it on in time to take in the seams.

The longer I stood there preening, the longer it would be before I found out whether or not Kalen would come. I hurried down the stairs and pulled on my warmest coat. I draped my scarf over my braided hair and wound the ends around my neck, then retrieved my gloves from my coat pocket and pulled them on as I left the house. Mother was only just ahead of me and she paused to wait while I caught up.

The sun was just setting behind the far off horizon and the sky was a riot of purple and orange. Tonight's festivities celebrated the start of spring. The long days of winter were almost at an end. The ewes were heavy with lambs, the snow was starting to melt and tiny buds had already appeared on ash and birch and beech.

The first cartloads of guests had just arrived and they went straight to where a huge fire had been built some distance from the lodge. They helped themselves to mugs of ale from the long tables and milled around, drinking and greeting friends and generally making lots of noise. Inside my gloves, my palms grew sweaty. Shadows were creeping in and I couldn't see the faces of those on the far side of the fire clearly enough to know whether Kalen was there.

"Eithne, don't go too far." Mother tucked a stray strand of hair back behind my ear. "You're still not very strong."

"I'll be fine, Mother. I'm going to see if I can find the Three Trees girls."

"Stay near the fire. Make sure you eat something and go back to the house if you start to get chilled."

I forced a smile at her and left. I was not a child who needed to be fussed over. I was seventeen summers old, which made me a grown woman and old enough to be married. I wove through the folk gathered around the fire, searching for the familiar pale face. Normally I avoided crowds as much as possible. Their clamour made my head hurt and I always feared being trampled. But Kalen would hardly show himself if I stood next to Mother all night.

The scent of sizzling roast meat and fresh bread filled the air but I wasn't hungry. The only thing I wanted right now was to find Kalen. I was almost knocked to the ground by a man who flung his arm out to the side as he spoke. He grinned an apology at me and then turned back to the woman he was speaking with. She smiled up at him, an obvious invitation in her eyes.

My twisted foot was starting to ache so I looked around for a bench. Finally I spotted a vacated seat where two girls had been sitting a few moments before. I sank down onto the bench gratefully and removed my gloves, tucking them into the pocket of my jacket. Someone sat next to me, a little too close for my liking, and I edged over slightly to put more space between us. Then I noticed the long, pale fingers of my companion.

"Kalen."

In the flickering light of the fire, his pale skin and too-red lips weren't quite as obvious as usual. He wore darkly coloured clothes and a thick cloak.

"I've been looking for you," I said.

"I did not expect this many people."

"It's Imbolc. Spring is on its way."

"It does not look all that different from our festivities."

"I wish I could see them some day." I spoke without thinking.

"I could take you there now."

"You know I can't."

"Why not?"

"I can't just disappear. Mother would worry."

We sat silently for a while. I couldn't tell whether he was irritated or just being quiet. A fiddler started a merry tune and I caught myself tapping my toes in time with it. Folk paired up and began dancing. I shot a sideways glance at Kalen. If I were a different person, I might have asked if he wanted to join them, but folk would stare if they saw me dancing and Mother would worry that I exerted myself.

My clenched fists were resting on my knees and Kalen slid his hand over them. His fingers were cool and barely touched mine.

"Come, Eithne, dance with me."

My mouth fell open. For someone who didn't want to be seen, now he wanted to dance with me in public?

"I don't know whether that's a good idea," I said, although my feet longed to move and I wanted nothing more than to throw myself into the crowd and dance until I was sweaty and exhausted. Not that it would take long.

He tugged gently on my hands. "I can't stay. One dance and then I must go."

Before I could think too hard about it, I stood. He took my hand and pulled me into the crowd. I was familiar enough with the steps from all my years of watching and Kalen picked them up quickly.

I hadn't been this close to him before and he was taller than I thought. The top of my head barely came up to his shoulders. He held my hands lightly, his cool fingers gentle. I felt tiny next to him, although he himself was slender. Only a couple of handspans of air was between his body and mine. I wanted to lean in against him and feel his warmth. I wondered what it would be like to kiss him and quickly banished the thought from my mind lest he read it on my face. My heart pounded, as much from excitement as from the exertion.

We moved together, now closer, now farther apart. The steps were quicker than I had expected and I could barely keep up. Kalen released my hands briefly as we each took a step backwards and spun in a quick circle. We came back together and he took my hands again before my fingers had time to grow cold.

The tune was only halfway over before my feet began to slow and my breath came in gasps. I kept moving though, determined to last the whole dance, although now I was a beat or two behind the melody. Our dance seemed to last for hours and at the same time, it passed in moments.

The song ended and the lingering notes of the fiddle faded away. After a moment of silence, the next song started and Kalen pulled me back through the crowd. Our vacated bench had been claimed so he paused in a shadowy spot a little distance from the fire.

"It is time for me to leave, Eithne. I am glad we were able to dance together tonight."

"Me too." I smiled up at him, still trying to catch my breath and wishing I could look more elegant as I did.

He released my hand and I felt a pang of disappointment.

"Farewell," he said and stepped back.

"Will I see you tomorrow?"

"Of course."

Kalen touched one cool finger to my lips. Then he was gone, melting away into the dark. Nobody looked at him as he slipped through the crowd. Perhaps he used a charm of some sort to render himself unnoticeable. The old tales told of the fey doing such things.

I pressed my fingers to the spot where he had touched my lips. It hadn't been a kiss but it was something close. I pushed my way through the crowd until I found a vacant bench close by the fire. I settled in for the rest of the evening. Mother would worry I was ill if I left so early so I would sit by the fire, watching the dancers and thinking about Kalen.

SUMERLED

*K*alen doesn't know I follow him. When he slips away through the woods that separate our world from that of the mortals, I sneak along behind. I can't figure out why he is so fascinated with them. They are weak and boring with tepid lives and indifferent deaths. Yet still he watches.

At first it was just every now and again. Then his forays into the mortal world came every few days. Now he goes to them every day, or rather, he goes to *her* every day.

I follow and hide. The woods are my home so I know how to move silently. I know just where to put my foot to avoid the crackle of leaves or the snap of a twig. I know how to move so silently that the woodlarks don't sing a warning. He is not far ahead of me as I crouch behind a holly bush and peek through. I'm certain Kalen doesn't know I'm watching until he sneaks up behind me and grabs me by the scruff of my neck.

"Sumerled," he hisses. "What are you doing here?"

Started, the woodlarks begin warbling.

He yanks me up, his hands rough. My teeth slam together as he deposits me on my feet.

"Following you." My voice is petulant and I refuse to look at him.

"Why?"

"Felt like it."

Kalen grabs me by my shoulders and shakes me. I taste blood where I have bitten my tongue.

"Why are you following me, boy?"

"Why do you keep going to her? She's just a boring mortal."

He shakes me again, so hard I think my head might fall off.

"What have you seen?" he says. "What do you know of her?"

I clamp my jaws shut. I will not tell him anything. He pushes me away and then turns and strides off. I hesitate but only moments pass before I am scurrying after him, stumbling over a fallen branch in my hurry.

"Kalen, wait for me."

"Go away."

"I bet I know something about her that you don't."

He hesitates, mid-stride, then keeps walking. "Tell me then, and prove yourself useful. Otherwise, go away."

I pause. What to tell? And what to save in case I need it later? I tell him my best secret.

"She is deformed. You could have at least picked one that is whole and sound."

"She's not deformed."

"Her foot-"

"I know about her foot." He whirls around and grabs me by the shoulder which already feels bruised from his previous abuse. "Sumerled, why have you been following me? Did someone tell you to?"

"I'm not telling."

He snarls and releases me, then storms off.

"Kalen-"

"Go. Away."

I try to follow but the woods are just as much Kalen's home as they are mine. He slips between beech and oak, and is gone. I look for signs of which direction he took — a patch of disturbed leaf litter, a broken twig, a heel print in the mud — but there is nothing. And I suddenly realise that if he does not want to be found, I cannot find him. He knew I was following all along. He waited for me to reveal myself. Perhaps if I had, our encounter would have been different. He might have trusted me. But I hid and thought I followed in secret. I was trying to protect him but instead I pushed him further away from me.

GRAINNE

*W*aking up beside Caedmon each morning was still something to be savoured. I was aware of his presence before I opened my eyes, even when his body wasn't touching mine. He warmed the bed beneath our blankets and his breaths, when he slept, were long and deep.

I treasured these moments for it would not be long before I would once again be waking up alone. Imbolc had passed and winter drew to a close. But we had some time together yet: a sevennight, maybe two if I was lucky. Already beech and ash bore tiny buds that would soon open into new leaves. The days were a little warmer and the nights less frosty. When I looked out the window, snow blanketed the fields all the way to the horizon but that would soon melt, the rivers would thaw and Caedmon would leave.

We had chosen a site for our home and Caedmon had already hired some men to build it. His brother Sitric, who intended to become a scribe once their father could spare him, had documented the details. In this way Caedmon could ensure our lodge would be exactly as he envisioned, even if he wasn't present for its building.

I was well pleased with the location, for the lodge would have a sunny aspect with a fine view of rolling hills from my work room.

There I would oversee the running of our house and do small chores such as darning socks. I would have a servant woman — Agata had already offered one of the women bonded to Silver Downs. We would be well out of sight of both the main lodge and also Eremon and Niamh's home, although both were only a short walk away. Here, surrounded by hills, we would have the illusion of privacy while being close to help and companionship.

Once Caedmon left, I would continue to live in his childhood home until our own was built. My heart froze whenever I thought about his departure. The long trek back to the campaign front would take ten days. The journey would be cold, and lonely for a man who travelled alone. I had asked Caedmon if he worried about sleeping outdoors, whether he feared robbers or wild animals, but he laughed and said nothing much scared him.

Beside me, Caedmon's breathing changed, signalling he had woken. I rolled over to face him. His short hair was dishevelled and when he first woke in the mornings, he always looked a little confused at finding me in his bed.

"Good morning, sleepy head," I said. "I thought soldiers woke at the crack of dawn. Aren't you supposed to get up early to practice or something?"

Caedmon smiled and reached out to push aside a lock of hair that had fallen over my face. "I'll be resuming my training soon enough. I can afford a few late mornings in the meantime."

"Do you know when you might come home again?" I regretted it as soon as the words left my mouth, for I had promised myself I wouldn't ask. After all, he had made it clear that our handfasting was based on practicality, not love. But still, my stupid heart yearned to know.

Caedmon's hand stilled in my hair. He closed his eyes briefly and inhaled deeply.

"I know you have to go," I said quickly. "And I'm not asking that you don't. I don't mind, truly. It would just be easier if I knew when you might return. You have only ever come home when you were injured. I wondered whether your commander might give you leave to return more often now that you are handfasted."

"There's something I need to tell you," he said, and his gaze skittered away from mine and his hand withdrew from my hair. "I would have told you before I left anyway, but you might as well hear it now, since you asked."

"What is it? You sound so serious." My heart stuttered, but no, it couldn't be anything bad. It wasn't possible.

"A few months ago, I had a strange dream." Caedmon's voice was calm enough, but he didn't look at me as he spoke. "I saw myself lying in a ditch, with my throat slit. Dead."

A chill ran through my body and I edged a little closer to him to feel his warmth. "That's horrible."

"It was a true dream."

"How do you know?"

I felt, rather than saw, his shrug beneath the blankets.

"I just know. I saw my dead body and I looked no older than I do now."

"Does this have something to do with why you decided to handfast?" Damn my stupid heart. A tiny part of me had hoped that maybe somewhere, buried too deep for him to notice, were some feelings for me.

"Death approaches, my dear Grainne. I don't believe I will come home again, not alive at any rate. I did not want to die without having handfasted. I wanted, just for a little while, to experience this. I hoped to leave behind an heir, even if there is no time for more. I can die without regret if I do not produce a soldier and a druid, but it would mean a lot to me to have an heir. I've been well paid for risking the dangers of a soldier. Enough for you to be comfortable for a good long while. You and our son."

"I don't care about how much money you have." I fought to keep my voice steady. I would not cry in front of him. "Why didn't you tell me earlier?"

"I'm sorry. It was selfish of me, I know. But I thought you would not want me if you knew."

I bit my tongue, for if I said anything right now, it would probably be that I loved him. That I would take whatever he had to offer, no matter how little it was.

"Say something, Grainne." Caedmon's warm hand touched my cheek ever so gently. "Tell me what you are thinking. If you are angry with me, it is no more than I deserve."

"I'm not angry. I just don't believe it was a true dream. I can't." My voice wavered on the last word and I rolled onto my back so he wouldn't see the tears that welled in my eyes.

"I didn't mean to hurt you. I thought I knew something about having a wife from watching my parents, but it seems not. I'm sorry, Grainne. I did not expect you to take it so hard. I should have told you from the start but I knew you wouldn't take me."

"I would have." I bit my tongue again before I said too much.

He wrapped his arms around me, drawing me into his warmth. I leaned my head on his chest, drinking in his scent and the sound of his heart beating beside my ear.

"Forgive me," he said.

"I already have."

He kissed me and it was some time before either of us thought of leaving the bed. Eventually Caedmon rose. I lay under the blankets, watching beneath my lashes as he washed in the basin. It was still surreal to think that this bedchamber in which he had grown up was now mine too. Caedmon leaned over to kiss my cheek.

"Do you want me to start the fire before I go?" he asked.

"No, I'll be quick."

"I'll see you downstairs then."

I waited until the door closed behind him before I climbed out from under the blankets. I was still somewhat shy about him seeing me unclothed. It was a relief to be able to wash and dress without wondering whether he watched, although he always closed his eyes and pretended to sleep.

I found Caedmon downstairs at the dining table, halfway through a bowl of porridge. He was all hard muscle from years of soldiering and ate enough for two people. I brushed away a sprinkling of crumbs that the servant had missed. Evidence that someone, at least, had eaten here earlier this morning. Shouts in a boyish voice came from outside. One of Eremon and Niamh's twins, most likely.

"I wanted to show you around the estate some more today, if you don't mind a walk. Introduce you to the tenants," Caedmon said between mouthfuls. "I'm sorry there aren't many women your age here. Just Eithne, although she's a year or two younger than you."

"Only a year? She seems much younger." I nibbled at my bread but Caedmon's words about his dream had ruined any appetite I might have had. The honey tasted sickly sweet on my tongue.

"She won't be much of a friend for you, I'm afraid." He scraped out the last of his porridge. "You know she is often ill and confined to bed. But she will be company every now and then, if nothing else."

"I'm sure Eithne and I will be firm friends."

"I worry that you will be lonely once I am gone."

I tried to keep my face calm. "You're not to worry about me. I don't want you distracted from your duties. I am perfectly capable of making myself useful and keeping busy. Eithne will be my friend and my sisters are not all that far away. I will speak to Agata about giving me some chores. There's little else I need."

Except you, my heart whispered. *The only other thing I need is for you to come back to me safe.*

GRAINNE

A few days later Caedmon took me to view the progress on our house. As we lingered by the river, we discovered that the ice near the edge had softened and was fast turning to slush.

"It's time," Caedmon said and squeezed my hand.

I said nothing as I stared at the melting ice, for my throat was tight with a sob I didn't want him to hear.

"When will you leave?" I asked at length, when I thought I finally had my voice under control.

"Tomorrow." His tone was regretful. "I'm sorry, I know it will be hard for you once I'm gone."

"Don't worry about me." I forced a bright voice, although to my own ear it didn't ring true. "I'll be just fine and waiting for you to return."

Caedmon took in a long shuddering breath and turned to face me. "Grainne, I need you to believe me. I won't be coming back. I'm sorry we have been handfasted for such a short time but I don't want you to live with false hope. You are a fine woman and I wish I had thought to hand-fast with you earlier."

"Do you expect me to handfast with someone else?" My voice was light for I didn't believe him, even if thoughts of his dream still gave me chills. I would miss him, and I would worry for his safety every minute, but I did not believe in his omen of impending death.

"You are young, Grainne. Too young to live the rest of your life as a widow. But if you choose to, Papa and Eremon would never turn you out of Silver Downs. You will have a house. I have quite a lot of coins saved; Sitric has the details. It should last you many years if you are careful with it. When the coin runs out, I suppose you will either need to take some work or handfast. It will be up to you."

I fought to shake off the gloom his words cast over me. "Come," I said. "I'll race you back to the house, but only if you give me a head start."

He laughed. "I will count to ten and then follow. You had better be fast if you think to beat me."

I took off running, pounding my legs as hard as I could through the melting snow. The breeze in my hair made me smile and his words of dire warning were little more than a memory by the time he caught up to me.

That evening the family gathered at Silver Downs to farewell him. We sat around the long table and feasted on roasted wild boar and honeyed winter roots. The food smelled rich and wonderful, but tasted like ash in my mouth. The brothers were all there. Fiachra offered no explanation for his extended presence and I never heard anyone ask. Fionn and Agata were no doubt simply happy to have the family complete for a short time.

Agata was pale and quiet that evening. She found it hard to say goodbye to her soldier son, no matter how many times it had to be done. Fionn was jovial. If he felt the same sadness as Agata, he hid it better.

Diarmuid appeared to be in a more agreeable mood than usual, even answering a question from me with a brief twist of the lips that might have been a smile. He had been strange recently. Or perhaps he was always like that; I didn't know him well enough to tell. I had sensed a growing rift between him and Caedmon. Usually they were inseparable while Caedmon was home but some argument had happened around Midwinter. Caedmon wouldn't speak of it, except to say he regretted the situation. Diarmuid wouldn't even look at him. They appeared in the same room together only at mealtimes and only long enough for Diarmuid to gulp down his meal. He missed a number of opportunities for tale telling, which struck me as odd, given he was supposed to be a bard.

After the meal, we retired to the family room and gathered around the fireplace. Eremon built up the fire, although this close to spring it was hardly needed. This was the last time the family would be together for many months. Caedmon and I, sitting close together on a bench, his arm around my shoulders, my hand resting on his thigh. Eremon and Niamh and their boys. Marrec and Conn towards the back of the room. Fionn and Agata. Sitric. Fiachra. Eithne, in a prime position close by the fire.

"We want a stirring tale tonight, Diarmuid," Fionn said, his voice still light.

I shuddered as Diarmuid took his place in front of the fireplace. I had no desire to hear another of his twisted tales. He and Caedmon exchanged a long look. Diarmuid was the first to look away.

Beside me, Caedmon's body was tense. The arm which had been draped loosely across my shoulders now gripped a little too tightly. I leaned against him, hoping he would take comfort in my nearness.

Diarmuid stood silently for a long time, fists clenched at his sides. He looked like someone preparing for battle, not a man about to tell a tale. We waited in silence and I shifted uneasily.

"There was once a soldier," Diarmuid said. "A simple man. He knew nothing but war and fighting. At length he decided it was time he took a bride so he returned home and chose a girl. They were handfasted in a ceremony under an ancient oak tree."

I was suddenly too hot and my stomach churned. Diarmuid's voice was cold and filled with power. If I had not known otherwise, I might have mistaken him for a druid rather than a bard.

"The night before the soldier was due to return to the campaign, he woke long before dawn. A strange state came over him and he became something that was not like himself. He beat his new bride bloody. He nipped at her tender skin with his teeth and tore handfuls of hair from her head. He slapped her face and bruised her body. When dawn came, he kissed his bride goodbye, picked up his pack, and set off on the long walk back to the campaign.

"When the bride's family learnt of what had befallen her, her father and brothers agreed they could not leave such a crime unpunished. They set off after the soldier."

My stomach rolled and I swallowed hard against the urge to vomit. I knew exactly where this tale was headed. Obviously Caedmon had shared his dire premonition with Diarmuid and the bard thought it clever to work it into a tale. I tried to think of more pleasant things: summer skies, fish leaping in a running stream, Caedmon's strong arms around me, the babe I hoped I carried within me. Block out the words. Don't listen. Don't let his awful tale get inside your head or you will worry until Caedmon returns again. Don't listen. Don't listen.

But I couldn't stop myself from listening. I had to know the soldier's fate. Sure enough, the bride's menfolk caught up to the soldier and beat him. They slit his throat and left him lying in a ditch by the road. He died, alone, looking up at the sky.

The tale ended and the silence was loud. Diarmuid looked uncomfortable now. Gone was the proud lift of his head and the arrogant smirk. Now his shoulders were slightly hunched and he shifted from foot to foot.

"You all right?" Caedmon murmured in my ear.

"How can he tell such a thing?"

"Telling tales is what he does. But yes, some of them are awful. Don't let it affect you. They are just tales."

I noted the odd tone to Caedmon's voice. He too was disturbed, more than he let show. I reached up to squeeze the hand that hung over my shoulder.

We all sat in silence, shifting uneasily in our seats. I inhaled a shaky breath and the scent of flames and pinecones caught in my lungs. Several of the brothers darted sideways glances at me. The silence stretched uncomfortably, broken only by the crackle of the fire.

"Not exactly an uplifting tale with which to send me off, little brother," Caedmon said, finally.

"It was a different sort of tale," I said, my voice wavering somewhat.

Diarmuid shot me a look that might almost have been grateful and Caedmon squeezed my shoulders.

At length, Eremon offered to share a tale. He moved to the front of the room. Diarmuid sat alone, neither brother nor sister choosing to sit with him for the evening's entertainment. I wanted to love my new family but when it came to Diarmuid, I was torn between revulsion and something like fear.

GRAINNE

*W*e lingered in the family room for some time after Diarmuid's tale, although when I next looked for the bard, he was gone. Eremon shared a tale about the hounds of Annwn and Sitric told a funny little tale about a man whose sole aim in life was to catch a fish.

Caedmon and I were sitting too far away from the fire to feel its heat and despite the warmth of his body beside me, I still felt chilled. The image of a soldier lying dead on the ground, throat slit and eyes staring sightlessly, would not leave my mind. Every time I blinked, I saw him. When I looked at Caedmon, I saw the dead soldier. Damn Diarmuid for putting such thoughts in my mind. Caedmon noticed my restlessness and squeezed my shoulders. A lift of his eyebrows asked whether I was all right.

"Did you tell him about your dream?" I murmured.

"Yes, although I gave sparse detail. I am sorry if his tale disturbed you."

I shrugged and didn't answer. I didn't want to ruin his final evening at home by being argumentative. Caedmon was soon absorbed in conversation with his brothers. I was content to sit beside him and hold his hand. Eventually tiredness began to cloud my head and Caedmon noticed me restraining a yawn.

"I intend to leave early in the morning," he said to the family. "So I will make my farewells now."

They gathered around, Agata and Eithne hugging him hard, Fionn and the boys slapping him on the back. Caedmon didn't hurry through his farewells but took time to speak a few words to each person. Eithne, in particular, he spent long moments with and her eyes glistened as she left the room immediately afterwards. There were tender words for his mother and a joke for each of the boys. His father, Fionn, was the last, and his face was haunted.

"Take care of yourself, son," Fionn said as he embraced Caedmon.

"Look after Grainne for me," Caedmon said. "Eremon will manage the men building the house and Sitric has my finances, but anything else she needs..."

"Don't you worry about her. She will be well taken care of. You know your brothers and I will not let you down."

"If..." Whatever else Caedmon intended to say went unspoken but Fionn nodded.

"I know. And I will."

"Thank you."

They embraced and then Caedmon and I went up to our bedchamber. I didn't ask what those last comments with Fionn referred to. If Caedmon wanted to speak of it, he would.

There were no final preparations to be done, for he had already filled his pack and left it leaning against the wall. I tried not to picture him shouldering it and walking away from me. Tried not to picture this chamber without him in it. My stomach clenched and tears filled my eyes. I blinked them away before he could see.

Caedmon had stirred up the fire, undressed and was already in bed. I changed into my nightgown and then climbed in beside him, gladly sinking down into the embrace he offered. He kissed me and I savoured the warmth of his body pressed against mine. It might be a long time before I could touch him again. We lingered over these final embraces and the night was late before Caedmon reached over to put out the lamp.

I lay with my eyes open, fearful that I'd fall asleep despite my intentions of remaining awake. I had a plan, a way I might save him from Diarmuid's tale. Caedmon lay on his belly with an arm draped across my chest and I watched him in the dim orange light from the fire, which sent shifting shadows around the room. His face was mostly in darkness but I knew every feature. I shifted a little closer so I could inhale his scent, trying with every breath to memorise it. Tears tracked down my cheeks, despite my best efforts not to cry, but I tried not to give myself away.

Caedmon seemed to take a long time to fall asleep but finally his breathing was deep and steady. I very slowly pushed his arm off my chest and slid out of the bed. He stirred and I froze, my heart pounding. But he merely murmured something and rolled over. His long, slow breathing resumed.

I tiptoed to the dresser. Hidden in one of my drawers was a small pouch Caedmon had never seen. I knew exactly where it was but wasn't sure I could retrieve it in the dark without making some noise. But the drawer that usually opened with a creak was soundless and my fingers reached straight for the pouch, hidden under my undergarments where I was sure Caedmon would never have reason to look.

It seemed the elements were working with me tonight for even the door didn't make a sound as I eased it open. I crept along the hall and down the stairs. No candlelight shone from under any of the doors as I stole through the lodge. If only I could do what I needed to before anyone found me.

I tiptoed into the kitchen and set the pouch on a work bench while I fumbled for a candle. Before I could find one, a light flared behind me. Heart pounding, I turned. The druid brother, Fiachra, stood there, a candle in his hand. He set it down on the bench, near enough to my pouch to indicate he had already seen it.

"Be careful, Grainne," he said. "You tread a dangerous path."

"How much do you know?"

"Nothing for certain. I see you are on the cusp of a decision. A very dangerous one."

"So what should I do?"

"I cannot make your decision for you. I can only warn you. Be very careful in what you ask, for a simple request can have consequences one could never have dreamed of."

There was no point in pretending I didn't know what he meant and perhaps he could advise me. I was certainly in need of wisdom.

"I must keep him safe. Or at least try."

"Good intentions do not mean the outcome will be as you intend."

"I can't let him leave tomorrow unprotected."

"I'm not suggesting you don't try, or even that you do. I am simply warning you to be cautious."

"Do you know what I intend to do?"

"I see choices only. I cannot know what decision you will make, but be sure you can accept the consequences before you act."

"What are the consequences? Either I manage to protect him, or I don't. I succeed or I fail. There are no other possibilities."

I might have expected Fiachra would smile at my blunt assessment but his face was solemn. From a pocket within his robes, he produced a black feather and held it out to me.

"Include this in your ritual."

The feather was light and silky in my fingers. "A raven feather? What is the significance in this?"

"If you do not know what a raven signifies to our family, this is not the time to reveal tightly-held secrets. The raven is a mysterious and powerful creature. The raven this particular feather came from even more so. It will add strength to your ritual. And strength is something you will need much of."

"Thank you."

He nodded and turned to leave without another word.

"Fiachra," I said softly, just before he slipped out the door. He turned to face me. "Would you stay with me? Help me?"

"I'm sorry, Grainne, I can't. This is your journey. I can only watch." Then he was gone.

I shook off his strange words. I needed to move swiftly for every moment I dallied was another moment in which Caedmon might wake and come looking for me. I unwound the ribbon sealing the pouch and spilled its contents onto the work bench. There was a very small bronze bowl with a suitably sized grinding stone, some dried herbs — sage, yarrow and rue — and a small vial of water that had been blessed by a druid.

I placed the herbs in the bowl and swiftly ground them. Once they were reduced to a fine powder, I added a few drops of water from the vial, then laid the raven's feather across them. How had Fiachra known that a token of air was the final element of my ritual? For I had herbs from the earth, blessed water, and a candle's flame for fire. I had intended to add my own breath to represent the air.

I tilted Fiachra's candle down into the bowl and set fire to its contents. Despite the water, tiny flames caught immediately. I took a deep breath, steeling myself.

"Beings of earth and air, beings of water and fire, I implore you." My voice trembled a little and I took another breath, trying to steady myself. "Watch over my love. Keep him safe and return him to me again, whole of body and sound of mind."

The burning herbs were pungent, their scent magnified as the fire consumed them. The feather was the last item to be devoured. A flame danced along its length, taking its time with this final gift. Once there was nothing left to eat, the flames died down and with a gentle puff of my breath, they were gone.

I wrapped the pouch around the bowl, careful not to burn my fingers. It was done. I had invoked the elements to request their protection. If they found my offerings acceptable, they would give what I had asked. There was nothing else I could do.

As I turned to leave, I noticed a figure standing in the shadows in the corner. At first I thought it was Fiachra, come back to watch and maybe even to help, despite his words. But as the man stepped forward into the meagre candle light, I realised I had never seen him before.

He was tall and thin with sickly white skin and lips that looked far too red. His cheekbones were high and his face was somewhat pretty although foreign. My heart pounded and I was sharply aware that I was alone in a dark room with a stranger.

"Who are you?" I demanded. "You shouldn't be here. Come another step closer and I will scream for my husband and his brothers."

His smile was slow and lazy. "They will not hear you scream, pretty one. Go ahead if you feel you must."

"What do you want?" I took a couple of steps backward, toward the door, in case I needed to flee swiftly.

He gestured towards the pouch in my hand, his long, slender fingers making the simple gesture somehow appear both elegant and obscene.

"That was an… interesting ritual."

"You had no right to watch. That was private."

"Perhaps next time you wish for privacy, you should check whether anyone watches."

"How long have you been here?"

"Longer than you. Longer than any mortal."

So he was fey. I was in more danger than I had thought.

"I meant, how long were you standing in the corner, watching me?"

He shrugged. "Perhaps it was long enough. Perhaps it was too long. Who can say?"

"What do you want?" My fingers tightened on my pouch. I wasn't sure I wanted to hear his answer.

"Your ritual was one of protection."

"My husband may be in danger."

"So you try to shield him."

"I am his wife." My tone was fierce. "I will do anything I must to protect him."

"Even if he doesn't return your love?"

His words stung. How could he know such a thing?

"He hasn't had time to learn to love me. He will, one day, if I can keep him safe long enough."

"What would you give if I could guarantee his safety?"

I held myself very still. Even though I had not grown up with a bard in my family as Caedmon had, I was still familiar enough with the old tales to know that pacts with the fey were not to be undertaken lightly. "Tell me exactly what you mean."

"I mean what I say. No more and no less. I could take your husband to a safe place, where the danger you fear cannot find him. But there is always a cost."

"What would the cost be?"

"What do you have to give?"

"I have nothing. No jewellery or riches. No fine fabrics or elaborate embroidery."

"Everyone has something. A price they can pay."

"I have only myself."

"Is that your offer?"

"Myself? What do you mean?"

"You offer yourself in exchange for your husband's safety?"

My heart stuttered and then continued at double speed. "Do you intend to kill me?"

"Kill you? No, I intend to ravish you."

His tone was devoid of emotion and the words chilled me. I took a step back, longing to flee but needing to see this conversation through to the end. "What exactly do you mean?"

"You do not understand the concept?"

"I want to be very clear as to what you are suggesting."

"I'm suggesting nothing more than to take advantage of the price you are willing to pay. You offered yourself. I am tempted to accept."

"And how long would this arrangement last?" Thank the gods I had learned enough from the old tales to ensure I did not agree to some endless contract.

"How long do you want your husband to be safe?"

"Until the tale his bard brother told has no power over him."

"And how long do you offer yourself in exchange?"

I hesitated. What would be a fair deal? "One night. From now until the sun comes up tomorrow."

"That is a paltry exchange, for the night is already half over."

"That's my offer. If you don't want it, I'll find another way to protect him."

"I accept. Go to your bedchamber. I will take your husband away."

"Can I see him first? To say goodbye."

"That was not part of our contract."

"Please?" I was near tears now, panic rising in my throat. What had I done? Had I cursed Caedmon to be sent away forever? Had I damned myself to spend the rest of my life without my beloved?

"I will return presently. Tell nobody."

"I've changed my mind." Fear smothered my lungs and stifled my heart. "I want to re-negotiate."

"You have already agreed. The terms are fixed."

"Wait," I called, but he was gone.

Forgetting to be quiet, I raced through the lodge and up the stairs. Along the hallway. Into our bedchamber. The bed was empty, the covers tossed to the floor. Caedmon was gone and the fey man waited there for me.

"Where have you taken my husband?" My breath caught in my throat and I could barely speak.

"To a safe place, as we agreed. And now it is time for your payment."

The door closed behind me. I reached for it, turned the knob, but it was stuck fast.

"It won't open until I allow it." His voice came from close behind me.

I didn't answer but pounded on the door, hard enough to bruise my hands.

"Nobody can hear you in here. I have set a charm of silence on this chamber. You can scream, if you wish, and they will still not hear. Scream for me, Grainne."

Scream I did and I pounded on the door until blood ran from my fists. But nobody came. At length I stopped and fought to compose myself. My breathing was rapid and my heartbeat erratic. I wiped tears from my face, smearing blood on my cheeks as I did so. Once I was suitably calm, I turned back to the fey.

"Do you have a name?"

"Of course I do."

"Tell it to me. If we are to be intimate, which I assume is your intention, the least you can do is give me your name."

"The least I can do, Grainne? After having taken your loved one to a place where he will be safe? After guaranteeing that so long as you uphold your end of our agreement, he will continue to be safe?"

"You may only have me for one night. But you will keep Caedmon safe for as long as is needed. That was the agreement."

"It was. You drive a hard bargain."

"Your name."

"You may call me Lunn."

"Is that your true name?"

"What does it matter? You need a name to call me by, a name to scream. Lunn will do as well as any."

"Fine. Lunn. Now what do you want of me?"

Lunn inched closer, his gaze never leaving mine, his grin predatory. When he came close enough to touch me, he reached out one slender-fingered hand and trailed it along my throat and down between my breasts. I could barely restrain my shudder. I had never thought to have another touch me in this way, not after my handfasting. *It is for Caedmon,* I reminded myself. *I will do anything if it keeps him safe. Anything.*

Lunn leapt at me, hands outstretched although later in my nightmares I recalled them as claws. He tore my nightgown from my body, slashing it into long strips that drifted to the floor with a casualness I could not imitate. Once I was naked, he dug his fingernails into my soft skin, tearing it almost as easily as my gown. Blood seeped from the wounds.

He leaned in closer, closer. I thought, for an instant, he intended to kiss me. But he turned his head at the last moment and bit me on the shoulder, hard. His teeth sank into my skin, almost to the bone. I screamed.

I screamed again as he hit me. As he dug his nails into the soft skin where my limbs joined my body. I screamed as he tore the hair from my head in clumps, letting them drift slowly to the floor where they lay in splatters of my own blood. I screamed as he abused me in ways I could never have imagined. When I could scream no longer, I sobbed silently, the tears falling from my face to land, burning, in my wounds.

At times the night seemed endless and I thought I would die before he finished. Sometimes I wished I was already dead. But the sun always rises and it did, finally. As the first rays streamed in through the window, Lunn left without a word.

I lay on the floor in my own blood and hair, curled into a ball. I couldn't even cry anymore. No one pain was distinguishable from the others. Everything hurt. Everything bled. My soul was bruised. But Caedmon was safe. Whatever it had cost me, I had saved him.

GRAINNE

I lay on the floor as sunlight brightened the room. My body was bruised and battered. The woven mat under my cheek was wet through with my own blood but I didn't have the strength to move. My ears rang, either from my seemingly endless screams or because Lunn had hit me there.

I hurt everywhere. I tried occasionally to rise but my limbs seemed boneless and I could do nothing more than lift my head. The room around me blurred. I didn't know whether it was because something was wrong with my eyes or merely because I cried. My heart beat slowly and weakly, and every now and then it seemed to pause for a long moment. Was it possible to experience so much pain that one's heart simply stopped? After what seemed like an aeon, somebody rapped firmly on the door.

"Caedmon, you lazy boy, are you getting up today? I thought you intended to leave at sunrise."

I didn't have the strength to voice a reply but I must have made some noise for the knock came again, louder this time.

"Caedmon? Is everything all right in there?"

"Help," I rasped, my voice little more than a whisper. It was enough though. The doorknob rattled and then Sitric crouched beside me.

"Gods, Grainne," he gasped, then grabbed a blanket from the bed to drape over me. He returned to the doorway to call for aid.

Only moments passed before feet pounded along the hall. Other brothers crowded in. Somebody lifted me and deposited me on the bed. It felt like the softest thing I had ever lain on. The blanket was wrapped more firmly around me. I blinked and it seemed that three of Sitric hovered over me, his face tight and worried.

At length, Agata came and her face paled when she saw me. "Everyone out." Her tone was so firm that nobody dared argue. "Sitric, send for hot water and clean rags. And somebody find Niamh."

The brothers exited and the door closed. Agata sat on the edge of the bed and lifted one trembling hand to touch my face.

"Oh Grainne, how did this happen?"

The pain was so great, I could barely think. But one thought ran through my mind: Lunn had said to tell nobody. He hadn't said what the consequences would be, but I could safely assume it would invalidate our pact.

"Grainne?"

My face was so swollen I could barely move my jaw. Inside my mouth, my tongue was thick and blood still dripped down my throat. I must have bitten my tongue, or perhaps I had lost teeth. It hardly seemed to matter right now.

"I can't tell you," I managed eventually.

Agata flinched as if I had slapped her. She withdrew her hand, instead clasping her fingers in her lap and staring down at them. Perhaps she prayed for strength. At length she spoke again.

"Grainne, this family has secrets, of which you might not be aware. Sometimes, strange things happen. It is clear somebody ill-treated you last night. Will you tell me who it was?"

"I can't."

"Was it Caedmon? Tell me that much at least. Put a mother's mind at ease, if it wasn't."

I shook my head. The room blurred and a vicious throbbing started behind my eye. "I will not speak of it. Please don't ask."

Agata stared me in the eyes for a long time before she nodded. "Very well then, Grainne. I will never ask again. But if you need to talk, I will listen. You are my daughter now. And Caedmon is my son."

My brain was slow to process her words. "What did you mean, secrets?"

"Caedmon has not told you?"

"No."

"He should have, if you are to live with us, but it is not my tale to tell."

"I should know."

"I agree. But I can't speak of it. I will ask Fiachra to talk with you, once you are recovered."

I nodded, unable to find the strength to speak any further.

Niamh bustled back in with an armload of cloth, followed by Sitric bearing a large bowl from which steam rose. Between the two of them, they drew up a chair beside the bed and set the bowl on it. Then Sitric was hustled back out of the room and the door closed firmly behind him.

Niamh sucked in her breath at the sight of my wounded body. I should have been embarrassed at being naked in front of them but I barely cared. Nothing felt real anyway. Not the night I had endured. Not my injuries. Not the fact that Caedmon was gone, taken someplace where I would never see him again.

Agata and Niamh were as gentle as they could be, but even so their ministrations pained me terribly. They washed the blood from my body and cleaned out the bites. Niamh had brought a bag of herbs and potions and she applied a soothing paste to my bruises and wounds. Soon they began to numb.

After an endless age, I was clean and wearing a nightgown. Niamh took away the bloody cloths and red water. Agata stayed with me. She said nothing, for which I was grateful.

When Niamh returned, she brought a steaming mug. I smelled the herbs as soon as she entered the room although I was too addled to make sense of what they were. Willow, possibly, for pain. Maybe henbane to make me sleep. She held the mug up to my mouth and helped me drink the bitter brew. I sipped what I could of it although my bruised lips were clumsy and I kept spilling it. Niamh wiped up the mess without comment.

Soon numbness spread through my body and my tense muscles began to relax. When Niamh judged I had drunk a sufficient quantity, she put the mug on a stool drawn up close to the bed, then helped me lie down. She drew the heavy curtains and left.

Agata sat on the chair by the bed I had shared with Caedmon and folded her hands into her lap. She looked as if she was settling in.

"You don't..." Did it always take so much effort to speak? "You don't have to stay."

"I will sit with you," she said. "You shouldn't be alone right now. Close your eyes and sleep, and know that either Niamh or I will be here, should you need us."

A surge of gratitude rushed through me and tears sprang to my eyes. "Thank you."

"Should I send for someone? Your mother, perhaps, or one of your sisters?"

Caedmon was the only one I wanted but I might never see him again.

"Not yet. Let me... let me heal a little first."

Agata nodded and her face held no judgement. "Sleep then. I will sit with you."

I knew I wouldn't be able to sleep. I would see Lunn every moment I closed my eyes. Feel his teeth sinking into my skin, and his fingers in places nobody but Caedmon had ever touched, and all of the other dreadful things he had done to me. But Niamh's potion was strong and as soon as I closed my eyes, I was asleep.

EITHNE

The house was quiet when I woke. At first I thought I must have slept late, that everyone was out in the fields working, or in the barn. But a glance out the window told me the sun was not long risen and when I went downstairs, my brothers were still there. They tiptoed through the house with tight expressions on their faces.

I couldn't find Mother anywhere or Caedmon. I had been sure he wouldn't leave without saying goodbye. But it seemed he had already gone for he was not in the house, the herb garden, or out in the fields, as far as I could see from the doorstep. I wasn't strong enough to search further for my blood was running hot and my skin was cold. I had been through this enough times to know I was about to succumb to the fevers.

The thought of breakfast made my stomach clench and bile rise in my throat. I settled into my chair by the fireplace, my feet tucked under me and a blanket wrapped around my shoulders. There was no fire but no matter, I would wait. One of my brothers would come along soon enough and they would surely light it when they saw me sitting by a cold hearth.

Fear teased me, lingering and waiting. Something had happened overnight. There was no point in asking for nobody would tell me. They never told me anything. They forgot that although my body might be frail, my mind was as sound as anyone's. But I always heard what was going on eventually. If I sat very quiet and still, people didn't see me. So I sat and waited.

Eventually Sitric came to light the fire although he didn't speak to me, only muttered to himself. I couldn't quite make out his words. Something about Caedmon, something about someone else whose name I didn't catch, and somebody needed to do something. He left as soon as the fire caught, still muttering, his eyes sombre.

It wasn't until Niamh hurried past that I started to understand. She carried a bowl and she walked carefully, which indicated the bowl wasn't empty. Tucked under one arm was a bundle that looked like blood-stained cloths. So someone was injured and my guess was Grainne. It seemed that one of Diarmuid's tales had finally come true.

Diarmuid's ability was one of those things I wasn't supposed to know about. Nobody ever spoke of it and I wasn't even sure all of my brothers knew. Eremon did, and probably Diarmuid for surely somebody had warned him after he first announced himself as a bard. Fiachra, maybe, because druids tended to know things they shouldn't. But perhaps not the others.

Diarmuid had been pale and pinch-faced for weeks and the tension between him and Caedmon was obvious to everyone. So this was his ill-considered revenge. He made Caedmon beat his new bride half to death and Caedmon by now was probably dead himself.

My chest constricted and tears welled as I pictured Caedmon dying in the manner described in Diarmuid's unlucky tale: alone, throat slit, empty eyes staring up at the sky. I swallowed my sobs. Damn Diarmuid. I hoped he never told another tale. In the meantime, though, perhaps there was something I could do to comfort Grainne, for it was likely that she was badly injured and also newly a widow. Here, at last, was a task I could undertake, at least until the fevers became strong enough that I was confined to my bed.

I left my warm spot by the fire and crept up the stairs. My legs were shaking by the time I reached the top. The door to Caedmon and Grainne's bedchamber was firmly closed. I knocked, my hand tentative, for I didn't know whether Grainne would welcome my presence. I barely knew her, after all.

The door opened just the slightest bit and Mother peered out. The lines around her eyes were deeper than usual. The astringent odour of some herbal concoction wafted into the hallway.

"I'm sorry, Eithne, Grainne is not feeling well," she said. "This is not a good time for visitors."

"I can sit with her." I tried to peer over Mother's shoulder, for she was not much taller than me but she had positioned herself where I could see nothing.

"I don't think that's a good idea. No visitors today."

"I know what it is like to be unwell. I won't talk but it might make her feel a little better to have someone sitting with her."

"I will sit with her. I'll tell her you came to check on her though."

Mother started to close the door and I surprised myself by inserting my foot in the doorway.

"I know what happened, Mother. You don't need to try to keep it from me."

Mother looked at me for a long moment, her grey eyes steady. At length she sighed and opened the door wider. "Keep your voice down so you don't disturb her. She is gravely injured."

I had not been inside Caedmon's bedchamber for many years, but it looked much the same as I remembered, except that he now had a larger bed. The heavy curtains were closed, making the room dim, and a comfortable chair was drawn up next to the bed. Mother's shawl lay abandoned across the back of the chair.

I approached the bed. Even in the shadowy light, I could see that Grainne was bruised almost beyond recognition. Her hair was clumped and matted around her face. The blankets drawn up to her chin hid whatever horrors had been inflicted on her body. Mother and Niamh had obviously washed her and tended her wounds but they hadn't touched her hair. I picked up Grainne's comb from the dresser and began to untangle the knots. I worked gently but the knots were tight and many would need to be cut out. I tried to pretend I hadn't seen the streaks of blood woven through her dark hair.

"Mother, would you fetch me some embroidery shears?"

Mother looked like she wanted to say something but she merely nodded and left. I worked in silence while she was gone. Grainne's eyes were open but if she knew I was there, she didn't react. Her hair was silky beneath my fingers. She had had beautiful hair.

When Mother returned, we helped Grainne to sit with pillows positioned behind her shoulders so that I could work on the back of her head. I was tiring already and the fever was making sweat drip down the backs of my legs but I couldn't bear to leave Grainne with her hair so bedraggled.

"You don't need to stay," I said to Mother. "I can stay with Grainne for a while."

"You shouldn't tire yourself," she said.

"I will send for Niamh when I am too tired."

Mother frowned at me. She opened her mouth as if to protest again but only shook her head and left. I continued to work silently, combing out what tangles I could and snipping off the rest. I tried to catch the falling strands so Grainne wouldn't see, but some landed in her lap before I could grab them. She touched them with a trembling hand.

"Do I look hideous?" Her voice was quiet but steady.

"Not hideous, no. You look like a strong woman who has survived much."

Her shoulders shook as she began to sob and I had to stop my work for fear of cutting her.

"Do you want to talk about it?" I asked.

Grainne shook her head. "I can't tell anyone what happened."

"I'm good at keeping secrets."

"Then tell me a secret this family keeps. Tell me one of the things I should have known before I married Caedmon."

"Caedmon is a good man." I felt like I should hug her but I didn't know how badly she was injured beneath the blankets. I rested a hand very gently on her shoulder. She flinched when I touched her and my throat tightened.

"That's no secret. I wouldn't have married him were he not."

Grainne's sobs had stopped so I resumed cutting out the matts. Once that was done, I tried to disguise the fact that handfuls of hair had been ripped out but there was little I could do. She would need to cover her hair with a scarf if she didn't want folk to stare.

"There are many secrets in this family," I said, eventually. "I'm sure I don't know them all."

"I bet you know more than people think you do."

I hesitated. "That is true."

"Then tell me a secret, for we are sisters now. What does this family hide?"

"Some of our menfolk have a special ability," I said, slowly, for I didn't quite know how to tell this secret. I had thought I would never share it. But what Grainne didn't know after last night, she had probably guessed. "In our family, when the seventh son of a seventh son is a bard, he is able to bring his tales to life. Not all of them though, and nobody quite knows how the power works."

"Diarmuid is a seventh son," Grainne said. "And I presume your father is too."

"Yes, only all of his brothers are dead. He does not talk of what happened to them."

"The tale Diarmuid told. The one of the soldier and his wife. Do you think it could come true?"

My hands stilled in her hair. "It would seem it already has."

"Don't think that. Caedmon would never do such a thing."

"Then who? Caedmon is gone and you have been beaten. You know what folk will think, even if they don't know of Diarmuid's ability."

"I can't say. Only trust in Caedmon. He is a good man."

Again I saw him lying dead by the side of a road, eyes blank, blood pooling beneath him. "Do you think he is alive?"

"I hope so. I have done what I can for him."

I didn't question her. She had her secrets, and I still had mine, for there was another more precious secret that I would not share with her. Not yet, anyway.

EITHNE

*A*s Grainne healed, I spent most of my waking hours in her room. Sometimes we spoke. More often we sat in silence. I would open the curtains and drag the chair to where I could warm my skin in the sunlight. I had some small items of embroidery in a little basket and I would work on my stitching for a short time until I was too tired. Then I would simply sit and look out of the window.

The illness had held off for several days although I could still feel it there, lurking, slumbering, waiting. The fevers came and went but they were mild enough that I wasn't confined to bed. My hands would tremble for a while and my legs would shake, but that too passed without growing worse. I wanted to believe my body was finally learning how to fight back, but such thoughts were futile. I would succumb sooner or later. In the meantime, at least I was strong enough to be out of bed and able to support Grainne in some small way.

Grainne's face looked worse before it got better. Two days after she was injured, her face was swollen round like a pumpkin and her bruises were the dark purple of storm clouds. She could barely speak for the swelling around her jaw. I never saw the damage to her body for Mother always sent me from the room before tending to Grainne's injuries. But I had seen enough to guess the extent of injury to both body and mind.

Then came a day when I had barely been out of bed for an hour before fatigue gripped me and I began to shiver. When Mother came to check on Grainne, she found me trembling and flushed. With a typical lack of fuss, she summoned Marrec and Conn to carry me out while she tended to Grainne. Afterward, she came to my room and rested a cool palm on my burning cheek.

"Eithne, my dear, you have exhausted yourself."

"The sickness has been coming for several days," I said. My mouth was dry and my throat hurt when I spoke. "I wanted to sit with Grainne for as long as I could."

"She will be fine. Niamh and I will care for her. You need to worry about yourself now. Concentrate on getting better."

"Do you think he did it?" I felt like a traitor but I asked only because I wanted to know what she thought.

Mother's face was serious and she didn't ask what I meant. "I hope not. I believe I raised my sons better than that. But the tale was strong and it may have left him with no choice but to act in accordance with what was foretold."

"Why does Diarmuid still tell tales, if he knows what he can do?"

"He doesn't understand it, my dear. I don't think he believed it until now." She sat on the chair next to my bed and folded her hands in her lap. The dark shadows under her eyes told of her exhaustion and I regretted that I would add to that over the next few days.

"He hasn't even come to visit her. To see the product of his own handiwork."

"It seems he has gone on a journey of some sort."

"To where? And for what purpose? Has he not caused enough problems without disappearing too?"

"I know only as much as Fiachra told me and he was sparse with the details."

I was lost to the fever shortly after, but that was fine with me because it meant time with Kalen. I had not been able to walk out to the beech trees since Grainne had been injured although I had longed to see him. No longer did he merely stand in the corner of my room and watch with dispassionate interest. Over time he had crept closer and now he actually sat in the chair where Mother had been sitting earlier. It was a plain wooden chair, not of the fine standard the fey must be accustomed to.

Kalen talked to me sometimes, small tidbits of information about his life. He didn't seem to mind that I never replied. I stored up every morsel of information, determined not to forget anything so that when the fever was gone I could linger over every detail.

There had been a lonely childhood. If he had siblings, he never spoke of them. An animal, a pet of some sort, although I didn't recognise the word he used and I had no sense of what kind of creature it might be. Lessons learnt in the forest, both practical and philosophical. He was an outsider, shunned by others of his kind, although he didn't specify what offence he had committed.

The things of which he spoke were mostly wonders of the physical world: a fiery sunset, a majestic storm, the pleasure of walking barefoot on soft grass. He made me want to see all those things too. As his words painted pictures in my mind, I added myself in. He and I together watched the sun set from a mountainous perch. We sought shelter under a stately oak from an unexpected spring storm. We walked over grassy hills and stopped to pluck the yellow tulips that grew in a hollow. The images were so real, I could almost smell the perfume from the tulips.

Kalen left when the fevers subsided. As I began my slow recovery, it was easy to believe we really had done all the things I remembered. We had still had only a handful of real conversations but I began to feel like I knew him so much better than that.

Another week passed before I was able to very slowly make my way back to Grainne's room. Although it was just down the hall from mine, my legs trembled with exhaustion by the time I rapped softly on her door. I breathed in great gasping pants. I could still smell the illness clinging to my skin. Grainne lay in bed, staring up at the ceiling. She started to sit up when I entered.

"No, don't trouble yourself," I said between gasps, and sank down into the chair. It was drawn up close to the bed rather than in the sunny spot I favoured by the window but I did not have enough strength to move it. The room smelled of healing herbs although they were different to the ones Mother burned in my room when I was ill.

Grainne was thinner than I remembered and her eyes sadder. Large splotches of faded yellow bruises covered her face and the swelling was much reduced.

"Are you recovered, Eithne?" she asked, and her once joyful voice was tight.

"Somewhat. It will be some days until I regain my strength." I drew my feet up under my nightdress and rested my head against the back of the chair.

"These illnesses, they occur often?"

"Too often. I have been sick for most of my life."

"That's terrible." Grainne's voice was genuine.

"Don't pity me. I hate being pitied. It is what it is." My tone was brusquer than I had intended but it was too late.

"Are you dying?"

Nobody had ever asked that before. I myself had only dared voice the question once. But I had never doubted it.

"Probably." I tried to keep my tone as matter of fact as hers. But it is hard to speak of one's own death and my voice broke on the last syllable. "I don't really talk about it."

"I'm sorry. I didn't mean to upset you, not after you've been so kind to me."

"I'm not upset. I'm still very weak. I can't talk for long yet. I really just came to sit with you."

"I appreciate that. I don't really want to talk either."

"Then we shall sit here in silence and both be perfectly happy with that."

EITHNE

*T*hree more days passed before I saw Kalen again.

Three days in which I wondered whether he would come again.

Three days in which I berated myself for fearing that he wouldn't.

Any woman who forms an attachment to a fey is a fool; I knew that. The fey don't understand hope or horror, joy or sorrow, love or pity. Life is a game to them, and well they can afford that, for they live many hundreds of years. Lingering over each word, puzzling out unsaid meanings: those are the things a woman does when she is besotted. They are not things a mortal should think of a fey. That can only lead to unhappiness.

I regained my strength slowly. I wasn't yet recovered enough to walk farther than from my bed to Grainne's chamber, but I persuaded Marrec and Conn to carry me out to my rock beside the beech trees. I even managed to convince them to leave me alone for an hour — one precious hour in which perhaps Kalen would come to me — before they returned to carry me back. The wind smelled of fresh, spring air and trees and grass, which was a relief after so many days confined to the lodge.

I could not see Kalen as we approached the trees, but of course he would not appear with my brothers there. Marrec and Con deposited me on the rock and I wrapped myself in the blanket Mother had insisted I bring. Then my brothers left, assuring me they would return in an hour. Conn pressed a wooden whistle into my hand.

"If you need us to return earlier, blow this," he said. "We will listen for it."

"I will be fine. You can go now."

As they departed, I didn't dare turn around and look behind me. As long as I didn't look, I could pretend he was there, waiting. I looked out towards the hill that hid the lodge from sight. The fields were patchy with melting snow and contained nothing but trees and cows and sheep all the way to the horizon. In summer these fields would be emerald green but now they were a quilt of white and brown.

Marrec and Conn were soon out of sight and yet I waited. The beeches around me were still and silent. The wind had died and not even a stray breeze disturbed their branches. There were no birds calling, no rustle of tree-dwelling creatures. If Kalen was there somewhere, he was utterly silent.

I took a deep breath. I would be sad if he did not come, but I would survive. I was not some weak-willed woman who had fallen in love with one of the fey. I was merely intrigued. He was a bright spark in an otherwise dull life, a splash of colour on a canvas of grey.

Still no sound behind me. But perhaps he waited for me to speak, to indicate it was safe to come out. I would call him, just once. If he did not come, I would wait for my brothers and I would not allow a single tear to fall. I would not waste another thought on him. My life would return to its previous drabness and I would be no poorer.

"Are you going to hide all afternoon?" I said, finally. "I have only such time until my brothers return."

Leaves rustled behind me and my heart pounded loudly. I didn't turn to face him but continued to stare out towards the snow-capped mountains of the horizon.

"I was not certain you wanted to see me," he said.

"I was hoping to talk to you. It's the only reason I came out here today." I phrased my words carefully, lest I give him the wrong impression. I didn't want him to think I had feelings for him. For he was fey and that made him dangerous to a mortal woman. Extremely dangerous. And interesting.

"You are recovered."

I wasn't sure whether he intended a question or a statement. "I feel better. It will be some days yet before I am fully recovered though."

"And then you will be ill again."

"Yes, there is never more than a few weeks between episodes."

"Is there no cure?"

I finally turned around. Kalen leaned against a silver-trunked beech. His hair was the same ruined cut as always and his dark clothes hung as if only a skeleton was beneath them. His face was as imperturbable as ever. If he was as pleased to see me as I was him, he gave no sign of it.

"Apparently not. I have seen several wise women and healers, and even a druid, but they could suggest nothing other than herbs and rest."

"That makes you sad." Kalen tilted his head as if examining a curiosity.

"Just a little. It is the only way I know to live. I have been like this all of my life. It would be much harder, I think, to be healthy and to be struck down with such an illness. For then one would already know what it is like to live without such a thing."

"What if you could go somewhere where the illness didn't affect you?"

My heart did a funny little leap. *Be careful here, Eithne. Be very careful.* "There is no such place. Not for mortals anyway."

"There is no illness in my realm."

"Your kind are very fortunate then. Would that we had the same fortune."

"If you came there with me, you would not suffer any longer." His face was emotionless, giving no indication that he understood the importance of what he offered. He continued to lean against the beech, although now he crossed his arms across his chest.

"I cannot go to your realm. I could not survive there."

"Of course you could. Your illness would no longer affect you. You would be whole and hearty."

"But mortals cannot live there. We cannot eat your food and drink your wine, or we can never leave."

"You would not go unless you intended to never leave."

"I could not do such a thing."

Kalen's face darkened as if I had angered him but it passed swiftly. "Why? You would be well."

"I could not leave my family."

"They barely notice you. You sit in your chair by the fire and they pass you by with barely a glance. Would they even notice if you were no longer there?"

Irritation flashed within me. "That's an awful thing to say."

"How can the truth be awful?" Kalen's voice was as bland as ever.

"It's not the truth. Not really. You're twisting it." I felt flustered now. My cheeks heated and I twisted my fingers together and tucked them into my skirt to hide the way they trembled. I hated to argue with anyone and I particularly didn't want to argue with Kalen.

"I only ever speak the truth."

"Well, sometimes you shouldn't. Sometimes you only make things worse by telling the truth."

"You would rather I lied to you?"

"No, I just don't want you to tell me awful things, even if they might be true. Besides, when were you watching me sit by the fire?"

"I often watch you. You know that."

"I know you sometimes watch when I am ill. I didn't know you watched me at other times, and in other places."

Kalen tilted his head and seemed to listen although I heard nothing. "Your brothers return."

"Already? They were supposed to give me an hour."

He shrugged. "I pay little attention to time."

"When will I see you again?" I hated how needy I sounded. I would not be one of those desperate women who falls in love with a fey and is devastated when they lose interest. He was merely an interesting friend.

"When can you come back here?" he asked.

If Kalen felt anything for me, I neither saw it in his face nor heard it in his voice, but the question gave me hope.

"Tomorrow. I will return at the same time tomorrow. Will you be here?"

"Tomorrow," he said with a funny little tilt of his head. Perhaps it indicated agreement.

He melted away into the trees just as Marrec and Conn came into sight. My brothers chattered about nothing much as they carried me back to the house. I let their conversation flow over me, too busy analysing every word Kalen had said, and everything he didn't.

I would see him again tomorrow.

SUMERLED

*K*alen has been spending far too much time visiting the disfigured mortal. Every time I ask why he continues to go to her, he stomps off without answering. So I do the only thing I can think of. Kalen will be furious but it is for his own good.

I go in search of the underground cave Lunn has made his own. I don't dare go inside but instead linger nearby. There is a stream where I have sometimes seen him. He sits by it for hours and stares at nothing with a pensive look on his face. I am never quite sure what he is doing and I certainly never interrupt.

I overhear many a comment about him as I wander — Kalen calls it skulking — around, listening to whatever someone is careless enough to say without checking nobody can hear. A perversion, they say. An aberration. His penchant for mortals is well-known — he has taken many mortal lovers, both female and male — and nothing else is so disdained by the fey as consorting with mortals. Lunn seems to have no interaction with anyone else, even at feasts where he is little more welcome than Kalen.

I hide behind a thick bramble bush. The stream is meagre with just a handspan of water but even so it gurgles as it sweeps over the stones. A hare comes to drink from the flowing water. A sprite sails past in an oak leaf boat and yells a challenge to the hare. Birds chitter overhead and a soft breeze waves the branches of oak and ash. Water bugs skirt the surface, and nothing pays any attention to me. I am used to that.

Time has little meaning in the fey realm so it might be hours or days that I wait. Sometimes I sleep but otherwise I just sit and wait. Eventually Lunn appears. I wait until he has settled himself in a patch of lush, velvety grass on the stream's bank before I rise, very slowly and quietly. I stand there, not moving, waiting for him to see me. He does at last.

"Boy," he growls. "Get out of my sight."

"I have something to tell you," I say and despite my best intentions, my voice trembles just a little. I am well familiar with Lunn's style of punishment.

"Not interested," he says. "Go away. Unless, of course, you'd like to come closer so I can finish drowning you."

"I'm fine over here. Will you listen?"

He glares at me once more and then lies back in the grass. "No."

He doesn't seem inclined to rise though so I decide to tell him anyway. He'll be pleased when I do, I know it. He might not reward me but surely he'll at least stop trying to drown me every time he sees me.

"Kalen has a secret," I say.

Lunn doesn't respond but I feel his sudden interest.

"He has been sneaking off to the mortal world."

Lunn sits up slowly and looks at me. "Go on."

"He has been visiting a mortal woman."

Lunn raises one eyebrow and his lips very slowly curl up into a grin. "Has he now. How interesting."

"I knew you'd want to know." I creep closer. "Have I done well?"

"You forget yourself, half-breed." Lunn's tone is suddenly cold. "If you come near enough for me to grab you, I'll throw you in the stream and hold you under until you stop breathing."

"But I told you Kalen's secret," I say, wounded. "I thought you'd be pleased."

"Oh I'm pleased," he says. "But that doesn't change what I think of you. Now get out of my sight."

I hesitate for a moment, my mouth open and ready to plead my case, but he glares at me so fiercely, that I turn and run. My chest is tight and a hot tear drips down my cheek. I wipe it away with the back of my dirty hand before anyone sees. Full-blooded fey don't cry.

EITHNE

I met Kalen by the beech trees every day for a week. Winter had broken and spring's presence was everywhere. Buds covered the branches of the beech, the woodlarks began to sing again, and glossy grass sprouted where snow had melted. The days were warmer, with just the faintest scent of summer. Despite all that, I would have stayed huddled in front of the fireplace were it not for the entice-ment of time with Kalen.

The house was still in uproar and nobody questioned my sudden interest in sitting on my rock, alone and out of sight. Diarmuid had disappeared on some secret quest and it seemed only Fiachra knew where. There had been no word from Caedmon. He should have reached the campaign front by now but it might be weeks before we received any message from him. Mother was distracted, but at least it meant she paid little attention to me. Even Papa's normally relaxed face became pinched with tension.

When I wasn't with Kalen, I spent most of my time with Grainne. Broken ribs were gradually healing and soon she would be able to breathe without pain. I knew it was horrible of me to not wish her back to full health but I would have less freedom when she was ready to leave her bedchamber. We had become friends during those hours I sat by her bed. Maybe we had even become sisters. But she still didn't know my secret.

During the stolen hour Kalen and I spent together every day, we talked about all sorts of things. My childhood memories. Incidents with my brothers that had made me laugh or cry or, one time, so mad I punched Marrec in the nose. Kalen talked little of his own life. He never mentioned siblings or friends. There were irregular references to his queen, Titania, who I understood he feared, even if he never said so in as many words. The things of which he spoke were mostly occurrences of nature. The finding of a bird's nest containing three abandoned hatchlings. The discovery of a field of bluebells. The recent pleasure of a nap in soft grass beneath a shady tree, savouring the perfume of nearby honeysuckle.

"Spring has barely arrived," I said. "How is it that flowers already bloom in your realm?"

Kalen shrugged. "Seasons are not the same there as here. Titania's whim determines whether it is winter or summer."

"The queen controls the seasons?" It was an unfathomable idea, but Kalen shrugged it off.

"We had almost a decade of winter once because she was mad about something. It snowed for years before she could be placated."

"How awful."

"She is the queen. She can do what she pleases."

"What else does she do?"

But he wouldn't say much about Titania and I did not want to press too hard. Better that I let him choose what he would tell me, for when it was something that excited him, he would talk willingly. And it was detail I longed for.

I wanted to understand his life, to picture the things of which he spoke. The endless fields of flowers. The portals to my own world. The strange creatures that inhabited the woods, unseen and unheard. It all fascinated me. The more Kalen talked about his home, the more I longed to see it with my own eyes. I had never expected adventure but if

I could have just a few minutes in the realm of the fey, I knew I would spend the rest of my life thinking about it.

My brothers' return always came too soon. I felt like I had barely settled on my rock before Kalen cocked his head and looked in the direction of the hill that hid us from sight of the lodge.

"Already?" I asked.

"Tell them to give you longer tomorrow. Two hours."

"They won't leave me alone for that long. They are only willing to do this because I have convinced them no harm can come to me in such a short time while I'm in the middle of our own lands and just barely out of sight."

"Persuade them."

I laughed, although I was somewhat irritated at the forcefulness of his tone. "I told you, I can't. But I will return tomorrow. Will you come?"

"Of course." Kalen took my hand and gently kissed my palm, his gaze never leaving mine. "I look forward to it."

Then he melted away into the trees, just as my brothers came into sight, and I had no time to savour the feeling of his lips against my skin.

"You have the strangest look on your face, Eithne," Marrec said with a laugh.

"What do you do out here all alone?" Conn asked.

"Talk to squirrels?"

"Coax birds down to sit in your hair?"

"Perhaps she has a secret lover?"

"He must be very secret," Conn said.

"For we have seen neither hair nor hide of him," finished Marrec.

"Enough," I said. "Take me back now."

I returned at the usual time the next day. Marrec and Conn deposited me on my rock and then hurried back to the house, for there was some chore Papa wanted completed urgently. But before they left, they checked I had the whistle and reminded me to blow it if I needed them.

The rock was warm from the mid afternoon sun and its heat seeped through my clothes and into my skin in the most pleasant manner. I felt quite drowsy and my head nodded once or twice but I made myself sit up straight and keep my eyes wide open. I did not want Kalen to arrive, find me napping, and leave. I could not bear the thought of passing a day without speaking with him.

Minutes passed. He was always already here when I arrived, although he never showed himself until Marrec and Conn had left. Perhaps he waited for me to call him. A game, although I didn't find it amusing.

"Kalen? Will you come out now?"

There was no response.

"Kalen, this isn't funny. You are wasting our time together."

Still nothing.

"Kalen!" I was irritated now. I hoped he was not merely hiding and watching. For the fun of it, or to make me mad, or some other fey intention that was incomprehensible to me. But still he didn't speak and I detected no sign of his presence.

Eventually Marrec and Conn returned. They didn't notice that I said nothing as they carried me back. I made them put me down when we were halfway home so I could walk the rest of the way. My progress was painfully slow and I didn't have the strength to hide my limp, but they pretended not to notice.

I was panting and my legs trembled by the time we reached the lodge. I collapsed into the first chair I reached. Many minutes passed before my lungs breathed normally again and it was even longer before I felt like I could stand without fearing my legs would immediately collapse beneath me.

Kalen hadn't come. For the first time I realised what I had refused to admit, even to myself: I was in love with him. How had this happened? I did not intend to become one of those women who fall in love with a fey and whose lives are destroyed when their beloved loses interest. I would not cling and hope he would return. I would not spend my time agonising over what might have prevented him from coming. I would simply forget him, for Silver Downs breeds its children strong and tough. Our blood is tinged with magic. How else could our bards bring their tales to life? I was just as strong as any other child of Silver Downs, despite the frailty of my body and my own lack of magic.

My resolution to forget Kalen lasted no more than a hundred heartbeats before a paralysing fear washed over me. Had something happened to him? He had given no indication that he tired of me. In fact, if I analysed his every word and action, he had seemed as infatuated with me as I was with him. Yesterday he had promised to meet me. He had kissed my hand. If today he did not come, then something had happened.

I worried throughout the rest of the day and barely slept that night for all my tossing and turning and fretting. When afternoon finally came again, Marrec and Conn carried me out to the beech trees and left with the usual injunction to blow on the whistle if I needed them. I waited only until they were out of earshot before I called.

"Kalen, are you there? Kalen?"

Woodlarks chattered above me. Branches rustled in the wind. But Kalen did not come.

When my brothers returned, I allowed them to lift me without a word. I made them set me down a little farther from the lodge this time and again I painstakingly lurched the rest of the way. Two days. Two whole days.

Still, on the third day, I waited at the rock. Again I called for Kalen and again he did not come. It was only then that I was certain. Something might prevent him from coming to me once, perhaps even twice, but not thrice. Thrice was deliberate.

This was one of the times when I desperately wished for a sister. Someone to confide in, someone who could advise me, perhaps hold my hand as I cried. At length I remembered I did indeed now have a sister. I had been tempted many times, as I sat beside Grainne's bed, to tell her about Kalen. But I had held my tongue for I did not want her to think me foolish.

I slowly made my way up to Grainne's bedchamber. My legs trembled and I coughed repeatedly. I couldn't seem to get enough air into my lungs. My twisted foot felt like it was on fire. It would be some days yet before I was well enough to walk all the way from my rock to the lodge. But now, of course, there was no reason to go.

Grainne was alone and sitting up in bed when I limped into her bedchamber. She smiled when she saw me. She seemed to genuinely enjoy my company, even if I was usually lost in my own thoughts and said little. Most of her bruises had faded by now although she said her ribs and jaw still ached. I had trimmed her silky hair well enough that it was not too ragged. It was far shorter than a woman would usually wear it and there were places where I could not disguise the handfuls that had been torn out, but I had done my best.

"Eithne, did you enjoy your walk?" she asked.

"I must tell you something." I closed the door and settled into the chair beside her bed, still trying to catch my breath. My limbs shook uncontrollably and I was grateful to be able to sit at last.

"Is something wrong?"

I had resolved to be calm and logical, but at her words, I burst into tears.

"Eithne, tell me." Grainne sounded alarmed. "Whatever is the matter?"

"I have done something very foolish," I said. "It is so foolish, I am embarrassed to tell you."

"I will listen without judgement." She leaned back against the pillows and folded her hands in her lap. Her face was calm and composed, although her eyes were shadowed and weary. "You can tell me. Whatever it is."

"Do you promise you will tell nobody?"

"I have grown up with sisters. I am very good at keeping secrets."

I waited until my tears subsided. When I thought I could speak without crying, I began. "I have fallen in love. It is a foolish, foolish thing and I swore I would never do it. But it is done and I do not know what to do about it."

"Why is this a bad thing? Falling in love is the most wonderful thing in the world, unless he does not return your feelings. And even then, there is hope. As long as there is life, there is hope."

Grainne studied her hands as she spoke. How much of her words were intended for me and how much were a reminder to herself? Perhaps they were both.

"I do not know whether he feels the same," I said. "I had thought perhaps he felt something for me. But if he once did, it seems he does no longer."

"Will you tell me who the lucky man is? Do I know him?"

"His name is Kalen."

"A good Celtic name."

"He is... not mortal."

Grainne looked at me for a long moment, her dark eyes steady and considering. "They are not like us, Eithne. I wish you had fallen in love with one of our own kind."

"I know. I am ashamed."

"Love is never something to be ashamed of. You cannot help who you fall for. But tell me, what has happened to upset you so? Has he told you he does not love you?"

"We have never discussed it. We have been meeting every day. He tells me of his world and I tell him of ours. But he has not come to me now for three days."

"And you have no indication of why?"

"None. He promised to meet me the next day and never came again. Three days I have waited."

"Do you have any way to send him a message?"

I shook my head. "I do not even know where he lives, save there is a portal to his world somewhere in the woods on the edge of Silver Downs. Father forbade any of us from entering the woods, for people disappear in there and never come out again, or they return changed, their minds broken."

"So what will you do?"

"What can I do, other than try to forget him?"

Grainne merely shrugged and returned to staring at her hands. I began to suspect she saw some other solution but was hesitant to suggest it.

"What would you do?" I asked. "What if it was Caedmon?"

Grainne answered immediately and she looked me right in the eyes as she spoke. "I would search for him. I would search every day and every night until I found him. And once I found him, I would never let him go again."

My mind was awhirl. "I need to rest. I'm sorry to leave you alone."

"Go. I will be fine. Rest and we can talk later."

GRAINNE

I hardly knew what to make of Eithne's news. Why did the fey have such interest in this family? I had never known anyone who had seen a fey, let alone encountered one myself, until I came to Silver Downs. In fact, I hadn't even entirely believed they still existed. But Eithne spoke as if it were of no great significance that she had been secretly meeting one, except in as much as she felt foolish for having fallen in love.

As a married woman, I knew I should offer advice. Something sound and intelligent. But what could I say? Reason suggested I encourage her to forget him, but how could I tell her to do what I could not myself?

I spent the evening puzzling over the situation. I briefly considered telling Agata, but dismissed the thought almost immediately. Eithne had confided in me and I would not breach her confidence. I might perhaps be able to convince her to seek advice from Fiachra. Surely her druid brother would be able to say the words I couldn't find.

I had plenty of time alone to think, for I had yet to leave my bedchamber since the night with Lunn. At meal times, Agata or one of the serving women would bring me a tray. Agata had been coaxing me to eat with the family. She said it would be good for me to do something normal again. But I had grown accustomed to being alone and was not yet ready to face the stares and questions I would encounter downstairs.

My hand mirror showed that the bruises were almost healed. My ribs hardly hurt anymore and running a hand over the back of my head told me that my hair was still somewhat ragged, but it would grow eventually. Of the child I had hoped I carried, there was no sign. Perhaps he had not survived Lunn's abuse, or perhaps he had never existed. I would rather think the latter than that my effort to save Caedmon had resulted in the loss of his heir.

Eithne bustled in early the next morning with a determined look on her face and her movements as awkward as ever. I was still lying in bed in my nightdress. My breakfast tray was balanced on the chair where Eithne usually sat. The odour of uneaten porridge was making my stomach roll and I was relieved when Eithne moved the tray to the floor.

She sat on the chair and tucked her feet beneath her so that her skirt covered her shoes. She often sat like that, as if to occupy the smallest space possible. Perhaps to make herself invisible. I had seen the way folk took little notice of her. She would hold herself still and quiet, seemingly barely even breathing, and they would look right past her. It was a curious thing. I was sure her family did not intend to be cruel, for that was not the sort of folk they were. And yet unless she spoke, or moved, they did not see her.

"I have made a decision," Eithne announced. Gone was the pinched, worried look from yesterday. Instead she looked calm, resolute, and I already knew her decision.

"I intend to find him," she said.

I wasn't sure what reaction she expected but I hid my sigh of relief. It grated at me that Eithne accepted her presumed fate so readily. She fully expected to live a short life, enduring brief periods of wellness interspersed with days where she was confined to her bed. She acknowledged that she would die from this illness, and likely soon. I would never understand how she could reconcile herself to this and if she had decided to also passively accept the fey boy's disappearance, I would have been irritated beyond words.

"I see." My voice was carefully detached although my heart had begun to pound. I hadn't dare let myself hope she would come to this decision. Or think of what I would do if she did.

"I can't believe he feels nothing for me. I won't believe it. So if he no longer comes to me, it is because he is in some sort of trouble. I will go and find him and rescue him."

"What if he does not want to be found?" I carefully pulled a dangling woollen thread from one of my blankets. I rolled the coarse thread between my fingertips. "Or rescued."

"I don't believe that."

"Eithne, I am sure you have heard as many tales of the fey as I have. More, probably, since you come from a line of bards." I kept my expression neutral so she wouldn't see how desperately I wanted her to ignore my words. "The fey are fickle. They do not love the way we do. What may have seemed to you to be a deep connection might have been no more than a passing fancy to him. Something to occupy a few hours of boredom."

"I can't think that. I don't believe it. Something is wrong and I must go to him."

"What exactly do you intend?"

"I will go to the woods and find the portal."

"The woods are large. Do you intend to wander without direction until you stumble on the portal? How will you even recognise it for what it is?"

"If I am meant to find him, I will find the portal."

"How will you get there? Surely you cannot walk so far."

"I must, so I will." Eithne's face was determined. Looking at her now, all fire and strength, it was hard to believe she regularly couldn't leave her bed for days at a time.

"Eithne, be sensible. You are not well enough for such a journey. The woods are a half day's walk for one who is physically sound. It would take you a day or more, if you even have the strength for such a thing."

"Grainne, I have no choice. I must find him. Something is wrong."

I sighed as if forced into a decision I did not want. "Fine then. If you are determined, I will go with you."

"You will?" The surprise and delight on Eithne's face shamed me, for she had no idea of my selfish motive. "Grainne, I did not expect this. Will you really come?"

"I can hardly let you go alone. I suppose you do not intend to tell anybody else."

"Of course not, for they will only say I cannot go. And I will not be stopped."

"Someone has to keep an eye on you, I suppose. It would be unseemly for you to go alone."

Eithne wanted to set off immediately, but I convinced her we should commence our journey in two days. I had no idea how she would walk so far. She breathed too heavily from merely walking up the stairs and along the hall to my bedchamber. But she had come to this decision on her own, mostly, and that gave me a reason to go with her. If Caedmon was really somewhere Diarmuid's magic could not reach him, then he was most likely in the realm of the fey. And if Eithne was determined to go there, I would go with her. I would find Caedmon and bring him home.

GRAINNE

*E*ithne and I discussed our plan numerous times over the next two days — not that there was much to it. Walk to the woods. Hope we stumbled over the portal, for neither of us had any idea what such a thing would look like. Pray we somehow found Kalen and could rescue him from whatever situation had befallen him. Trust that any fey we encountered would be sympathetic. Probably the worst that might happen was to be forced to leave without completing our quest. Of course my own aim remained unspoken: find Caedmon and a way to avoid Diarmuid's magic, and bring him safely home. Every time I was tempted to confide in Eithne, Lunn's words echoed through my mind: *tell nobody.*

Eithne sat in her usual spot, her legs tucked beneath her skirt. The sun was high in the sky and she had positioned the chair where the sun could warm her through the window. After so long confined to my bed, I was starting to crave the feeling of sun on my skin and fresh air in my lungs.

"You need to tell somebody," I said.

"But who would I tell? Mother would worry, Papa would forbid me. Eremon would go straight to Papa. Sitric has gone back to Maker's Well.

Diarmuid has gone off on his own journey. Marrec and Conn might be persuaded to keep a secret, but I can't be certain."

"So tell Fiachra."

"I barely know him," Eithne said. She was chewing her fingernails, a habit I hadn't noticed before. "And he always looks so stern. I don't know what he would say."

"He is still your brother and you must tell someone. If I disappear, folk will assume I have returned to my family. But they will worry if you leave without explanation."

"But what would I say?"

"Tell him the truth. He is a druid. He might know something that can help you."

"I'll think about it," she said although her tone indicated she intended no such thing.

A knock on the door interrupted our discussion. I bid the knocker to enter and Fiachra appeared as if we had somehow summoned him. My heart ached at the echoes of Caedmon I saw in his stance and his face.

"I came to see how you fare," Fiachra said. "Both of you."

His face showed no indication of his thoughts and I could see why Eithne professed to be afraid of him. But behind his serious eyes, I thought I detected the tiniest hint of a smile. He knew how to laugh, this druid brother. Eithne was staring intently at her hands so it seemed I must respond lest he think us both either rude or stupid.

"I am almost healed," I said. "My ribs still hurt a little, but otherwise I am fine."

"And what of your mind?" Fiachra asked. "For that does not heal quite as easily as the body."

Tears came to my eyes unexpectedly and I didn't know how to respond. I had consented, in a way, to everything done to me. It had seemed a fair trade to ensure Caedmon's safety. I did not doubt that Lunn would uphold his side of our agreement, for the fey might twist the truth, or omit a crucial detail, but they did not lie. Or at least that's what the old tales said. Although I had said nothing, Fiachra nodded.

"I see," he said. "Time heals most wounds, whether we intend it or no."

There seemed nothing left for me to say. Although I was inclined to like him, I wasn't sure I could trust this druid brother of my husband. Fiachra's inquiry of me was obviously concluded, for he turned now to Eithne.

"Sister." He offered her a brief smile and, to my mind at least, it seemed almost tender. "You have made a decision."

"I don't know what you mean." Eithne shrank back into her chair, shoulders hunched as if to make herself invisible.

Fiachra stretched out his hand and touched her gently on the forehead. "Travel safe, dear sister. The one whom you seek is unreliable. You will need to keep eyes and mind open. Stay alert, for that place is fluid and dangerous. Do not trust anyone."

Eithne's face was pale but the way she held her mouth said clearly that she would not be dissuaded. "I will do what I must. I am not afraid."

"You should be," he said. "Most mortals do not return from there, and those that do are forever changed."

"There is risk in all life," Eithne said. "That does not mean one should sit at home and be afraid to step outside."

Fiachra smiled, and it seemed there was sadness in the expression. "Our family has been blessed, and cursed, many times over. Some of those blessings are physical, like the fertile land around us. Others are invisible to the eye, but powerful none the less. That is why they watch us. Our ignorance is intrinsic to their aims. If our family ever understands the truth, what they aim for will be much harder and they may well fail. Diarmuid is not the only one in this family with power. You will not unlock your own ability until you understand its source."

Eithne's forehead wrinkled. "I don't understand."

"You will," Fiachra said. Then he turned back to me.

"Grainne, you have been brave thus far and it seems you must continue to be brave for much longer. You have thrown your lot in with the family of Silver Downs. Whether you understood what you were doing is no longer relevant. You have made your choice and choices have consequences."

"I will face whatever I must." I clenched my hands together so he would not see the way they trembled.

"He is safe, for now. Get to him as fast as you can."

My heart lurched and I wanted to jump out of the bed and shake Fiachra until he told me everything he knew. "Are you certain?"

"He will be much changed from the man he was."

"Where is he? How do I find him?" My voice cracked.

Fiachra stepped back towards the door. "If you look, I believe you will find him, for your will is strong and your heart is pure."

He left, closing the door softly behind him. Eithne and I sat in stunned silence.

"How did he know those things?" she asked finally.

"He is a druid. I would not assume anything is secret from one such as he."

"What did he mean, the things he said to you?"

I hesitated. I was not yet ready to talk about Caedmon or what I had done. When I didn't answer immediately, Eithne shook her head.

"You don't need to tell me. I don't mind if you have secrets."

"I feel like I should tell you. After all, you have shared your secret with me. But I can't."

"You can tell me when you are ready. I won't pester you about it."

We fell into silence. I was occupied with thoughts of Caedmon and what Fiachra might mean about him being changed. At least I knew he was safe.

We agreed to leave after breakfast the next day and Eithne retired to her bedchamber. I took the pack Caedmon had intended to take with him and tipped out its contents, sorting through them carefully. I had not been able to make myself empty it until now. It had seemed too much like an admission that Caedmon would never need it. The pack didn't contain much: a spare shirt, a blanket, a water flask, flint, a small purse of coins, a knife. If that was all Caedmon had thought he would need, I would trust it would be sufficient for our journey too.

As dusk fell and I ate yet another lonely dinner from a tray, my memories of Caedmon were so strong I could almost feel him there with me. The room still held the faintest trace of his scent and if I closed my eyes and concentrated, I could just smell it.

"I'm coming, my love," I whispered into the empty room. "Wait for me. I will find you."

GRAINNE

*a*fter breakfast the next morning, I lifted my pack and left my bedchamber for the first time since the night Lunn had locked me in. Although I had walked no farther than the length of the bedchamber for some weeks now, I felt stronger than I had expected as I tiptoed down the hall.

I hoped to slip unnoticed through the house, for there would undoubtedly be questions and exclamations if anyone saw me and I didn't know how I would answer them. The brothers must have already left to start their day's chores though and the only voices I could hear were of Agata and the servant women, and they were at the other end of the house.

Eithne already waited at the back door, looking wan and delicate in sturdy boots and a thick coat. A large pack sat beside her on the floor.

As I pulled my coat off its hook, she hefted her pack. She hesitated a little and I swiftly reached for it, twisting it from her arms with little effort. It was far heavier than mine.

"Here, you carry mine and I will take this one," I said.

"I can manage." She reached for her pack, but I slung it over my shoulder.

"Don't be foolish, Eithne. You won't last an hour carrying this. Take mine, it's much lighter. What on earth do you have in here?"

"Food, mostly. Bread, cheese, dried meat, fruit. The tales say mortals should not eat the food of the fey or they will never be able to leave."

We departed and I set a slow pace, aiming to conserve her strength for as long as possible. What we would do when she could walk no further, I didn't know. Nights would be cold with only my one blanket between us, but we had our coats, and flint. I could survive a couple of early spring nights. It was Eithne I worried about. We had been walking for only minutes before her breathing grew heavy and she began to favour one leg.

"Have you hurt your foot?" I asked.

She shook her head, too breathless to speak. Her face was red and covered with a sheen of sweat.

"Let's stop for a few minutes. We both need to catch our breath."

There was nowhere to sit, other than the dewy grass and patches of half-melted snow, so we stood with the morning sun beating down on our heads. Although we had a long journey ahead of us yet, I felt free. Lighter. Every step brought me closer to Caedmon. When Eithne's breathing sounded more even, I set off again.

"What is wrong with your foot?" I asked, noting that she still seemed to limp.

"It is deformed." Eithne's tone was somewhat defensive. "It twists inward. I was born like this."

"I've never noticed you limp before."

"I don't, usually. But when I am tired, it is hard not to."

I didn't comment further although I wondered what else she kept hidden.

Again and again, we walked until Eithne was straining to breathe, then we stopped to rest, standing in a field. When our stomachs started to rumble, we ate bread and cheese. The bread was cool but fresh and the cheese was sharp and crumbly. My appetite was stronger than it had been for weeks.

The sun was starting to sink as we finally reached the edge of Silver Downs' land. The woods loomed ahead of us, far larger than I had imagined. I could see nothing past the first few trees, which were a mix of ash, oak and birch. The darkness within was like a blanket, thick and obscuring, despite the mostly naked branches of the trees on the edges. I quailed a little and if my journey had been for any purpose other than to find Caedmon, I might have turned around and gone home. But I did not intend to let my husband down.

Eithne's face was pale and she trembled with exhaustion. When she caught me examining her, she lifted her chin in a manner I had come to recognise as Eithne deciding to be brave.

"I am fine," she said.

"We will need to make camp soon. Should we go into the woods or find a suitable place out here?"

"Let's keep going. We are close to the portal, I can feel it."

"What do you mean?" I felt nothing other than apprehension about entering the woods, the creeping coldness of night approaching, and fatigue from walking all day.

"There's a... pull," Eithne said. "It's like something tugging on my insides. Drawing me closer. Whatever it is, it wants me to find it."

So we entered the woods. They were dark and still but not as cold as I had expected. In fact, within their shelter, the air was rather warmer. If the woods held a consistent temperature, the nights might not be as unpleasant as I had feared.

Once we passed the outer trees, the light inside the woods seemed brighter than the sinking sun outside. In fact, the farther we walked, the brighter it became until I would have sworn we walked through a shady patch of trees in the middle of the day rather than through woods at dusk. Somewhere high above me, a woodlark sang a merry tune.

"Strange," Eithne murmured, and I finally realised she had stopped some distance behind me.

"What is it?"

"The birch already has catkins. And look, blackberries."

"It is warm in here. Perhaps winter has not touched these woods as much as it has affected us outside."

Now that Eithne had drawn my attention to our surroundings, I noticed that the naked branches of winter were gone and so too were the buds of early spring. The oaks were decked in their summer finery with glossy green leaves and small acorns. The ash bore tiny purple blossoms. A small flying creature fluttered past my face, its colourful wings drawing my gaze, and landed on the branch of a birch not far from us, as if to watch our progress.

Eithne breathed more easily now and her limp was less pronounced, despite how exhausted she must be. My pack didn't seem quite as heavy and my feet hardly ached at all anymore. There was something invigorating about these woods.

I was about to ask whether Eithne still felt the pull of the portal when the ground began to vibrate and a thundering echoed through the woods. It sounded like horses. A stampeding herd, perhaps? An unusual thing to encounter here, but then these woods were strange anyway.

Eithne looked as confused as I. My thoughts whirled. What should we do? My first instinct was to climb a tree, to get out of the way before the herd crushed us to death. But I could not climb wearing a long skirt, and Eithne would not have the strength to, so I grabbed her hand and we backed up against an oak. I held my breath and prayed the herd wouldn't notice us.

They were elegant white beauties, heaving from their run. But this was no spooked herd. They carried fey riders: tall and thin with hair the colour of the dark of the moon and lips so red they looked like gashes in their pale skin. They clutched long spears and wooden clubs. Running along with the horses were hounds, brown and slender with long necks and eager legs.

They would have rushed right past if it weren't for one of the hounds who stopped to sniff at us, perhaps curious about our foreign scent.

"Go away," I hissed quietly. "Please, go."

One of the riders reined in his horse to check on the hound and then they were all pulling up, surrounding us. They sat straight-backed on their horses, their dark clothes giving them a grim appearance. Their faces were angular and cruel and filled with suspicion. The horses and hounds were unnaturally silent and still.

"What have we here?" asked the one who had stopped to check on the hound.

Eithne squeaked in fear and it was obvious I would have to do the talking.

"We are merely passing through." My voice trembled almost as much as my legs. I clutched Eithne's hand tightly, as much to stop her from running away as to remind myself I was not alone. "We mean no harm."

As one, the fey all laughed.

"We mean no harm," one said in a falsetto clearly intended to mimic my tone.

"Merely passing through," said another.

"You are trespassing," said the one who had found us. "How did you get here?"

"We walked. The woods border our lands on one side."

"You walked from there to here?" He lifted an eyebrow as if to suggest he did not believe me.

I did not respond for I didn't know what to say. How else did he think we got here? By flapping our arms and flying like birds?

"How did you find the portal?" he asked.

"We didn't. That is, not yet. We were looking for it."

A low hiss arose from the rest of the party and was silenced immediately when the one speaking to us, clearly their leader, held up his finger.

"Do you mean you passed through the portal without even knowing?" His tone held a dangerous message.

Eithne and I looked at each other.

"Is this… is this the realm of the fey?" I asked when it became clear he intended to wait for however long it took us to respond.

Again the fey laughed and once again they were silenced at the slightest gesture from their leader.

"You did not even realise you were no longer in the mortal realm? Why must mortals be so stupid?"

"How were we to know we had passed into your lands?" Anger rumbled within me. "There was no visible portal. We simply entered the woods and found ourselves here. There was no transition, nothing to mark the passing from one place to another."

"You did not recognise that woods as lush and bountiful as these could not exist in your own realm?"

"I have never been in any woods before. How am I to know whether these are unusual?"

The fey twittered and even their leader laughed this time. They all stopped in the same instant.

"Bring them," the leader said, his voice casual. He tugged on the reins, turned his horse, and rode away.

Before I had time to wonder what he meant, one of the fey leaned down from his horse to grab me. His fingers dug painfully into the soft skin on the undersides of my arms. He hauled me up to sit behind him. There was no consideration given to the practicality of riding a horse while wearing a dress and consequently my skirt was bunched around my hips, displaying an inappropriate amount of leg.

"I suggest you hold on," he said.

I barely had time to grab his waist before we set off. The horses thundered through the woods. The hounds kept pace, baying from time to time. I had no hope of remembering the path we took, for we travelled so swiftly that the trees were merely a blur. I couldn't see Eithne and panic began to well within me. Surely they didn't leave her behind? But eventually I caught sight of her dark hair. She too was lodged behind one of the riders. Then the horse I rode jumped over some obstacle and I could think of nothing other than clutching the shirt of the fey man in front of me.

We rode for hours. As the terror wore off, I became tired, for we had walked all day and it must be late night by now, even though the light never changed. My eyes grew heavy and my arms and legs ached from holding on so tightly. I dozed off several times, waking with a start as my head nodded and my desperate grip on the fey man slackened. Still we rode, the horses and hounds never tiring.

Occasionally one of the riders let out a blood-curling scream. I couldn't see anything but the back of the fey in front of me. Whatever quarry they pursued must have finally escaped, for all of a sudden, the horses veered off. I clung to the fey rider as his horse turned sharply. If I fell, I would be trampled beneath the horses' hooves.

After what seemed like several more hours, the horses finally slowed. We halted in a large clearing, a dozen horses and half as many hounds. Their sides heaved as they panted and strands of white foam draped from their mouths. I wondered what they really were, for no ordinary horse could have run so long.

The fey slid down from their mounts, and boys — mortal boys — emerged from somewhere behind the trees that ringed the clearing. They took the horses' bridles and led them away. A mortal woman appeared and although she said not a word, the hounds gathered around her and followed her back into the woods. The fey too melted into the trees, except for their leader and the riders with whom Eithne and I had travelled.

"How dare you," I spluttered, finally able to speak now that my feet were on the ground and my skirt covered my legs. "What right have you to abduct us?"

The leader was unperturbed at my outburst. "We do not suffer mortals to trespass uninvited in our realm."

"I already told you we did not know we had passed through the portal."

"You also admitted you were searching for it. The portal chooses who it allows through. Some may search their entire lives and never find it. Others find it immediately."

"So how it is our fault if this portal chose us and let us through? That hardly counts as trespassing."

He shrugged, looking bored. "I will not debate with you. The queen will decide your fate." He snapped his fingers at the two riders and stalked away without another word.

One of the riders grabbed me roughly by the arm and dragged me with him as he strode through the woods.

"Could you at least slow down?" I struggled to keep my feet beneath me as we hurried over twisting roots and rocks and slippery patches of leaves.

He didn't look at me nor slow his pace, and all I could do was try to keep up. I had little time to wonder how Eithne fared. We stopped beside a large oak, its mighty girth and spreading branches bearing testament to its age. The fey pressed his palm to the trunk and it swung open. He flung me into the cavity within the tree.

By the time I got my feet back under me and managed to stand, Eithne was on her hands and knees beside me. The trunk closed and we were left in darkness.

GRAINNE

*T*he darkness was absolute and panic gnawed at my stomach. I had never liked the dark.

"Grainne?" Eithne's voice was thin and full of fear. "Where are you?"

I swallowed down my fear. I was the older of us, the married woman. I had to lead by example.

"I'm here." My voice wavered only a little. "Stand still and I will find you."

I stumbled around until I crashed into her and we clutched each other. She felt small and fragile in my arms. The space in which we stood seemed too large for the inside of a tree, even one the size of a great oak. The air was a suffocating mix of mustiness and damp earth. I closed my eyes and tried to pretend it was only dark because of that. But still my heart raced and my breathing was ragged.

"What do you think they mean to do with us?" Eithne whispered.

"He said we will be presented to the queen. I suppose that's Titania." I breathed deeply, in and out. I had to stay calm for Eithne's sake. "We will have an opportunity to make our case and then, when she realises we have done nothing wrong, we will be released."

A small sob was Eithne's only reply.

"We should sit," I said. "Get some rest. Who knows how long we will be waiting here and surely we have been up all night."

Still clutching each other, we sank down onto the floor. It felt to be made of hard-packed dirt, scattered with small remnants of something that might have been hay.

"Lie down and put your head in my lap," I said. "You may as well try to sleep."

Eithne said nothing but she lay down. I stroked her hair, which was tangled from our ride. Eithne's shoulders shook occasionally, although she tried to suppress her sobs, but eventually her breathing became deep and even. My fear of the dark returned once I no longer needed to be brave for her sake. I continued to smooth her hair slowly, forcing myself to inhale and exhale in time with the motion.

I tried to stay awake but my eyes were heavy despite my fear. I woke with a start each time my head dropped, my heart thudding as I listened for any sign that the fey returned. Hours passed and my fear receded a little. My bladder began to ache and my stomach growled. Hunger and thirst warred with fatigue. Finally Eithne stirred and sat up. The darkness was so complete that I couldn't see her, even though she was right beside me.

"How long did I sleep?" she asked.

"A long time."

"I feel a little better. You should sleep now."

I lay down and rested my head in Eithne's lap. Her skirt smelled of horse and sweat. The earthen floor was cool and hard beneath me.

I woke as light poured in, burning my eyes and leaving me blind. I struggled to sit up but my feet were tangled in my skirt.

"Get up," someone said.

Eithne and I stumbled to our feet. My muscles were stiff and I moved slowly. I bent to pick up my pack but somebody grabbed me by the arm and hauled me outside.

"Wait, my pack," I said, but they paid no heed.

Again they hauled us through the woods, caring little whether we kept our feet beneath us or were dragged behind. By the time my eyes adjusted enough to see, there were no familiar landmarks.

We stopped in a large clearing; the same as yesterday or a different one, I couldn't tell. Dozens of fey waited. A crowd of mortals would be fidgeting, chatting, quieting noisy children, but the fey were silent and still. They stared as we stood at the clearing's edge, our guards beside us still grasping our arms.

"Can we not have some time to make ourselves presentable before we speak with the queen?" I asked the fey who held me. He wasn't the one with whom I had shared a horse yesterday.

He clearly heard me, for his gaze flicked towards me briefly but he didn't acknowledge my words in any other way.

"Please?" My voice was as meek and placid as I could make it. "I'm rather-"

"Silence," he said with a tug on my arm so firm, I wondered that it didn't pop out of its socket. "You are not permitted to speak until you are told to."

"Not permitted?" I forgot all thoughts of being meek and placid. "How dare you! We have been brought here, unwillingly, by force. Kept in a dark room for hours, and now you tell me I am not permitted to speak?"

He turned to me and looked me in the face for the first time. His midnight eyes blazed.

"You will be silent. If you wish to see the queen, you will do as you are told. Otherwise I will return you to your quarters and you will wait until the queen expresses a desire to see you. And that may be a very long time."

I opened my mouth but Eithne caught my eye. Her face was pale and streaked with tears and I suddenly remembered why we were here. I closed my mouth with a snap and directed my gaze at the ground so he would not see the hatred I was sure burned in my eyes.

We waited. I was beginning to wonder how much longer I could hold my bladder when a company of guards marched into the clearing. Following them was a fey woman. Tall and luminescent, with the white skin and black hair typical of that race, she exuded power and cruelty and I was suddenly very afraid. Afraid for our safety, afraid she might not allow us to do what we came for, afraid we would spend the rest of our lives locked in that dark hole in the tree.

Titania settled herself on a golden throne I would have sworn wasn't there earlier. She wore a long scarlet dress that flowed like blood over her legs and pooled at her feet. She raised one hand and our fey guards dragged us forward. We were deposited in front of the throne. Titania eyed us up and down, distaste apparent in her cold gaze.

"Kneel," my guard hissed. When I hesitated, he grabbed me roughly by the shoulders and forced me down. Side by side, Eithne and I knelt in front of Titania, the grass damp and cold beneath our knees.

Finally, Titania spoke. "What have we here?"

"Two mortals, my lady," my guard said. "We found them on the edge of the woods."

"They passed through the portal without aid?"

"So it seems, my lady."

"What is your purpose here?"

For a moment I didn't realise Titania's words were directed at us. I glanced at Eithne, for this was her story to tell. My purpose would remain a secret for as long as possible lest I jeopardise Caedmon's safety.

Eithne's mouth trembled but she straightened her shoulders and lifted her chin, much the way her bard brother composed himself before he began a tale. My heart pounded as I waited for her to speak. Her words would determine our future.

EITHNE

"My lady, we apologise for the intrusion." I wasn't sure whether I was permitted to look at the queen but when I dared to raise my head, nobody shoved it back down again. I was proud of the calm in my voice. "We stumbled through the portal without realising, although it is true we were searching for a way into your realm."

"Explain yourself." Titania's voice was as wintry as her eyes. The fey around us were silent and I didn't dare look away from her to see whether they stared at us.

I darted a glance at Grainne and she nodded. Whether she meant for me to tell the truth, or merely intended encouragement, I didn't know. We should have spent the time we were shut inside the tree figuring out what to say to our captors instead of sleeping. I took a deep breath and continued.

"We came to search for someone. One of your folk. His name is Kalen."

Titania made a sound I couldn't interpret and her face screwed up as if she had tasted something sour. "What makes you think he wishes you to find him?"

"Do you know him?" My heart leapt. This might be easier than I had expected. "Can you tell me where he is?"

"I ask the questions. How do you know him?"

I hesitated. If I told the truth, Kalen might be in trouble but I couldn't think of a plausible lie quickly enough. "I've met him. In the mortal world."

"So why do you seek him here, if you can see him in your own world?"

"Because he has stopped coming to visit me and I am afraid it means he is in trouble."

Titania raised one eyebrow and continued to stare at me. The guards flanking her throne smirked.

My knees were starting to ache, but I didn't dare stand. I was confused by the guards' reaction.

"Why is that funny?" I asked.

"Many mortal women have been in the same situation as you find yourself now," she said, and if I had thought her stare cool before, it was even colder now. "They fall in love with a fey. They think themselves to be special. They believe their fey lover's promises to always be true. And when he loses interest, the mortal fails to understand. She searches for her lover, determined to find him and reignite his interest. But the truth is that the attention of the fey is fickle. We forget far easier than mortals do. If he has stopped coming to warm your bed at night, the only thing you can do is forget."

"It's not like that. He is not my lover. And I don't believe he has merely forgotten me. Something is wrong."

"And you think you can solve his problem? You, a mortal woman?"

"Without knowing what the problem is, I can't say. But I have come to find him and to help however I may."

Titania's face shifted and I thought for a moment she would laugh. But her voice was still as unforgiving as stone. "There is no problem. He has merely lost interest. Go home. I will have you taken back to the portal if you promise to leave immediately and never return."

Beside me, Grainne stiffened. Was this what she wanted? To turn around and go home? I couldn't ask with Titania glaring down at us. But

Grainne knew why we had come. Surely she would not expect me to leave yet.

"I am here to find Kalen," I said. "Will you give me leave to search for him?"

"Search for him?" Titania's voice rose. "How do you think to find him? Do you plan to wander aimlessly through my realm, hoping you might stumble upon him?"

Yes, that was pretty much what I had intended.

"Do you know where he is?"

"I know everything that happens in this realm."

"Would you send someone to fetch him? Give me a chance to speak to him? If what you say is true, that he has merely lost interest, I will return home without complaint and will never come back. But please let me just talk to him."

"He will not be interested. He has probably already taken a new lover and forgotten about you."

"If that's true, I will accept it. But I will not believe he has forgotten me unless I hear it from his own lips."

"What would you give to speak to him?"

"I don't understand." I wiped my sweaty palms on my skirt. The ache in my knees was almost unbearable and the damp from the cold grass soaked my skirt.

"You think to come uninvited to my realm and demand to speak to one of my subjects? For nothing?"

"Tell me what you want."

"You must complete a task."

"Name your task."

"You will serve as a slave to my people — for one hundred years. At the end of that time, you may speak to him."

My heart dropped. For a moment I could hardly breathe. One hundred years? I would not age in the fey realm, or I would age very slowly, but life would continue in my own world. By the time I left, everyone I had ever known would be dead. I could never return to my old life.

"And if I refuse?" Papa always said one must understand the consequences before making a decision.

"You will be a slave anyway. Until I choose to release you."

"And you will allow Grainne to return home?"

"If you refuse, you will both stay as slaves."

I heard Grainne's intake of breath. I couldn't condemn her to an endless period of slavery at the whim of the fey. No matter the consequence for me, Grainne must be free. She had come out of friendship, or perhaps loyalty to her husband's family. The reason was irrelevant. It only mattered that she was able to leave safely.

"The agreement is that I will serve as your slave for one hundred years, after which time I will be able to speak to Kalen, and then you will allow me to go home?"

"Correct."

"Then I agree."

Titania nodded once, the movement short and sharp. "Take them away."

The guard seized me once more by the arm and hauled me away, his fingers digging into already-bruised flesh. Beside me, Grainne was subjected to the same treatment. There was no time to protest. I didn't have breath to speak as long as I was trying to keep my feet beneath me. We stopped in front of a tree and the trunk opened, revealing a dark interior. Whether it was the same tree as before, or another, I couldn't tell. I was tossed inside with Grainne close behind me. Then the door closed and I could see nothing more.

"Wait," I called. "Grainne is supposed to go home."

On my hands and knees, I stumbled back to where the door was. My skirt, wet from the grass, wrapped around my legs. I found the door and banged on it with my fists. It felt as solid as any tree trunk and my fists quickly bruised. "Come back. You have to take Grainne home."

"Eithne, Eithne." Grainne's hands were on my shoulders, pulling me back from the door.

I turned to her and we wrapped our arms around each other.

"She was supposed to send you home," I said, stifling a sob.

"She did not say she would. Only that she would not allow me to go if you refused."

"I did not intend to agree for both of us. She knew that." I could no longer hold back the tears. My sobs came thick and fast.

"Ssh." Grainne stroked my hair. "What is done, is done. There is nothing we can do about it now."

"We can ask to see her again. Explain I wasn't speaking for you."

"It's too late, Eithne." Only now did Grainne's voice break and her hot tears fell on my arm. "It's done and it can't be undone."

"I would have never agreed if I knew."

"There was no choice. She intended to keep us as slaves no matter what you said. At least this way, we know when our imprisonment will end."

"One hundred years. How will we survive that long?"

"We will survive because we must."

All I wanted to do was cry into her shoulder, but Grainne was being so strong that I tried to collect myself. "You're right. We mustn't lose hope. But how will we mark the passing of the days? It is impossible to tell in here, and out there, the light is always the same. Already I don't know whether we have been here for one day or several."

"I don't know. We will find a way. But for now, let's see if we can figure out what we have in here. My bladder will burst if I don't empty it shortly."

With outstretched hands we felt our way through the darkness. In one corner we found a meagre pile of hay. Elsewhere was a clay pot that stank of urine. Nothing else. If our packs had been here, they were no longer, but perhaps this was not the same place we were kept in previously.

"Nowhere to sleep," I said, my voice forlorn, "unless the hay is intended as a bed."

"I suspect it is." Grainne's voice was brisk. She was much better at coping, at just getting on with things, than I was. I resolved to learn from her example. "It seems they think us little more than pigs so they have given us hay to sleep in and a dark hovel."

"I wouldn't treat a pig this badly."

"At least we have a chamber pot."

I heard the rustling of skirts and then the sharp ping of liquid hitting the base of the clay pot. The stench of urine reached my nose.

"Do you need the pot?" Grainne asked.

We fumbled around, searching in the darkness for each other, before she finally managed to pass me our chamber pot.

"We need somewhere to keep it," she said. "Where we won't knock it over."

There weren't many options. The area in which we were confined appeared to be roughly circular. The complete absence of light left no direction for navigation. The only feature that might serve as a landmark was the pile of hay and we decided to stand the chamber pot against the opposite wall. It was still possible, perhaps even probable, that one of us would knock it over, but it was the best we could do.

"They could at least have left us some food," Grainne said.

My stomach growled in response. My pack had contained food enough for a couple of days but if we were to remain here for a hundred years, we would have to eat their food sooner or later. And eventually we would learn whether the old tales were true.

EITHNE

*G*rainne and I curled up together in the hay. We left our boots on for fear that we would not be given time to put them on when the fey returned and might lose them forever. With both our coats draped over us, we huddled close together for warmth.

I dozed for a while but mostly I lay awake, cursing myself for getting us into this mess. If only I hadn't allowed Grainne to come with me. If only I had been more specific when I agreed to Titania's offer. I should have stipulated that Grainne was to be returned safely home immediately.

I went over and over everything that had been said, both my words and Titania's. What else had I missed? The wording of the pledge seemed simple enough: *The agreement is that I will serve as your slave for one hundred years, after which time I will be able to speak to Kalen, and then you will allow me to go home.* No matter how I picked and prodded, I could find no loophole Titania might exploit, except perhaps that I had agreed to speaking *to* Kalen instead of *with* him. My words indicated clearly that I spoke only for myself.

But as Grainne said, what was done was done. I couldn't blame her if she was furious with me. If she refused to speak to me for the next hundred years, that would be no more than I deserved. I could see why Caedmon chose her. A soldier needed a wife who was strong and composed and not given to fits of hysteria. And that was Grainne. He would be proud of her. Tears pricked my eyes again. I could not afford to think about Caedmon. I would likely never learn his fate now, not if I was kept here for a hundred years.

After hours had passed — certainly longer than a single night — the trunk silently cracked open and light flooded our prison. Grainne and I sat up, arms shielding our eyes from the sudden brightness. A draught flowed in and I suddenly realised how stale the air had become. Hay stuck to my skin, making it itch, but before I could brush it away, a woman spoke.

"Get up," she said. Something landed on the dirt floor with a thud. "Eat and make yourselves respectable. It is time for you to work."

Still mostly blind, we scrabbled around in the dirt. I found it first, my fingers closing around a half loaf of bread. I tried to tear it in two but it was stale and hard.

"Here, let me." Grainne took the bread from my hand and ripped it apart. She handed me half and started nibbling on hers.

I gnawed ravenously, hungry enough to ignore its strange taste and odour. As my eyes adjusted, I finally saw what we were eating. The bread was not only stale, it was covered in large blotches of moss-green mould. I gagged, spitting out the mouthful I had yet to swallow. My stomach spasmed.

Grainne tossed the mouldy bread to the floor and then leaned over to retch loudly. When she had finished, she wiped her mouth with the back of her hand and then turned to the fey woman who waited in the doorway.

"We cannot eat that," she said. "That is not fit for human consumption."

"It is fit for slaves," the fey said, her voice bored and uninterested. "Eat it or not. There will be no other food."

"But it will make us ill," I said.

The fey shrugged. "If you are finished with your meal, it is time to leave. If you walk nicely, I will let you walk on your own feet. Run, or do anything else to annoy me, and I will have you carried like sacks of turnips." She waved a hand in the direction of two large men who waited just outside.

They did not have the tall thin stature of the fey, nor their pale skin and black hair. Rather they were broad, one tending to fat, with pasty complexions, straw-like hair and blank faces. If they recognised us as fellow mortals, they gave no indication of it. But still, seeing them gave me a small surge of hope. There might yet be someone who could help Grainne escape.

Grainne vomited again, a foul-smelling clear liquid that splashed over the bread on the floor.

"We're ready," she said.

We followed the fey woman as she led us on a winding path past birch and beech, fallen branches, and holly bushes laden with shiny red berries. I tried to remember landmarks, but it seemed we walked in circles, for a birch tree with a distinctive silvery knot seemed to be everywhere and we kept passing a log that held the nest of some small forest creature. A raven squawked from the branches of a beech, his harsh cry a challenge to those who disturbed the woods.

I was so intent on remembering our path that at first I didn't notice that it was no effort to keep from limping. My twisted foot seemed straight and I walked evenly.

The two mortal men followed, their footsteps loud in the silence of the woods. The fey woman walked ahead of us, soundlessly gliding from spot to spot. I tried to walk as quietly as she did.

"What is your name?" I asked at length.

"That is irrelevant."

"How is your name irrelevant? I just want to know what to call you."

"You call me nothing, for you will not speak unless I tell you to."

I said nothing further. There was no point wasting breath on her. I had hardly slept for what felt like days and had eaten nothing more than a few nibbles of mouldy bread. My limbs were weak and my head fuzzy. My tongue felt fat and thick, and my mouth tasted bitter.

Eventually we stopped in front of a large oak. My head was swimming by then and my vision was starting to waver. Grainne reached out and took my hand.

The trunk cracked open soundlessly, spilling out light and heat and the tantalising scent of fresh pastries. My stomach growled loudly. The fey woman waved us inside.

"You will work in here until I come to collect you."

Grainne and I hesitated and she huffed, indicating again for us to enter.

"Go. Hurry up."

Side by side, we entered the tree and the trunk closed behind us. Sweat immediately began dripping down my back, for the room was uncomfortably hot. Like the oak in which we had slept, this one seemed larger than it should. It was equipped as a kitchen, with a row of wood ovens along one curving side and a vast wall of food-laden shelves against the opposite side. A long work bench in the centre took up most of the rest of the space. Four mortal women worked frantically at the bench, sweat dripping from their faces right into the pastries they were preparing.

"Hurry up then," said a woman standing near the ovens. "Get to work. There's no time to waste and I won't have dawdlers in my kitchen."

She was definitely mortal, small and almost as round as she was high. She glared at us over a glistening red nose and a tray of pastries hot from the oven. My mouth watered.

"You there." She dropped the tray on a bench and pointed at Grainne. "Get over there and start peeling the turnips. And you-" She pointed at me. "Start sweeping."

"Could we-" I motioned towards the tray of pastries. "We haven't eaten since we were brought here."

The woman drew herself up to her full height, which was only about as high as my shoulder, and gave me a withering glare. "Slaves do not eat the food we prepare. You ought to get that straight first thing. You get caught eating this, the penalty is harsh. First offence is a whipping. Second offence, your hand is cut off. So get any thoughts of tasty pastries out of your head and start sweeping."

I was too scared to say anything else. Trying to ignore the tantalising scent, I took up a battered broom leaning against the wall and started sweeping the wooden floorboards. The floor though was charmed for I would clear one patch and start on another, and when I turned back to the first area, it would be just as dirty as before. I paused to wipe away the sweat dripping into my eyes.

"Sweep harder, you lazy wench," the fat woman said. "You think you're ever going to clean the floor at that pace?"

"It doesn't matter how fast I go, it's always just as dirty," I said.

She rolled her eyes and started transferring the hot pastries to cooling racks. "Every new slave says the same thing. Lazy, you all are, and don't think I don't know it."

"Are you not a slave?" Grainne asked. She stood at the far end of the long bench and I could barely see her above the enormous pile of purple turnips. She used a knife to scrape a turnip, dropping the skin into one tub in front of her and the peeled vegetable into another.

The fat woman huffed. "I am no slave. I am kinswoman to one of the fey. Half sisters, we are."

"Why do they make you work in here then?" Grainne asked.

"Make me?" The fat woman's voice was incredulous. "This is a privilege. And you will understand that before you ever leave here. Those turnips ain't going to peel themselves, so I suggest you move faster."

As harsh as the fat woman's words might have been, her tone wasn't quite as fierce as when she had spoken to me. I resolved to keep my mouth shut. Perhaps Grainne would be able to win her over. If the woman sympathised with us, she might help us escape, or at least give us some food. We worked in silence for a while before Grainne spoke again.

"Is there a name we might call you by?"

"You can call me Treva," the woman said and now her voice was almost kind.

"Well met, Treva. My name is Grainne and my sister is Eithne."

"You won't need names here, girl. The fey consider their slaves to be worth less than livestock. A few more years and you'll be thanking them for keeping you alive. So forget your names and focus on doing what you're told."

Grainne didn't speak again and I kept my head down, sweeping, sweeping, always sweeping, as my eyes blurred with tears. What had I done?

EITHNE

I could barely stand by the time the surly fey woman came to collect us. I had no way of marking the hours but surely we had laboured for at least the time between dawn and sunset. We were marched back to the tree they kept us in when they had no use for us. The two mortal men again followed.

The fey woman stopped at the tree. She handed Grainne a small jug of water and half a loaf of mouldy bread.

"I suggest you eat it this time. The next time you throw your food on the floor, there will be no more until you finish it."

We stumbled into the tree. There was just enough time to see that vomit still stained the earth although the uneaten bread had been removed. Then the door closed and we were in darkness. The room reeked of sickness and I breathed through my mouth in an attempt to avoid smelling it.

"They could have at least given us something to clean that up with." Grainne's voice was a mix of irritation and sadness. "I'll try to loosen some dirt to cover it or we'll end up walking through it."

She managed to hand me the bread and jug and then I heard her scrabbling at the ground. I stood still, clutching our poor meal, for fear that if I set it down to help, I would either knock it over or put it straight into the vomit she sought to cover. My legs shook and I swayed. My stomach had stopped growling, which was a blessing, but my throat felt so dry I could barely swallow. Finally Grainne was finished.

"Hand me the jug, Eithne. I know we have precious little water but I need to rinse my hands. I will drink less to make up for it."

"No, we will share whatever is left," I said, or at least that was what I intended, but my mouth didn't seem to work properly.

Grainne fumbled for the jug and I released it into her grasp. Water splashed on the earthen floor as she rinsed her hands. Then she took the bread and passed me back a portion.

"We have to eat it." Grainne's voice was determined. "Perhaps if we do, they will give us something better next time. And if they don't, at least we have something in our bellies. It is better than starving to death."

The darkness made the bread easier to eat, for I could more readily ignore the smell of mould than the sight of it. It tasted earthy, as if the loaf had been covered in dirt. We took a long time to eat, for it was so hard and stale that we could only gnaw at it. When we had finished, we took turns sipping from the jug. All too soon the water was gone.

"We may as well sleep while we can," Grainne said. "Who knows how long they will leave us here this time. Now that we have work to occupy us, they will likely give us less time to rest."

Irritation stabbed at me. Why did Grainne think she could make all the decisions? But I was too tired to fight with her so I said nothing. We lay on the hay with our coats draped over us. Although my stomach still felt empty and I was too thirsty, I fell asleep quickly. If any of the fey passed by our tree, I never heard a thing. I was still in a deep sleep when light flooded the interior.

"Get up, get up." It was the same fey woman who had escorted us yesterday. "Lazy creatures. You should be up already."

"How are we supposed to know?" Grainne asked. "There is no light in here and no way of marking the hours."

"You have food and water and a safe place to rest. You don't need anything else."

"But you said we should have known it was time to get up."

The fey exhaled, a short, sharp huff. "Get up already. I don't have all day to wait on you."

"If you could show us how to find the kitchen, we could make our own way there tomorrow," Grainne suggested.

I stumbled to my feet and tried to pick some of the hay off me as my eyes adjusted to the light. Beside me, Grainne did the same.

"Oh yes, give you a chance to escape? Wouldn't the queen be pleased with me."

"Why does she hate us?" I asked, sourly. "We haven't done anything wrong."

"You think she hates you?" The fey woman raised her eyebrows and looked genuinely surprised. "She feeds you, protects you, gives you work to do. Do you think she would do that if she hated you? I am starting to understand why they say mortals are too stupid to reason with. Follow me and keep close."

She turned and strode off. Grainne and I hurried to catch up. The two pasty-faced mortal men followed.

Treva greeted us with something that might almost have been a smile. "Turnips." She pointed at Grainne. "Sweep," to me.

The kitchen looked exactly the same as the previous day. The four mortal women were already at the work bench, shaping small pieces of pastry and filling them with something that might have been stewed fruits. My stomach grumbled loudly at the scent of cooking pastries.

Just like the day before, no matter how hard I swept, the floor was never any cleaner. And the pile of turnips next to Grainne never grew any smaller, despite the tub that filled with peeled vegetables.

Grainne tried to strike up a conversation with Treva, but the fat woman seemed ill inclined to speak today. She tried also to talk with the other mortal women but they did not even acknowledge her.

It was stiflingly hot in the kitchen. Treva kept a steady stream of pastries going in and out of the ovens. I couldn't tell what purpose there was to Grainne peeling so many turnips as I never saw Treva actually use any of them. But I was learning not to ask questions, only to watch. Watch and listen and look for an opportunity to get Grainne out of here.

Each day passed much the same. Some days stretched forever and others seemed like only a few hours before the fey woman came for us. The nights were as variable as the days. Some seemed as long as the span from one dawn to another, and on others we barely had time to eat our mouldy bread and fall asleep before the light streamed in and the fey woman yelled at us to get out of bed.

The hem on my shirt began to fray and I had caught my skirt on sharp branches often enough that it hung in tatters. The sole of one of my boots was near coming off. I didn't need a hand mirror to know I had lost weight I could ill afford to lose. Grainne's face was pinched and pale with dark shadows under her eyes. Her frame now looked much like mine, all angles and edges. I had to keep reminding myself that I was doing this for Kalen. Survive long enough and Titania would let me speak with him. And Grainne would be able to go home.

I began to wonder how much longer we could live like this. The erratic pattern of days and nights. Eating nothing but mouldy bread and a few mouthfuls of water. Being locked in the dark when we weren't required to work. I could barely remember what it felt like to sleep in a bed with a soft pillow beneath my head and woollen blankets piled over me. To sit in a comfortable chair drawn close by a fire. To eat a proper meal, with meat and vegetables and fresh bread. To drink ale or spiced wine. To be comfortable and clean. Things I once took for granted were all distant memories.

Every time I slept, I dreamed of Silver Downs. In my dream, I lay in my own bed, clean and well fed and comfortable. In my dream, I would wake as sunlight slipped in through the gap where I hadn't quite drawn the curtains. And then I would open my eyes and find myself in darkness, lying on a pile of hay, with Grainne beside me and our coats for blankets.

How much time had passed in the mortal world since we left? The old tales said time did not run to the same path in the mortal and fey worlds. I held onto the slim hope that although our slavery might span one hundred years, perhaps it wouldn't be that long in our own world. I might yet return home while my parents lived. But one hundred years here might be many more in our own world. My parents would probably die still wondering what had happened to the daughter who disappeared so many years ago. We might return to find Silver Downs crumbled to dust, generations of my family dead and gone.

Time was monotonous. Maybe it even stopped here. My hair and fingernails didn't grow and my monthly cycles, although always irregular, had ceased. Or maybe we had been here no more than a few days and that was why I saw no evidence of time passing.

My one hope was that Fiachra would come looking for us. His druid ways had clearly given him some insight into our journey for although I had told him nothing, he knew anyway. I doubted he would tell anyone where we were, even if they thought to ask, but perhaps when enough time had passed and we didn't return, he might come searching for us.

Every time I woke, I worried that my illness would return. For a few moments my stomach would tense and my heart would beat in double time. For what would the fey do with a slave who was too sick to work? But I had no fevers or sweats, no sudden faints. I was weak from lack of food, too much work, and not enough rest, but I was not ill. The other odd thing was that my deformed foot didn't twist quite as much. I didn't need to concentrate on keeping it straight as I walked or on hiding my limp. I was too embarrassed to ask Grainne if she knew why, but if I had any small joy during these days, it was that my foot seemed almost normal.

Sometimes I woke in the middle of the night and thought I couldn't keep living like this. That nothing existed other than this dark hole in a tree. I would cry — quietly so Grainne wouldn't wake — until my nose was blocked and my chest was tight. Then I would wipe my face with the grimy sleeve of my coat and wait for either sleep or the fey who escorted us to the kitchen.

And still I swept. Every day, I took up the battered broom with the misshapen wooden handle that left splinters in my soft palms before they grew hard with calluses. I swept and swept and swept. The floor never looked any different, whether I swept it or not, just as Grainne's pile of turnips never grew any smaller. Finally, after many days of frustration and exhaustion, I asked Treva why.

She gave me a disparaging glare. "It's because you're doing it wrong.

Foolish girl. I wondered how long you would sweep before you thought to ask."

My mouth dropped open. "Why didn't you tell me?"

Treva shrugged. "Not my place to offer advice. Not if you don't ask. Here, do it like this."

She took the broom from me and demonstrated. With a little flick of her wrist, the dirt disappeared as the broom touched it. It took several tries before I could mimic the action. Pain stabbed through my wrists, but if I flicked the broom in a certain way, the floor cleared. I almost cried with relief as I worked my way around the room and the dirt melted away before me.

"Would you show me too?" Grainne asked. I couldn't see what Treva did, but before long the pile of unpeeled turnips was visibly smaller.

By the time the fey woman came for us, the kitchen floor was clean and Grainne had only a small pile of turnips left.

Treva nodded at me as we left. "Might finally be able to put you to work doing something useful tomorrow."

She was true to her word. The following day, I was given the task of shaping little pastries like the other mortal women. I had still never heard them speak a word. They clustered down the other end of the long work bench and worked furiously at their tasks.

Now that I knew how the magic worked, it didn't take long to figure out the little flick of the wrist I needed to use as I formed each pastry. The piles of pastry and bowls of preserved fruits for the filling steadily decreased as I worked. The pastry was soft and cool on my callused fingers and if I hadn't feared Treva's reaction, I would have sunk my hands into it for the satisfaction of such a pleasant sensation.

Grainne finally finished the turnips and now she worked beside me. Her fingers were defter than mine and she soon produced twice as many pastries as I.

"How many of the fey does this feed?" I asked Treva a couple of days later, my fingers flying as I moulded the pastry, working more by feel than by look.

Treva pounded away, making pastry and stewed fruits and overseeing the constant stream of trays going in and out of the ovens. The other mortal women hunched over their own piles of pastry.

"None."

I waited, sure I must have misheard, but Treva didn't offer any further information.

"What do you mean, none? We work all day producing pastries. Surely we must feed a small army."

"This food does not feed anyone." Treva didn't look at me as she spoke, instead focusing on a mound of dough that was receiving a particularly severe beating. "It disappears overnight and tomorrow we start again."

"I don't understand."

"These pastries, they undo themselves overnight, pulling apart into their original ingredients. And tomorrow we make them all over again."

"We make the same pastries every day?" Grainne asked and her voice sounded as dispirited as I felt.

"You could think of it that way."

"But why?"

"Why what? There are lots of whys and you will drive yourself mad if you try to figure them all out. Just accept it and get on with the task. That's what I do."

"Why are you here, Treva?" Grainne asked. "Are you here of your own will?"

"Do you think anyone in their sane mind would do this willingly?" Treva left her dough and stooped in front of an oven. She removed a steaming tray of pastries. Her face was flushed from the heat of the oven.

"What did you do?" I asked.

"It is of no consequence, and indeed I have been here so long, I hardly remember anymore."

"How long will they keep you here?" Grainne asked.

I held my breath as we waited for Treva's response.

"Until they tire of me," Treva said. "And then, if I am lucky, they will kill me. If I'm unlucky, they will take my mind and send me home."

Grainne and I were both shocked into silence. She was the first to recover.

"You would rather die than go home?" she asked.

"I would rather die than go home without my mind. You must have heard tales of folk who return from the fey realm, witless and dumb. That is no life. Besides, I've been here so long there's probably nothing left of my family or my home."

"What family did you leave behind?" I asked, trying hard not to think of my mother and father and brothers whose faces were starting to blur in my memory.

"A husband and two sons." Treva passed a hand over her face. I couldn't be sure whether she wiped away sweat or a few tears. "But enough years have passed that I doubt they still wonder what happened to me, or hold any hope of my return. They will have moved on. If they are even alive. Chances are, they are long dead and sent to their rest."

"I have a husband," Grainne said after a while.

"He'll forget you soon enough," Treva said. "Men usually do. We're the ones who spend our lives remembering."

EITHNE

*B*ack in our tree cave, once we had eaten our meagre meal of mouldy bread and water, there was nothing to do but sleep. Grainne and I huddled under our coats on the pile of hay. I no longer even noticed the hay that pricked my skin and clung persistently to my clothes and my hair.

Treva's comments about being sent home without her mind kept running through my head. I had assumed that when we were eventually sent home, we would be whole. It had not occurred to me that there might be more punishment to come. The thought was more than I could bear.

"I don't know how much longer I can do this," I said softly into the dark.

Grainne's hand found mine. "Be strong, Eithne. There is no other choice."

"A hundred years is so long. And we don't know how much time has already passed. Have we been here for a month? Six months? A year?"

"It has been months, at least. Who knows, perhaps a whole year has already passed. We might only have ninety-nine years left."

Somehow that sounded even worse than a hundred years. A few

tears slipped from my eyes and I tried not to sniffle. I didn't speak again until I had myself under control.

"I don't know how you stay so strong. I wouldn't blame you if you never spoke to me again."

"What would be the point in that, Eithne? We have to stick together until we can get out of here."

Although I knew her words were intended as encouragement, irritation nibbled at me from her forceful tone. Grainne hadn't cried since that first day we were locked in here. She wasn't losing hope. She was as confident and capable as ever. I might have felt less alone if she had shown some emotion occasionally.

"I can't live like this for much longer. I'll go crazy, if I don't starve to death first." I stared into the darkness, forcing my eyes wide to stop more tears from falling.

"Like I said, we have to stay strong." Grainne's voice was still brisk and firm.

"We could try to escape. We've been assuming we can't but what if we are wrong?"

"And what then? We are in a strange land, with no food or drink but what is given to us, no friends, and no means of navigation. What do we do? Wander around until we happen on someone who will direct us back to the portal rather than imprisoning us?"

"It would be better than being slaves for a hundred years."

"You think starving to death lost in some fey woods is better than being a slave? At least here we are fed and we are safe."

"That mouldy bread they feed us is hardly food," I said bitterly.

"You got us into this, Eithne. The only thing we can do now is endure."

Her words stung although I knew she was right. I stopped trying to provoke her. It never mattered what I said, Grainne still didn't show any despair or fear or even longing for home. Although with Caedmon dead, maybe she felt there was nothing worth going home to.

"I need to find Kalen," I said. "That's what I came here for. If we get away, you should try to find the portal, but I still need to find him."

"I'm not leaving you alone."

We were silent for a time. I concentrated on breathing evenly, still trying not to cry, and wished we at least had a proper blanket. I wasn't quite cold but I wasn't exactly warm either. The temperature in here, like so many other things about this world, seemed unchanging. Even the smell never changed. It was always earthy and dank with a faintly lingering odour of sickness. The kind of smell that lingered in the back of one's throat.

"We are always locked in," I said into the dark. I wasn't sure whether Grainne was still awake. "They guard us whenever we are outside. Our best chance might be to overpower the guards on the way to the kitchen."

"We assume we are locked in the kitchen," Grainne said.

The hay rustled as she shifted and I felt another stab of annoyance at her tone. If she knew so much, why hadn't she tried to escape already? "If the door is not locked and there is no guard, why are Treva and the other women still there?"

"We know little of Treva's story and none of that of the others. They may well have tried and failed. Or there might be something keeping them here, something that stops them from even trying to escape. Treva, at any rate, for she is the only one who still has her own mind. I think there is too little left of the other women for them to know, or care, where they are."

"That will be us eventually," I said, closing my eyes although it made no difference. The inside of my head was just as dark as the inside of the tree. "Mindless, care-less, just doing what we are told. Sleep when we are told to. Eat when we are told to. Make pastries when we are told to. A hundred years mightn't be so bad if I didn't have my own mind."

"Don't say that," Grainne said and at least now her voice held a spark of emotion. She grabbed my hand and squeezed my fingers so hard it hurt. Her fingers felt soft against my own calloused skin. "Don't ever wish you didn't have your own mind. You know they can take it from you."

"I hate Titania. She tricked me and now we find that even once we have served our time, they will take our minds. There was nothing fair about the deal she offered."

"We must stay strong and focused. We will watch for an opportunity to leave and see if anyone stops us."

"If they don't, what do we do?" I asked.

"We run."

GRAINNE

I tried not to be bitter with Eithne, but it was hard. I was trapped like a rabbit in a snare. Caedmon was here, somewhere, and maybe not very far away, and yet I couldn't search for him. We had seen nothing of this place except our tree, Treva's kitchen, the winding walk through the woods between them, and the clearing where Titania had pronounced our fate.

I tried hard to hide my resentment but it slipped through every now and then in my words or my tone. I felt bad about it — Eithne knew she was responsible for trapping us in this gods-forsaken darkness. The guilt ate at her constantly. But every day I thought about how I wouldn't be here if she hadn't agreed to Titania's ridiculous proposal. I would have found Caedmon and we would be back at home at Silver Downs. Our own home would be built by now. Perhaps we would even have a son. I ran my hand over my stomach, which caved in towards my spine. The fey gave us barely enough food to keep us alive. It was perhaps fortunate that the babe I had hoped I carried seemed to be no more. Or perhaps he had never existed.

As the months passed, Eithne sank deeper into melancholy. The only thing I could do was be strong and calm and confident we would survive, in appearance if nothing else. At least Eithne couldn't see into my mind where I too teetered on the edge of defeat every day.

The one weakness in our situation, it seemed, was Treva's kitchen. There was no visible guard, although we had no way of knowing whether she was under orders to ensure we did not escape.

Getting out of the kitchen would be difficult though, for we couldn't open the door and we wouldn't know whether there were guards outside until we tried to leave. No matter how carefully I watched the fey woman who escorted us there every day, I couldn't see how she opened the doors into the trees. No magical words were said and she didn't appear to use any special hand motion. I watched where she placed her feet, wondering whether perhaps she released a secret lever by standing on it, but she never seemed to stand in exactly the same place twice. It was as if she simply willed the tree to open. The fey who had first locked us in a tree had pressed his palm to the trunk but clearly that wasn't necessary.

I considered asking Treva if she would open the door for us, but she had made it clear that she herself was imprisoned. Reporting our intention to escape might win her some special favour. I couldn't risk it. So long as the fey believed we had no thought of escape, they probably didn't watch us too hard. Our only hope was surprise.

Day after day, for months on end, I stood at the long wooden work bench and my fingers flew as I shaped little pieces of dough into triangles and diamonds and squares. Dab the stewed fruit in the centre, fold up the corners, pinch, twist, turn, crimp the edges. Pastry after pastry. We became very proficient and between us we made thousands of tiny pastries every day. I had grown used to surviving on little food and my stomach no longer rumbled at the scent of the delicacies.

I had never heard a word from the other mortal women who worked with us. Treva rarely had reason to give them a direction but when she did, they swiftly obeyed. It was clear that at least some part of their minds remained. I had tried to speak to one or other of them at various times when Treva was busy with the ovens, but they never acknowledged me. I wondered whether they worked through the night, for they were always there when we arrived, and they remained when we were taken away.

Then came the day when Treva seemed distracted. We never spoke much as we worked, but I had twice asked her for more stewed fruit and she hadn't answered. From the corner of my eye, I saw that Eithne's fingers had stilled.

"Don't stop," I urged, for the pastry was fickle and would be ruined if we held it too long. Treva had hinted that our imprisonment could be made much worse if we were careless.

"Do you smell something burning?" Eithne shot me a glance. Her eyes glittered brightly and my first thought was that the illness had finally returned. Then I smelled the burning pastries. I kept working, although more slowly now, and tried to hide the way my body was tensed ready for flight.

"Treva?" Eithne said. "Is everything all right?"

Treva didn't respond. She was rearranging some pastries that had been set out to cool, although I could see no purpose to her task. Black smoke began pouring from one of the ovens. The air was suddenly thick and hard to breathe.

I flung my pastry down on the bench and raced to the oven. When I wrenched open the door, smoke poured out and heat blasted my face. I snatched up the towel that hung from a nearby nail, then squinting and trying not to breathe in the smoke, I fumbled around inside the oven. I managed to grab the tray of pastries. They were burnt to embers.

"Treva." Eithne's voice was urgent. "Quickly, open the door before Grainne gets burnt."

"Hurry, Treva, it's hot," I said.

Treva finally noticed me standing by the oven, clutching the tray of burnt pastries.

"Oh my," she said. "Oh dear. I am going to be in such trouble."

"Just open the door." I gritted my teeth and prayed hard. The tray was so hot that my fingers were already starting to burn through the towel.

The door swung open and fresh air streamed in. I raced for the exit, holding the tray out in front of me. As I stepped outside, Eithne was by my side. A quick glance around showed no sign of a guard. I threw the pastries, tray and all, on the ground, grabbed Eithne by the hand, and we ran.

GRAINNE

There was no sound of pursuit from behind us — yet. Perhaps Treva was busy clearing the smoke from the kitchen or something. We might have a precious few moments before she noticed our absence. I didn't let myself wonder what sort of punishment she would face for letting us escape. Treva was not my responsibility. My only obligation in this strange realm was to Caedmon. Eithne, I would keep safe for as long as I could, but now that we were free, Caedmon was my priority.

At first the woods seemed sparsely treed. Flight was easy and I ran too fast to think about where to place my feet. Step, leap to avoid a rock, slide in leafy ground cover, step, jump over a fallen branch, step, step, step. I dodged a startled raven who flapped his wings in my face in fear. My thighs were beginning to burn and my breath was short, but I kept going. As long as Eithne could keep running, I could too.

I had no idea what time of day it was. The light was noon-day bright as it always seemed to be in this place. We were moving too fast to be cautious about how much noise we made but I figured it didn't matter. They would pursue us anyway and our best chance was speed.

Just as my legs started to tremble and my lungs to heave, we were forced to slow to a jog. The trees grew closer together here, birch and ash and oak standing side by side. Every step now involved not just avoiding obstacles on the ground but also watching for branches that were ready to poke out an eye or stab us through the chest. Eithne lagged behind, although not so far that I felt obliged to wait. She gasped for breath, but continued gamely. No doubt if I could see her, her face would bear that expression I was now so familiar with, the one that said Eithne was determined to do something. Little sickly Eithne. If her brothers could see her fleeing the fey, how surprised they would be.

We splashed across a shallow creek. My well-worn leather boots filled with cool water, but there was no time to remove them and I dared not run barefoot anyway.

The trees gave way to thick holly bushes laden with shiny red berries. The leaf matter covering the ground disappeared and was replaced by a dense weed that wound around my feet. I paused to rip its sticky tendrils from my soggy boots, but they clung to my hand. When I tried to brush them off against my dress, they stuck there too. They tugged at my boots, threatening to tear them from my feet. The only thought in my mind was *keep moving.*

Eithne caught up when the sticky weed reduced my flight to a walk. Her breathing had an odd whistle and she wheezed.

"We should stop," I panted. "Rest."

Eithne shook her head. If she could continue, so could I, although my legs burned and with every breath I thought my lungs might burst.

The holly bushes gave way to enormous piles of tangled brambles. I forced my way through them. The strange weeds that clung to my feet now had more time to tighten their grip and I could no longer shake them off. I had to lift my foot and tug until the weeds broke. Then I could put that foot down and lift the other. Soon the brambles became too dense to push through and we could go no further.

There was no option but to go back. But when I turned, the brambles behind us were just as thick. We had left no trail, or perhaps the passage had closed.

"What is this?" Eithne asked between gasps.

"The woods have their own mind."

"They are alive?"

"I don't know. But they are surely trying to stop us."

"Do they mean to keep us trapped until the fey catch us?"

"Maybe."

The air was warm and thick like honey as I caught my breath. The woods around us were strangely silent. There were no sounds of pursuit but neither were there the usual sounds of woodlark or deer or badger. The only noises were our own ragged breathing. Eithne's hand slid into mine.

"Something is wrong," she whispered. "What do we do?" Her eyes were wide and her face too pale beneath the flush of exertion.

"We wait, I suppose. The woods have decided we may go no further."

My heart pounded and a sense of something sneaking up on us rose over me until I felt sure I would scream if I didn't do *something*.

"Perhaps we were going in the wrong direction," Eithne said quietly after we had stood there for some time. "Perhaps the woods don't mean to stop us, only to prevent us from going the wrong way."

We were surrounded by thick brambles that stood taller than we. If the woods wanted us to go in a particular direction, they gave no clue of it.

"Which way then?" I asked.

She shrugged and turned to the left. "I suppose we just try and see." She tried to step forward but the brambles remained solid and unyielding. "Not that way then."

But when we turned to the right, the brambles edged backward. One step, two. Our progress was slow but we were definitely moving. And the sticky weeds no longer latched onto my boots or wound around my legs.

"It's working," I said, too exhausted to be amazed.

"Do we keep going?"

"I can't see that we have another choice. We either follow or wait for the fey to find us."

She squeezed my hand and we moved forward together. The brambles gradually thinned and soon disappeared altogether, making way once more for the sparse woods in which we had started our desperate flight. We continued in the same direction, for fear the woods might rise up against us again if we didn't.

We walked until we could go no further and in all that time, I heard no sound of pursuit. But perhaps they did not need to pursue us. Maybe Titania had some magic that told her where any intruder stood.

Eithne finally threw herself to the ground. She covered her face with her hands and her shoulders heaved. I wasn't sure whether she was crying or just catching her breath and I didn't have the energy to ask. I lowered myself onto the blanket of fallen leaves. It was the softest seat I had had for months.

We sat in silence for some time. My eyes drooped but I dared not let myself fall asleep for fear the fey would sneak up and capture us again.

"We should keep moving," I said after a few minutes. My legs still trembled and, in truth, I wasn't certain I would be able to stand.

Eithne nodded and hauled herself to her feet.

"All right?" I asked. I stood, my movements stiff and awkward. My thighs burned and my feet ached and a long shallow cut stung my calf.

"I can't quite believe it yet. I don't dare believe for fear this is a dream and I will wake up in that horrid dark hole in the tree."

"We have to go. They might not be far behind us."

"But to where? We have no food or water, no shelter, no friends."

"I don't know. I'm just hoping that if we keep going, we'll figure something out. Or come across someone who can help us. Or stumble upon the portal. Perhaps if we go far enough, we'll find the edge of the woods and whatever is on the other side."

"There might be more than one portal." Eithne's voice was hopeful. "Although how we would recognise it, I don't know, given we never knew when we passed through the first."

"We just have to keep going. We managed to escape and the woods have helped, in their own way. If we go far enough, we will find something else, or someone, who can help us."

"Maybe we will find Kalen."

Or Caedmon, I thought, but I didn't say it.

GRAINNE

$\mathcal{A}$s soon as we had caught our breath, we started running again. I kept my gaze on the ground, partly to watch for obstacles but mostly because I didn't have enough energy to look anywhere else. The ground never changed: leaf litter, twigs and fallen branches, moss-covered rocks. I moved slowly now, too slowly.

Sunlight filtered in through the branches of oak and ash and beech. It could be mid morning or mid afternoon. I had long since given up trying to figure out what time of day it was, let alone the season. The woods hadn't changed at all during the months of our captivity. They were still lush with thick bushes and vines, mosses and the pleasant scent of decaying leaves. Shiny red berries blanketed the holly bushes. Catkins covered the birch trees. Woodlarks called from the branches of the trees, and under other circumstances, a walk through the woods would have been pleasant. But the relentless need to keep moving tore any joy from the fact that we were finally free.

Eithne stumbled and fell to her knees. I didn't ask whether she was hurt. I couldn't. Staying upright, breathing, keeping my feet moving — they were the only things I could focus on.

My wet boots rubbed my feet raw. Something dripped down the back of my boot — blood or perhaps pus. When I placed a hand over a stitch in my side, my ribs stuck out so sharply that I wondered why they weren't bursting through my skin. I was gasping for breath and moving slower and slower. We needed rest, sooner rather than later, and for that we needed shelter. A way to hide ourselves away from the sight of both casual passersby and those who might have reason to search.

I hardly noticed when our surroundings began to change again. It seemed that one minute we passed through normal woods spread with trees and bushes and leaf litter. Then all of a sudden, the trees were so close together that I had to turn sideways to slide between them. The leaf litter disappeared, replaced again with the strange tangly weed that reached up sticky tendrils to grasp my boots.

Brambles once again blocked our path and crept up behind us. They formed a solid wall taller than we stood. It was only then I noticed that the woods were deathly quiet.

"Why are the woods stopping us again?" Eithne's voice trembled.

"I don't know." I could barely make my mouth form words and I didn't know whether they were even comprehensible. I reached out and clasped her hand.

The ground began to vibrate. Eithne squeaked in fear.

"Ssh," I said. "Be quiet and still."

Within moments, the vibration became the recognisable thunder of hooves. I didn't need to see them to know that a herd of horses hurtled towards us. I was suddenly very thankful for the strange bramble wall that crept even closer around us until my legs could have given way and I would still have remained upright.

The horses thundered past, not very far away from us. Without the bramble wall, we certainly would have been seen. Were these our pursuers? Or other fey who just happened to pass by?

The sounds of the horses faded as rapidly as they had come. The bramble began edging away and soon we were able to continue walking. Eithne and I looked at each other. Her eyes were huge and dark in a face pale with exhaustion.

"Do the woods protect us?" she asked in a whisper. "Or does someone control the woods?"

I didn't have enough energy to reply.

We stumbled on. Surely at least a day had passed since we fled Treva's kitchen. A day in which we had not eaten or slept. We had drunk briefly from a stream, but that was hours ago. I had been watching for a suitable place to stop and finally I spied a tree with wide-leafed branches that draped down to the ground like a skirt. When I stopped beside it, my legs wobbled so hard that I didn't think I would be able to move again. I parted the leaves and peered inside. It would quite nicely fit one grown woman if she lay on her side and curled her body around the trunk.

"We can rest in here," I said. "Maybe we should split up. If one of us is found, the other might yet escape."

"We should stay together," Eithne said. "It's gotten us this far. I'll take the first watch. Lie down, Grainne. You look about to fall over."

Indeed I found myself swaying on my feet as she spoke. I should have argued, for Eithne was not as strong as I, but I couldn't. Instead I lay on the dirt with my hands under my cheek. The earthy aroma of my bed filled my nose. It smelled fresh and alive, not like the dank, stale smell of the tree in which we had been imprisoned. I was asleep almost before I closed my eyes.

I woke with a start, sitting up so quickly that blood rushed to my head and left me dizzy. Eithne sat with her legs drawn up, arms resting on them. Her face was pale and her eyes shadowed.

"Did I sleep long?" I ran my fingers through my short hair. It didn't seem to have grown at all in the last few months. At least it was mostly short enough that it didn't tangle.

"A while. Maybe a couple of hours."

"I feel much better," I lied. My mouth was dry but at least I had stopped feeling hungry. "Your turn."

Eithne obediently lay down and seemed to fall asleep almost immediately. I eased my boots from my feet. The leather had dried and the backs were stained with blood. I would have given almost anything for a hot bath and a change of clothes. After wearing the same gown for many months, it was so tattered and threadbare that the linen was almost falling apart. The fey must have noticed how neglected our clothes were and yet they had offered us nothing. I hoped the fabric would hold together until I could find Caedmon and get us out of this place. The boots would have to be forced back on my feet, although where we walked to, or for how much longer, I didn't know.

We could continue to walk if we had some supplies but we desperately needed to find food and water. Once Eithne woke up, we would make a plan. Perhaps we could forage in the woods around us. Surely there would be berries or nuts or mushrooms.

I sat up straight, legs tucked under me, and concentrated on staying awake. This was the first time in months that I had been able to sit in daylight, even if I was shrouded by branches. To just sit and be able to see seemed a precious thing after so long in darkness.

My eyes were heavy and although I kept telling myself I must stay awake, my head nodded. I would rest my eyes for just a moment although I would not let myself fall asleep.

SUMERLED

*T*he mortal women walk and walk, stumbling with slumped shoulders, barely picking up their feet. Why they do not stop to rest eludes me. They move with the force of much larger creatures, revealing their location to anyone who cares to listen as they step on twigs, crunch leaves, and frighten woodlarks into silence. I follow them easily for they make no attempt to cover their tracks.

In appearance, they are bedraggled and spent with pallid skin and greasy hair. Their clothes are threadbare, they limp, and they breathe far too heavily. I still have no idea why they fascinate Kalen. But right now they are my own delicious secret. He has no idea they are here. I had known from the moment they passed through the portal, for I had been watching even then. I have spied on them ever since without anyone ever being the wiser.

Keeping a secret is hard. It is even harder when the secret is so exquisite. I know why Kalen had stopped going to visit the mortal woman. I know she came here to search for him. And I know he doesn't know she is here.

When a group of fey come too close, I don't want the mortals to be discovered. I am having far too much fun sneaking along behind them, watching, and imagining Kalen's face when he discovers the mortal he is so fond of has been here for so long. I wouldn't help them in other circumstances, for nobody cares what befalls a pair of mortals trespassing where they should not. But if they are captured again, it will spoil all my fun.

So the woods rise up and shield them and the fey pass by without ever knowing how close they came to finding the mortals Titania had instructed the whole realm to search for. It would not do for my fun to end too soon and I know just how to make it last even longer.

EITHNE

I woke with Grainne's hand pressed over my mouth. Her
calloused fingers were rough against my lips.

"Don't make a sound," she breathed into my ear.

I froze, muscles tense and heart pounding, my cheek pressed into the
dirt.

Leaves crunched. A twig snapped.

Footsteps. Right outside our shelter.

They had found us.

Grainne was pressed close to me. She smelled of sweat and fear, and
her heart beat just as wildly as my own. I reached up to remove her
hand from my mouth.

The footsteps came closer. They stopped, right beside us. If it
weren't for the curtain of leaves that stretched down to cover us, we
would already be face to face with our finder.

A hand reached between the leaves and parted them. Somebody
slipped inside.

It was a boy, maybe eight years old. He was thin enough to be called
malnourished and his clothes were in tatters. His skin was pale, like
someone who had spent a lot of time indoors. He looked startled to see
us and swiftly held his hands up as if indicating he was no threat. Then

he put a finger to his mouth, signalling we should be quiet. He eased down onto the dirt and sat cross-legged.

The three of us were frozen, staring at each other, but there were no noises other than the normal sounds of the woods. My heartbeat gradually slowed, for the boy was obviously no threat and indeed it seemed he too was being pursued. I sat up slowly, trying to be soundless.

When the boy finally spoke, his voice was quiet and hesitant. "Do you have any food?"

Eithne and I looked at each other and I heard her stomach rumble.

"No," she said. "I'm sorry."

"I haven't eaten for days," he said.

"Who is following you?" Grainne asked.

His eyes were shadowed. "You know."

"Tell me."

"They do." He waved his hand, vaguely indicating something outside.

"Who?"

"Them that live here."

"The fey?"

He shrugged. "I suppose."

"What is your name?" I asked.

He looked at me seriously for a long while. His face was clean and pale. "Names are a funny business. Knowing a name gives you much power."

"It's just a name. Something to call you by."

Still he was silent, his mouth scrunched up as if thinking hard. Finally he said, "You can call me Sumerled."

"I'm Grainne and this is Eithne," Grainne said when it became clear Sumerled was quite happy to sit in the dirt and stare at us. "Where are you going?"

"Here and there. Away."

"Do you know how to get there?" I asked.

Sumerled considered me for a moment. "I might."

"Do you know Kalen?" Under other circumstances, it might have seemed a strange question, but there was something odd about the boy, something that made me feel like we were meant to meet him right here and right now.

"It depends on how badly you want to find him."

"Do you know him or not?"

Another shrug. One shoulder poked through a hole in his shirt. He was all bones and skin. Had he too been a prisoner of the fey?

"Can you take us to him?"

"Probably. Or maybe not. What do you have to offer?"

Beside me, Grainne stilled.

"What would it be worth to you?" I asked.

Sumerled considered me with squinting eyes. "It will be a dangerous journey. I could be injured, or even killed."

"Name your price and I will consider it."

"A promise."

"What exactly?"

"A promise you will fulfil at a time of my choosing."

"Eithne," Grainne said. "I don't think-"

I hushed her, rudely probably, but her cautions would only distract me.

"What would the promise entail?"

"Whatever I ask."

"That is too vague. It must be more clearly defined."

"You asked my price and that is it. We can leave right now to go find your Kalen or we can sit here all day, until they find us. They're looking for someone right now. Looking very hard."

"How do you know?"

"I saw them."

"How did you find us?" Grainne asked. In our leafy shelter, her face looked far too pale.

Sumerled smiled, a tight, controlled smile. "I have been watching you, ever since you left."

"You couldn't have kept up with us." Grainne's tone was scornful. "We ran for ages, and you aren't even wearing shoes."

I looked at his bare feet. They were clean. Far too clean for someone who had spent a day following us through the woods.

"Who are you really?" I asked, shuffling back a little, struck by a sudden need to get away from him.

"I'm just a boy. I can't hurt you."

Grainne and I exchanged a look. She didn't trust him. I hadn't decided yet.

"Are you mortal or fey?" she asked.

"What difference does it make? I am alive and so are you. But you won't be much longer if you stay here. I told you they search for some-one. They will find you soon. And what do you think they will do then?"

"Are you sure you can lead us to Kalen?" I asked.

Sumerled sniffed. "You're asking the wrong question. You should be asking whether I will."

"The promise must have a timeframe. A date by which you will ask for it or give it up."

"You must fulfil your promise before you return to the world of mortals."

"I will not harm any living being."

"Fine."

I didn't know what other limits to put on his promise. I had an expiry and an agreement that I would not be required to inflict injury. The promise was still too loose but I was too hungry to think clearly. I could only hope I wasn't dragging us into an even worse situation.

"If the Kalen you take us to is not the Kalen I seek, the promise is void," I said.

Sumerled yawned. "Agreed. Is there anything else?"

"Grainne has no obligation to you. She is not a part of my promise."

"Fine. Then you accept my terms?"

"I do."

Sumerled jumped to his feet. "Let's go then. The longer we dally, the closer they get."

EITHNE

*S*umerled went first, easing out from beneath the leaves that had sheltered us. He moved cautiously and quietly, and seemed alert for any sign of pursuit.

"I don't like this," Grainne muttered. "There's something peculiar about him."

Irritation flashed through me. This was the first time anyone had offered us aid and she knew I had to take it. "He says he can find Kalen."

She shook her head but said nothing further. We emerged from beneath the branches of the tree into the perpetual daylight of the fey woods. I heard only normal woodlands noises: little feet scurrying, birds chirping, leaves rustling. No sounds of pursuit.

We walked in single file, Sumerled leading the way and Grainne taking up the rear. Sumerled moved soundlessly, which seemed odd given he had made so much noise in approaching our hiding place. But he was my best chance to find Kalen — my only chance so far — and I dismissed my brief suspicion.

We walked for a very long time. Whenever Grainne or I asked how much further we needed to walk, Sumerled would say that we couldn't stop now, that the fey were right behind us. My thoughts wandered aimlessly and my legs trembled so much that I feared they wouldn't hold me up for much longer. My feet no longer hurt and I worried about what that meant.

"Sumerled, stop," said Grainne from behind me.

He stopped so quickly I almost walked into him.

"Would you give us a moment?" she asked. "I need some privacy and I'm sure Eithne must too."

He motioned to a nearby hawthorn bush. "You can go behind there. But hurry, because they are likely not far behind us."

Grainne grabbed me by the arm and pulled me behind the bush before I could speak. "Eithne, hush, listen. He is leading us in circles."

I noted the paleness of her face and the way her shoulders slumped. She was just as exhausted as I. Likely she was searching for a reason to rest.

"He's leading us to Kalen," I said.

"We have passed by this same bush several times. I know because the third time we passed it, I pulled a piece of thread from my shirt and draped it over a branch. It is still there."

"He's probably trying to lose the fey."

"Nobody is following us, Eithne. Don't you think they would have caught us by now at the pace we're moving? We would have heard them, if nothing else."

"You're only saying that because it was my decision to go with him."

She glowered at me for a moment. "He's trouble, Eithne. We need to lose him."

"He knows Kalen."

"He hasn't given you any proof of that. You asked if he could lead you to Kalen and he agreed. That doesn't mean he intends to, only that he *could* if he chose to."

"But I agreed to a promise. The fey take promises very seriously."

"He's trouble. That's all I know. He has been leading us in circles for hours. Nobody is following."

I ran my fingers over the prickly bush beside us. Its thorns dug into my fingertips. The pain grounded me and my foggy head cleared just a little.

"He might have an explanation for that. And what if he really does know Kalen? This could be my only chance to find him."

"Then ask. If Sumerled can explain himself, he must. If not, we leave him and find our own way."

My irritation at her bossiness suddenly fled. "I'm scared, Grainne. Scared we won't find Kalen. That we're never going to find a way out of this place."

"I am too." She wrapped an arm around my shoulders and I leaned into her. "But we can't let fear rule us. We have to be smart, cunning. And I think the smartest thing we can do is get away from Sumerled."

When we emerged from behind the hawthorn bush, Sumerled was tapping his foot impatiently, not that it made any sound in the leaf litter. He set off again as soon as he saw us.

"Sumerled, wait." I pitched my voice low in case someone really was following. "We need to ask you some questions."

"We don't have time to waste," he said. "They could catch up to us any moment."

"Who exactly are they?" Grainne asked.

"You know who they are."

"No more walking in circles," I said sternly, and stopped walking. "Tell us who you believe is following because we have neither seen nor heard sign of them."

"Don't believe me then. Dally here and let them catch you. Why would I care?" Sumerled kept walking, although he slowed as if reluctant to leave us behind.

"I don't think anyone is following us," Grainne said. "But I think you want us to think it."

Sumerled ignored her and looked only at me. "Don't you want to find Kalen? The longer we wait, the greater the possibility we won't. He might have moved on from where he was last."

"And where was that?" I asked.

"Where I'm taking you."

"You're taking us nowhere," Grainne said. "We've been walking in circles for hours. Why?"

"Because that's how we will find Kalen."

"By walking in circles through the woods?" Her tone was sceptical.

Sumerled shrugged. "I didn't make the way. Kalen did. I'm just following."

I didn't know what to believe. Sumerled said someone followed us; Grainne insisted there was nobody. Grainne said we walked in circles; Sumerled said it was because Kalen had. The only thing I knew was that I would never find Kalen if we kept standing here.

"Keep going," I said to Sumerled.

Grainne grabbed my hand. "Eithne, you can't be serious."

"What other choice do I have?"

"I don't believe him."

"I do. This is why we're here. I'm willing to believe him for a little longer."

Grainne sighed and rolled her eyes. "Fine. I'll be right behind you."

Now that I knew we walked in circles, I began watching for landmarks. A fallen log, two trees that grew in a tangle, the rotting carcass of some woodland animal. A fall of leaves masking a rock on which I caught my foot the first two times we walked over it. The signs were all around us. And we kept passing them by. When finally I could walk no further, I stopped.

"Sumerled, I need to rest. I need food and water and some sleep."

He turned back to us. "But we can't stop now. We're almost there."

"We are?" My heart leapt.

"Close. So close. We have to continue."

"Exactly how close are we?" Grainne asked.

"Almost close enough to see. Almost close enough to touch. We can't stop."

"If it's only a little further, I can keep going," I said, although I could hardly lift my feet to put one in front of the other. We walked for what felt like another hour. Twice more I asked Sumerled to stop and twice more he told me we were too close to stop.

Finally Grainne halted. "That's it. I am not going any further until I have rested."

"But-" Sumerled started.

Grainne cut him off with a sharp motion. "I said we're stopping."

I sank down into the leaves. They were damp and soft and smelled like rot. My head swam, I could hardly swallow, and the ground seemed to wobble and shift in front of my eyes. Beside me, Grainne sat with her knees drawn up and her arms and head resting on them.

"Grainne?" I managed to say.

"I'm fine," she said. "I just need to rest. And I need to eat but there's not much we can do about that right now."

"I can get you food," Sumerled said.

We both looked at him.

"From where?" Grainne asked and the suspicion had returned to her voice.

He raised a hand and indicated our surroundings. "The woods will provide."

He trotted off into the trees and returned a few minutes later with a sack.

"Where did that come from?" I asked.

Sumerled shrugged, which seemed to be his typical response to anything he didn't want to answer. He reached into the sack and pulled out a loaf of bread, thrusting it at me with quick impatience.

Grainne and I stared at each other. Doubt gnawed my stomach. The sack was one thing. He might well have had it tucked inside his shirt, but a whole loaf of bread? I turned the loaf over, its crust smooth beneath my fingers. It was soft and fresh. In fact, I fancied it was even still a little warm from the oven.

Sumerled produced a wedge of yellow cheese, ripe red apples, a handful of plump blackberries, a small knife. He laid the sack down on the ground with a flourish and piled the food on top.

"Eat," he urged, stepping back.

Grainne and I just stared. The aroma of fresh bread filled my nostrils and my mouth watered. After nothing but mouldy bread for months, this was a feast.

"Sumerled, where did this food come from?" Grainne's voice was stern.

I reluctantly tossed the bread down onto the sack as we waited for Sumerled's response.

"The woods provide."

"The woods did not just hand you a loaf of bread and some cheese," she said. "And you certainly didn't carry it all this way. Tell me where you got it."

Sumerled's mouth had a nasty set to it. "You said you were hungry. I got you food. You should eat it."

"We aren't eating a thing until you tell us where it came from," Grainne said.

I wanted to cry at the sight of that food and not being able to eat it. It took all of my strength not to snatch it up — any of it, all of it — and cram it into my mouth.

Sumerled's jaw clenched and his face reddened. "You have to eat."

"Where did it come from?" Grainne sounded just as stubborn as he.

Sumerled glared at her. "You shouldn't be so ungrateful. Bad things happen to ungrateful people."

Grainne rose stiffly to her feet. She stepped right up to Sumerled. He was only as high as her shoulders. "Are you threatening me, little boy?"

Sumerled's face was sullen and he turned his back on her. "I will not speak to you any further. You can find Kalen on your own."

"I don't believe you could lead us to him anyway," she said. "It's all just a game, isn't it? A big game of how long can you make us follow you. Round and round in circles, never going anywhere, never getting any closer to Kalen."

"That's not true," he said.

"Who sent you?" she asked. "Somebody knew where we hid and it wasn't you. You're too young to know anything."

"I am not. I'm older than I look."

"I doubt that." Grainne's voice was scathing. "You're just a boy. A mortal boy. You couldn't possibly know anything useful or important. I think you should leave. We will find Kalen faster without you."

I held my breath for fear that Sumerled really would leave. He was my only link to Kalen.

Sumerled turned back to us, his fists clenched. "I'm not mortal. I'm half fey."

"Oh, a half-blood." Grainne sounded bored. "How impressive."

"I'm the only one who can find Kalen for you."

"What makes you think you can find him at all, let alone that you're the only one who can?"

"Because I'm his brother."

Grainne and I froze.

"What did you say?" I asked. I awkwardly got to my feet and my thigh muscles spasmed. "Kalen never mentioned a brother."

"We have the same father."

"What about your mother?" Kalen had never spoken about his family so I had no way of knowing whether Sumerled lied. But now that I looked at him carefully, I saw echoes of Kalen in the shape of his chin and mouth.

"Our mothers were mortal. They are irrelevant."

"Kalen is half-mortal?" Why would he not have told me something so important?

"Why are you looking for him anyway?" Sumerled asked, and it was me he directed his words to.

"That's none of your business," I said. "You haven't managed to take us to him, so I don't owe you anything — neither explanation nor promise."

"I can take you to him. I know the secret place where he hides. Nobody else knows. Without me, you won't find him if he doesn't want to be found."

"Why wouldn't he want us to find him?" Grainne asked.

Sumerled's face closed again and he shrugged.

"How far away is he?" I asked. "We are exhausted."

Sumerled pointed over my shoulder. "That way."

"Exactly how far?"

A shrug. "A hundred paces. Maybe less."

I froze and my heart seemed to stop beating. "A hundred paces? Are you telling me we are only a hundred paces from Kalen? Why did we stop here?"

"You said you wanted to stop."

"You never said we were so near."

"I told you we were close."

"You've been saying we were close for hours," Grainne said. "How were we to know you were telling the truth this time? Not that I'm convinced yet."

"He is too. He's just over there."

"Prove it," she challenged.

He glared at her and then stomped away in the direction he had pointed. He disappeared from sight behind a birch tree.

The ground seemed to tilt from side to side and Grainne quickly took me by the arm.

"Eithne, sit."

"I'm fine. I can stand a little longer. If he's telling the truth..."

"He might not be. You should be prepared for that."

"But he could be."

Finally Sumerled reappeared. A few paces behind him was Kalen.

EITHNE

I lurched forward, barely aware of having moved. "Kalen!"

Kalen paled and his jaw dropped. He grabbed Sumerled's arm and shook him, saying something stern. The boy's face turned sulky again. Kalen released him with a shove and looked back towards me. His face was a thundercloud.

I stopped, suddenly unsure. He didn't look pleased to see me. "Kalen?"

"Eithne." He stopped in front of me and surveyed me from head to toe. He looked the same as always with his ruined haircut and dark clothes that hung loosely off his frame.

I was abruptly reminded of my threadbare clothes, my grimy and tangled hair, the stench that rose from my body. I wanted to reach out to him but instead I made fists of my dirty fingers. I had grown used to the filth that coated my entire body but Kalen was clean. He wouldn't want me touching him.

"You shouldn't be here," he said, his voice a little gentler now.

"I came to find you. To help you." I clutched my tattered skirt to stop myself from reaching for him.

"Help me with what?"

"You stopped coming to see me. I thought... I knew something must be wrong."

Kalen's laugh was hollow. "Surely, Eithne, you know enough to understand what it means when a fey stops visiting a mortal woman."

My heart plummeted. All these months I had never doubted his feelings. Never thought he would be anything but pleased when I found him.

"You don't mean that." My voice was a whisper.

"What did you expect me to say, Eithne? Did you think I would fall at your feet in gratitude that you risked your life to be here? What happened to you anyway? You look atrocious."

I covered my face with my hands and burst into tears. They dripped between my fingers and fell onto the leaves in grimy, grey splatters. Grainne took a step closer but didn't touch me.

"Kalen, why are you being so awful? You have no idea what I've been through to find you."

"I don't need you to rescue me, if that's what you thought. Go home, Eithne. Sumerled will show you to the portal. Get back to the mortal world before you draw unwanted attention."

"Titania already knows we're here."

Kalen sucked in a breath. "She does? Have you spoken with her?"

"Spoken with her?" My voice rose. I scrubbed the tears from my face with my fist and scowled at him. "She kept us as slaves. We've been locked in the dark and fed mouldy bread and forced to work in a kitchen where everything we make unmakes itself overnight."

Kalen's glare became even fiercer. "How long have you been here?"

"Months. She was going to keep us for one hundred years."

"That's a penalty Titania reserves for those who offend her the most."

"All I did was ask to see you. She said if I worked as a slave for one hundred years, she would let me. But I didn't know she would keep Grainne here too."

Kalen glanced towards Grainne for the first time. When he looked back at me, something flickered in his gaze. "You need to leave immediately. Both of you. Sumerled, take them straight to the nearest portal.

Don't linger for any reason. Keep quiet. Don't draw attention to your-selves. If you can get back to the mortal world, she isn't likely to come after you."

"We can't leave now," I said. "We've only just found you."

"You must leave, Eithne. You have no idea how much danger you are in."

"Kalen-" I stepped forward but he quickly backed up and I finally understood. "You don't want me here."

"You are in danger here."

"I came to help you."

"You can't help me. Nobody can."

"When will I see you again?"

"You won't. I won't be returning to the mortal world and you must not come here again."

A sob tore from my chest. "I thought you loved me."

"I'm sorry." Kalen's mouth twisted and his tone was almost regretful. "You have no idea how sorry, but you need to leave right now."

My heart was wrenched into pieces. My chest was too tight. I couldn't breathe. I turned and ran.

Grainne called out, "Eithne, wait."

I fled and if Grainne followed, she didn't catch me.

I crashed through the woods, tripping over logs and roots, blind to the direction in which I ran. When I could go no further, I collapsed onto the soft leaves. My chest heaved and tears dripped from my face. I was a fool. Every tale that tells of such a thing says the fey are fickle. We always feel far more than they. Kalen didn't love me. He never had.

I cried until there were no tears left. My nose was blocked, my eyes were swollen and my chest hurt. I lay in the leaves, the woods around me quiet and lonely. When I was with Grainne, I was ever conscious of the fact that we were possibly — probably — being pursued but even then I had not felt this vulnerable. But alone I was weak and fragile and scared. If someone indeed followed, they would need little effort to overpower me. Even Sumerled could probably do it, as weak as I was right now.

I shouldn't have run away. Shouldn't have left Grainne behind. But I hadn't been thinking clearly. All I knew was that I couldn't bear to look at Kalen for a moment longer. I had put both Grainne and myself through so much, and all for a fickle fey who had probably not given me a thought since we last met.

I sniffed and wiped my nose with the frayed edge of my skirt. I couldn't lie here all day, no matter how miserable I was. I stood, careful on wobbly legs, and began to stumble back to where I thought I had left Grainne. My stomach was tight and my heart ached. Kalen would be long gone by now but hopefully Grainne had stayed, waiting for me. I had led us both to the point of starvation and exhaustion. Kalen might not care about me, but Grainne did. We were sisters and friends. I would find her and we would make our way home together. And once we were safely back at Silver Downs, I would never think about Kalen again. I had learnt my lesson. No more fey. No more men at all. I would be content with my life, such as it was.

I stumbled through the woods, paying little attention to my surroundings until I smelled smoke. I stopped, realising for the first time just how loud I had been, carelessly putting my feet wherever they landed, paying no mind to the noise I made or the trail I left. Smoke could mean one of two things. It might be a wildfire or it might mean people, probably fey. I had better be prepared to run regardless. My legs trembled at the thought. I had already run so far.

I couldn't see and hear anyone but the acrid scent of smoke was strong. It was not far away. Slowly, softly, I walked another few paces, placing each foot ever so gently, freezing, my heart pounding when a twig snapped beneath my boot. There was no indication that anyone heard — no shouts of alarm, no feet running to investigate — so I kept moving as quietly as I could.

I waited for the woods to close in around me, to protect me as they had before, but the trees didn't move and the bramble stayed where it was. Even the tangly weed didn't appear. The woods had decided not to shield me this time.

I searched for another of the skirted trees that had sheltered us before Sumerled's arrival but they were scarce in this part of the woods.

The best I could find was a knotty bramble bush with a small hollow beneath it. It would not shield me from view if anyone passed on this side but it might hide me from someone on the other side, provided they didn't look too closely. I crawled into the small space. The earth was cool beneath my body.

I was well experienced in making myself unnoticeable. All of those times I had sat by the fire, being still and quiet, and folk's gaze would slide straight over me. All of the secrets I had heard while sitting in plain view because people stopped seeing me. I drew on those times now, curling my body into a small ball, making myself still and quiet. I waited.

With my eyes squeezed shut, I listened intently and soon began sorting the usual chatter of the woods from the noise of those I sought to avoid. The quiet murmur of voices; at least two, although whether they were mortal or fey, I couldn't tell. The crackle of a fire. A harsh laugh startled me and I stiffened in alarm. At length I heard movement. Snaps and pops as somebody stirred up the fire, and then footsteps heading in my direction.

Still and silent, I held my breath as he came closer. Clearly not fey, for he walked as heavily as I did. He stopped on the other side of the bush I hid beneath.

Still and silent.

A rustle of cloth and then a stream of liquid hit the bush. Warm droplets splattered my back.

I held my breath and hoped he couldn't hear my heart beating. Still and silent.

At length he was finished. Another rustle of cloth and he left, stomping heavily through the woods, back to his fire and his companion.

I remained where I was. I had no way of knowing how long the men might stay or in which direction they would leave. I also didn't know whether the fey watched them. I needed to be invisible until they left.

For hours I lay under the bramble bush. The earth beneath me was cool and I had just enough space to avoid the bramble's thorns. Occasionally a laugh reached my ears. The men, it seemed, had settled in for a lengthy stay.

A shout of alarm.

The noise of a brief struggle.

The sound of bodies being dragged away.

Still and silent, I waited.

GRAINNE

*W*hen Kalen told Eithne to leave, the cracks in the armour she had shielded herself with for so long finally broke open. The possibility of finding Kalen, of saving him from whatever she believed had befallen him, had sustained her through the months of darkness and slavery. I had never asked what she would do if she discovered it had all been a fantasy and indeed I now suspected she had never considered the possibility.

Eithne fled and I moved to follow but Kalen grabbed my arm.

"Let me go." I gave him my coldest glare and tried to shake him off.

"Let her run," Kalen said. "It might be her best chance."

"Don't be ridiculous. We need to stay together. If I can't find her again, we're both in even more trouble than we already are."

"She needs to be as far away from me as possible. If you are captured again, tell them you never found me." He finally released my arm.

"If you want her to be safe, then she and I should be together."

"You are here for your own reasons, not hers. She is safer alone."

My heart stopped and then stuttered wildly. I looked away and clenched my hands together so Kalen wouldn't see how they trembled. I tried to keep my voice casual. "Is he still safe?"

"More or less."

"How do I find him?" I kept my gaze on a handful of young hazelnuts growing on a nearby bush. My stomach spasmed at the thought of food and the constant smell of fresh bread was making me sick with hunger. I couldn't even look at the food lying on the sack for fear I would lose the last shreds of my control and throw myself on it.

"Are you sure you want to?" Kalen asked. His blue eyes were serious and gave no hint of betrayal.

"Of course I'm sure. Why would I come if I didn't intend to find him? I'm here to take him home."

"Why do so many of the women in your family think their men need saving?"

"Eithne is my sister but only by marriage. Do you consider yourself her man then?"

Kalen hung his head and his breath hitched. "She should not have come here."

"She loves you. She has spent months as a slave and all to find you."

"I'm protecting her." His words were hesitant, as he if didn't quite believe them.

"By sending her off into the woods alone? She doesn't need your kind of protection."

"Sumerled will find her easily enough. Go," he said to the boy who stood behind him, forgotten. "Take Eithne back to the mortal world."

Sumerled looked like he wanted to argue, but after a moment of hesitation, he darted off into the trees.

"Why did you let her think you don't care?" I asked.

"It's a long story."

"Tell me."

Kalen shook his head. "The more you know, the more danger you will be in. I am protecting her as best I can. That is all you need know."

We eyed each other warily. His jaw was clenched and one eyelid twitched. Clearly he was not as indifferent as he pretended to be.

"Where is my husband?"

"He lives with some of the wilder fey. They like to hunt and feast. They live large."

"Is he well?"

"As well as any mortal can be when exposed to such a lifestyle. He has probably long forgotten who he is though."

"How do I find him?"

"They will hunt tonight, for the moon is full. I can take you to a place where you can hide until then and wait for them to pass. He won't remember you though and he won't want to leave."

"How do I restore his memory?"

He shrugged and I saw echoes of Sumerled in the gesture. "He will choose to remember or not. But if you can convince him to leave, make for the edge of the woods immediately. You will need to find a portal and return to your own world before he changes his mind. You won't convince him a second time."

"He won't change his mind, not once he remembers."

"Perhaps, perhaps not. The delights of our realm are intoxicating to mortals. Most will not willingly leave, even if they remember."

I didn't let my mind linger on what delights Caedmon might have sampled.

"You should eat," Kalen said, indicating the food Sumerled had provided. "Sleep. Then I will take you to where you can wait for your man."

GRAINNE

I tried not to gobble, but it was almost impossible to restrain myself. The bread was fresh and soft, the cheese creamy and the blackberries juicy. I ate just enough to ease the ache in my belly, mindful of making myself ill, and then I lay down to sleep. Kalen leaned against a slender ash, lost in his own thoughts.

My dreams were strange and confusing. Times of darkness interspersed with periods of running through the woods. Sounds of invisible relentless pursuit. Treva's kitchen and the pastries that unmade themselves every night. Running, hiding. Darkness. Woods.

I woke feeling like I emerged from a deep sleep. My thoughts were woolly and a few moments passed before I noticed him.

He sat cross-legged about ten paces away from me, his back straight and his piercing gaze fixed on me. How long had he watched me as I slept? I sat up, pulling leaves from my hair, and trying to pretend I was not suddenly deathly afraid.

"Lunn," I said. "Why are you here?"

He looked at me in a way that made the hair stand up on my arms. "Why, Grainne, are you not pleased to see me? I am most delighted to see you."

Memories of his clawed hands on my body made my stomach roll. I pushed the thoughts away and repeated my question.

"I could ask you the same thing," he said. "I am surprised to see you here, but oh so happy that you are."

He moved quickly, his limbs a blur, and suddenly he crouched in front of me. I didn't have time to so much as blink before something wrapped around my throat. My fingers touched a thick wooden collar. It was attached to a bronze chain, the other end of which was wrapped around Lunn's wrist.

"What have you done?" The collar was too tight. I couldn't breathe. Panic swiftly welled within me. I tucked my fingers under the edges and tried to open it. "Get this off me."

Lunn's smile was slow and lazy. "You're mine now, Grainne. You shouldn't have come here."

My limbs went weak and when I spoke, my voice trembled. "Where is Kalen?"

"He's gone," Lunn said. "Did you think he would stick around to help you? Risk his own neck? No, he ran away as soon as I arrived."

I tried to push the panic down, to breathe normally. The collar was uncomfortable but it wasn't actually impeding my ability to breathe. Until Lunn tugged the chain. I choked and gasped. My panic was sharp and almost overwhelming. For a few moments I really couldn't breathe.

"You'll learn to do as you're told, Grainne," Lunn said. "And you'll learn quick, I promise, because that's just a taste of what will happen if you don't. Now get up, we're leaving."

He tugged the chain again, this time harder. I was pulled off my rear and onto my hands and knees.

"I said, get up." His voice was cool and impatient.

I climbed to my feet, my legs stiff and clumsy. Tears streamed down my cheeks and I hurriedly wiped them away. He had better hope I didn't have a knife in my hands when I finally escaped.

Lunn set off at a loping pace. I had to jog to keep up. We ran for a while and when I began tripping over my own feet from fatigue, Lunn allowed me a brief rest and then set off again. At long last, we came to a clearing. In the middle was a grassy hill about half the height of a man.

Lunn halted in front of the mound and it opened soundlessly. A yawning chasm led down into the ground. Lunn walked in.

"Wait." Panic welled again. It was dark inside, like the tree the fey had kept us in. "Stop. Lunn."

He paused and looked back at me. "Better follow, Grainne. I thought you would learn faster."

"I can't. Please don't make me go in there."

"Last chance. Follow or I'll simply drag you in. I don't care how but one way or another, you're coming in." He tugged the chain, not quite hard enough to choke me.

I forced my feet forward. My breaths were shallow and fast. A rushing noise filled my ears and if Lunn spoke again, I didn't hear him. He disappeared down into the darkness and I followed. I had no doubt that he would drag me in if I didn't.

The tunnel bore down sharply, but it wasn't completely dark. Instead it was filled with a dim green light that shone from some invisible source. I focused on breathing steadily and on not thinking about the earth piled above me and how I would be buried and smothered if the tunnel came tumbling down. The walls were made of packed earth with no supports that I could see. The air had a pleasant earthy smell, like a freshly dug garden.

We had only walked for a few minutes before Lunn stopped and turned to face the wall. An open doorway appeared in front of him and he walked through. I followed quickly.

I had expected another tunnel but this was a small earthen cavern decked out as a home of sorts. There was a bed and an assortment of chairs, a dresser, a table and a cupboard, all made of wood that looked as if it had simply grown into shape. I ran my fingers over a chair. The wood was smooth and if there were any joins, I could neither see nor feel them.

The wall closed behind me and when I turned, there was no sign a doorway even existed. There were no windows, no other doors, no means of escape. I forced myself to breathe slowly.

Lunn released my chain, letting it fall from his hands to land with a thud on the earthen floor. He gracefully lowered himself into a chair, crossed one leg over the other, and smiled at me.

"Well, Grainne, here we are."

I stayed where I was standing. "Why am I here?"

"You amuse me. I like things that amuse me."

"Where is Caedmon?"

"Hmm. Who? Oh, you mean the mortal you took such pains to save? And they were pains, weren't they, lovely Grainne? You suffered much for him."

"What have you done with him?"

"Don't you worry. I've kept my end of our agreement."

"Will you take me to him? I need to see him for myself. See that he is safe."

Lunn laughed. "No, Grainne, I don't think so."

"How can I believe you if you won't show me?"

"I don't care whether you believe me or not. I've done what I said I would and that's all that matters."

"It matters to me."

"But not to me, and that, my dear, is what is important. Now sit down like a good girl, Grainne. You may as well rest while you can. You can use my bed if you want to sleep."

"No thank you." I couldn't restrain my shudder.

Lunn noticed and seemed amused. "Suit yourself. We have a big evening tonight. A feast. It will be a late night."

Lunn settled back in his chair and closed his eyes. Whether he slept, or was just thinking, I couldn't tell.

I gingerly sat on the chair closest to me. It was surprisingly comfortable. I leaned my head against the back and closed my eyes. I was sure I wouldn't fall asleep, not with Lunn in the room, but I did. I woke when he tugged hard on my chain, almost pulling me off the chair. I choked and coughed and wheezed.

"You could have just spoken to me," I said, when I could breathe again.

Lunn didn't even look at me. "Get up. It's time to leave."

He had changed his clothes while I slept and now wore a blue shirt which flowed over his shoulders like water rippling in a pond.

"Can I wash first?" I was suddenly acutely conscious of how filthy I was. "And I need new clothes."

Lunn finally looked at me, a slow examination of my body. The edges of his mouth turned up slightly. "What you're wearing is quite appropriate. Let's go."

The door opened and he led me back out through the tunnel. A short walk through the woods led us to a clearing strung with tiny coloured lights — not candles, but presumably some sort of fey magic — and filled with long tables piled with food. Dozens of fey already sat at the tables, although nobody appeared to be eating yet. Conversation stopped when Lunn and I walked into the clearing.

"What ever have you found, Lunn?" a woman asked as she looked me up and down with a snide expression.

I glared at her but Lunn only laughed.

"A mortal, obviously. Wandering where she shouldn't be."

He led me to a table and settled himself into the sole empty chair. I stood behind him, close enough that the chain was slack between us. As much as I didn't want to be near him, I felt even more unsafe surrounded by so many fey. I endured several more unpleasant comments, including an offer to swap me for another mortal from a tall fey whose mouth twisted in a cruel expression. Lunn turned him down with a laugh. I scanned the fey but couldn't see Titania. Would anyone realise that I was one of the mortals she was searching for?

As one, the fey reached for the food and started feasting. Roasted birds, too big to be hens. Strange vegetables I had never before seen. Unfamiliar fruits and berries. Sauces and salads, puddings and wines. My mouth watered and my stomach growled. My simple meal of bread, cheese and berries felt like a very long time ago.

They feasted for hours while I stood behind Lunn, forgotten. Eventually I sat behind his chair on the ground and drew up my legs to rest my head on them. The grass was cold and damp but I was too exhausted to care. The chatter and clatter of the fey feast seemed to fade away as I dozed. Eventually the fey began to rise and drift away. Lunn set a plate of scraps down on the grass beside me.

"Eat," he said, and to my shame, I did.

I gnawed on half-eaten bones and finished vegetables with only a few bites taken out of them. The food was rich and spicy but strangely unsatisfying. When I had finished, I felt almost as hungry as I had been before. The clearing had emptied by the time I looked up. Lunn tugged on my chain.

"Up," he said.

I clambered to my feet, slowly and stiffly. We walked back through the woods without speaking. Twice Lunn stopped to wait while I picked myself up off the ground but he didn't comment. We entered the mound that led down into the tunnel and again came to the cavern where he lived.

The wall closed behind us and Lunn dropped my chain. He stripped off his clothes as he strode towards the bed and was naked by the time he climbed into it. His shoulders were narrower than Caedmon's and the muscles not as well defined.

"Find somewhere to sleep, sweet Grainne," he said. "You can join me in here, if you wish, but be warned you won't get much sleep if you do."

I quickly sat on a chair. The light in the room disappeared and soon soft snores came from the direction of Lunn's bed. I woke when the light came back on. Lunn stood in front of me, fully dressed.

"Time to get up, Grainne. We are going to watch the hunt pass by."

GRAINNE

*T*he woods were lit with the perpetual noon-bright light although my body told me it was late evening. We walked for some time before Lunn stopped beside a large oak. He leaned against the trunk, the end of my chain dangling from his fingers.

"Now what?" I asked.

"We wait. They will be along soon enough."

Mere minutes passed before the ground began to vibrate. I edged a little closer to Lunn. He both repulsed and terrified me but he was the closest thing to protection I had here.

"Stand against the tree," he said. "They will not stop if you get in their way."

Lunn had positioned us where we would have a clear view as the hunt swept through. Dogs came first: slender, baying hounds. I didn't see whatever quarry they pursued but the hounds ran as if they knew exactly where they were going.

Next came the horses, tall and sleek and white. Their riders were deathly silent, as focused on their quarry as the hounds. I thought I recognised some. One might have been the fey who sat opposite Lunn at the feast. Another might have stood near Eithne and I the day we were presented to Titania. Or perhaps not. It was hard to tell when they flew by so fast.

Then I saw Caedmon. He rode towards the back of the herd, crouching low over his horse's neck, his face intense and focused. He had aged from when I saw him last. Not like he had lived longer, but as if he had lived harder. My heart thudded and my palms went clammy.

"Caedmon!" I called, thoughtlessly stepping out in front of his horse. The beast didn't slow.

Lunn grabbed my arm and yanked me back a moment before the horse trampled me.

"Let me go." I tried to pull my arm away but he held on tightly. "Caedmon, it's me, Grainne!"

If Caedmon heard, he gave no indication of it. The horses disappeared into the woods. The ground still shook from the thunder of their hooves.

"Caedmon, don't leave me here," I called after him forlornly. I turned to Lunn and beat my fist against his chest. "Where are they going? Take me to them."

Lunn laughed and wrapped his hands around my wrist, holding it against his chest. If a heart beat within, I couldn't feel it. "You can't follow those who ride horses bred from our stock. They are too fast and can run far further than you."

"Why did you bring me here?" I wrenched my hands from his grip. "Why show me Caedmon like that? Was it just to gloat? You must have known he wouldn't hear me."

"It wasn't that he couldn't hear you, my dear. He didn't *want* to hear you. And why would he? Look at the life he enjoys now. He feasts and hunts and does whatever he wants. How can any life you offer compare to that?"

"He would want to go home."

"And what would he return to? Working the fields? Breeding children? Watching you grow tired and haggard and old?"

"He's a soldier," I said, my voice both fierce and proud. "A very good one. And family means everything to Caedmon. He would go home if he could. If not for me, then for his parents and his sister and his brothers. He does not want to be here."

"You saw him, Grainne. Did he look like a man who did not want to be here?"

"He looks like a man who is charmed. He only sees what you want him to."

"It sounds to me, my dear, like you are the one who only sees what you want. Now come along, I am tired and want to sleep."

"I won't go with you." I crossed my arms and gave him my fiercest glare. "I demand you take me to Caedmon."

"Oh he won't be found for hours yet. Not until the hunt finishes."

"Then take me to wherever he sleeps. I will wait there for him."

"For what purpose? He has forgotten he ever had a life before this. He won't even recognise you."

"Let me try, at least. If I can convince him to leave with me, let him go."

Lunn raised an eyebrow at me. "You are stubborn, aren't you? I am almost persuaded to let you try, just for the fun of watching. But no."

He tugged gently on the chain, just enough to remind me who was in charge, and we walked back to his chamber beneath the earth. Once inside, with the wall sealed up behind us, Lunn dropped my chain and went straight to his bed, peeling off his clothes as he walked.

"There is food on the bench if you need to eat," he said.

I glanced towards the wooden bench which grew out of the earthen wall. A small loaf of bread and a mug waited. The bread was fresh - I could smell it from here. I didn't feel like eating though, despite my constant hunger.

I sat on the wooden chair where I had spent the previous night. Or perhaps it was still the same night. I was tired, so very tired. For the first time, I felt old. I refused to believe Caedmon would not want to come home. He might not have had time to learn to love me, but I was his wife, after all. And I could give him the thing he wanted most in the world: a son.

As soon as Lunn woke, I asked again. "Take me to Caedmon. Let me at least try."

He dressed slowly, not caring that his naked body was on display to me the whole time. I kept my gaze on his face, refusing to show my discomfort.

"Leave him be, Grainne. He is happy here."

"He is not happy. He is charmed. He will be happy when he is home again."

"You should be pleased for him. He has the perfect life here, the kind all mortal men hope for."

"What do you know of what mortal men hope for?" I asked scornfully. "If this is what you think life is, you are sadly mistaken. Look at you. You live alone in this cave under the ground. You sleep alone. I haven't even seen you speak to another fey except at the feast. You have a sad, lonely, pathetic life."

Surprise crossed Lunn's face. "But I will live for many hundreds of years. Your kind will wither and die in my lifetime."

"A life like yours is not worth living, whether for one year or a thousand. I pity you."

He glared at me and I glared back.

"You should learn to guard your words, my dear," he said. "They will get you into trouble one of these days."

EITHNE

A very long time passed before I felt safe enough to leave my hiding place. The men and whatever attacked them had been gone for hours. I huddled under the bramble bush, too fearful to do anything other than stay still and quiet. But I couldn't stay here forever.

My body was stiff and my limbs numb as I crawled out. My legs failed to hold me as I stood, and I stumbled and pitched forward. On hands and knees, I listened for the snapping of twigs or rustling of leaf litter that might indicate someone coming to investigate. But I heard nothing to alarm me and at length I climbed to my feet.

Now that I knew the woods would not necessarily shield me, I walked carefully, although I was far from stealthy. I had paid little attention when I ran away and I could only hope I could find my way back and that Grainne would still be there.

Eventually I spotted a fallen log that may have been the one I tripped over on my heedless flight. Soon after, I spied a scrap of fabric dangling from a low branch. It was grey and nondescript, just like my own dress after so long without washing.

I sniffed the air as I walked, searching for any trace of smoke but there was nothing other than the usual scents of earth and trees and decay. A startled deer bounded away into the trees. A raven perched in a nearby oak eyed me curiously. I remembered Kalen's tales of other creatures that inhabited these woods but saw nothing out of the ordinary.

After what seemed like a very long time, I found a small clearing. It was empty of mortals and fey, but in the centre was a sack upon which sat the remnants of the meal Sumerled had provided. Without a second thought, I fell on the food. Never had bread and cheese tasted so good. The bread was fresh and the cheese was sharp and crumbly. I crammed them into my mouth and didn't stop until it was all gone. It wasn't until afterwards that I wondered why the food was even there, why it hadn't been eaten by the creatures of the woods.

With a belly that was blissfully full for the first time in many months, I sat back on my heels. I should have shown some restraint rather than gorging myself but it was too late. It was only now that I wondered about Grainne. Was it she who had eaten the rest? And where was she? Surely Kalen would look after her. He might not care for me the way I had thought, but I did not believe he would leave a mortal woman alone in fey woods. He had probably taken her to a portal. Grainne might already be back home at Silver Downs.

With that hopeful thought, my eyes drooped. Although I had dozed while hiding under the bramble, I had not slept properly for days. It would be unwise to sleep here without shelter from spying eyes. Anyone could sneak up on me. I would not sleep but merely rest for a few minutes. I lay down in a mossy patch with Sumerled's sack under my head for a pillow. I closed my eyes and sank down into sleep.

When I woke, I was lying on my side, curled up like a babe. I felt like I had slept long and deeply. For the first time in months, I felt refreshed and clear-headed. It took some time for my eyes to focus but when they finally did, I suddenly realised I had not been alone while I slept. Right in front of me, where before had been nothing but leaves and dirt, was a rock the size of my head.

There was nobody else here, neither mortal nor fey. And yet someone must have been here, for rocks do not move themselves. Again I became aware of my vulnerability. A lone woman, I was easy prey. And yet whoever it was had not disturbed my sleep. They had merely placed a rock beside me.

Was it a message? A warning? I couldn't even guess at its meaning. I heard nothing other than woodlarks calling, undergrowth rustling with the creeping of vole and badger, the distant bark of a deer. And yet sitting in front of me was inarguable proof that somebody else had been here, however briefly.

The rock was the grey of a winter's sky and had no markings. Nothing unusual. Nothing exceptional. Except that every time I looked at it, I could hear something buzzing. As soon as I looked away, it stopped.

Tentatively, I reached out my hand. My fingers shook just the tiniest bit, although I told myself I was being ridiculous if I feared touching a rock. I placed the tips of my fingers on its surface. It was warm and smooth. The buzzing stopped.

"That's better," a voice said, from somewhere very close to me.

I started and pulled back my hand. The buzzing resumed and I could no longer hear the speaker. I slid closer to the rock and touched my fingers to it once again.

"Took you long enough," the voice again. It was deep and gravelly and the words came slowly, as if the speaker stopped for thought after each one.

I looked around but I was still alone.

"Haven't quite figured it out, have you?"

"Who's there?" I asked, forcing a courage into my voice that I didn't feel. "Where are you?"

"I'll wait. You'll figure it out sooner or later. Time doesn't mean much to one such as I."

"Stop hiding. Come out and face me. It's cowardly to hide and try to scare me."

"Oh I ain't hiding, love. You just aren't looking properly."

"I don't like being teased. Show yourself or go away."

"Not teasing. Just waiting for you to figure things out."

I looked down at the rock and remembered the image from my fever dreams: the creature that looked like a rock.

"Think it through, love. You don't look all that stupid."

Maybe Titania had taken my mind after all.

"Perhaps I should sleep while you think? I'll warn you though, I don't wake easily. Once I nod off, you won't wake me again for, oh, a few hundred years."

"Are you the rock?" I felt like a fool but the voice was coming from nearby and I only heard it when I touched the rock.

"*Rock* isn't a very pleasant kind of word, is it? Rather harsh. But I suppose it will do as well as any."

"What are you if you aren't a rock?"

"I didn't say I wasn't a rock. Just that it wasn't a nice word. But yes, I suppose, to you I am probably a rock."

Gaining confidence, I pressed my fingers a little more firmly against its smooth surface. "Are you fey?"

There was a sound like a cross between a snort and someone clearing their throat. "Usurpers. Interlopers. Children."

Dimly-remembered snippets of ancient tales came to mind. Supposedly a species already inhabited these lands when the fey arrived. Older and smaller and not inclined to fight for their territory. The tales didn't say what had become of them, or if they did, I had never heard. I had always assumed they left. But perhaps they didn't go anywhere. Perhaps they were still here, waiting for the day the fey left — or died out.

"Why did you come to speak to me?" I asked.

"You have questions. I have answers."

"What kind of answers?"

"What kind do you want?"

"Where is my friend Grainne? She was right here the last time I saw her."

"Is that your best question? I might as well go back to sleep."

What information did I need the most? "Why does Titania hate me?"

There was a sound like rocks grinding together. Perhaps it laughed. "She doesn't hate you. She fears you."

"Me?"

"Well, not you, exactly. Your children."

"I don't have any children."

"Yet."

That made me pause. I had always assumed children would not be for me. That I would not be strong enough to survive a pregnancy.

"Why would Titania fear any children I might have?"

"A child that is part-mortal, part-fey is a dangerous combination."

"My children will be part-fey?" I hardly knew what to think.

"Just said that, didn't I."

"Who will their father be?"

"Can't tell you that. Have to leave some surprises."

There would be time later to dwell on this news.

"She watches you, you know. And your family. Has for generations."

"Does it have anything to do with the power the bards in my family have? If they are the seventh son of a seventh son?"

"Special thing, that, to be the seventh son of a seventh son. Powerful. Power like that could wipe out the fey, if anyone thought to use it right."

I stared down at the rock in surprise. "Why would we do that? The fey have never done anything to us. At least, not until now."

"Aah, but there's always potential, isn't there? Potential for someone to think a little bit harder than those who came before. But it's not just the menfolk who have power. You have some of your own."

"Me? I don't have any power."

"Oh, you do, all right. Might not have realised it yet, so I won't say too much. But you have your own power, girlie. Time's a-coming when you'll need to know how to wield it. Or maybe it won't be you. Might be your daughter or your granddaughter. Better figure it out while you have time."

"I don't understand."

"No, you probably don't. But I've said enough. Tired me out, all this talking. Time to go back to sleep."

EITHNE

*T*ry as I might, I couldn't wake the rock again. I should have asked for instructions on how to get back to the mortal world. I could have asked how much time had passed while we had lingered in the fey realm. There were so many things I should have asked had I been more prepared. These were fey woods after all. I should have expected the unexpected.

I set off through the woods, but stumbled, distracted. A woodlark rose from a nearby branch with a startled squawk. I forced thoughts of the rock away and concentrated on moving quickly and quietly. I searched for signs of Grainne but there was nothing. No footprint in the damp soil, no disturbed leaf litter. No scrap of fabric hanging from a branch. Nothing that said she had passed this way.

The skin on the back of my neck began to prickle and an uneasy feeling crept over me. I paused beside a birch and looked around, peering hard into the shadows between trees, but saw no evidence of anyone watching. I held myself very still and listened. No footsteps. No crackle of undergrowth. No snap of broken twigs. Nothing. Not even the usual sounds of the woods.

I continued walking but still couldn't shake the feeling that somebody watched. I spied a raven sitting on a branch, its beady gaze fastened on me. It tilted its head as I looked at it and seemed to look me right in the eyes. Relief surged through me. It was just a bird. The raven let out a caw and took off, its glistening black wings lifting it into the air with ease. I breathed a sigh and kept walking. But the sensation of being watched didn't abate.

The hair on my arms was standing straight up. A growing sense of doom rose within me and I fought the urge to run. Flee, something inside me said. Run, as far and as fast as you can, or something bad will happen.

A bug darted in front of my face. I swatted it away but it came right back. I walked a little swifter. A second bug arrived. I fervently hoped they did not bite or sting. A third joined those circling me and now my heart beat a little faster.

With every few steps, another bug appeared until within a minute or two a dark cloud surrounded me. I waved my arms, trying to keep them away from my face.

"Shoo," I said. "Go away."

A faint sound like a titter reached my ears and suddenly my palms were clammy. I stopped walking.

"What are you?" I asked. "What do you want?"

Something grabbed my boot. The finest thread, no thicker than a spider web, was draped over my boot. It sparkled in the bright sunlight. I tried to lift my foot but the strand held me fast to the ground.

A strand shot over my other boot and then something shoved me from behind. I fell to my hands and knees in the leaf litter. A second shove sent me to my stomach. The leaves were cool against my face and when I inhaled, everything smelled fresh and earthy. Down here, the trees towered over me, impossibly tall.

My hand rested on a tree root that ran along the surface of the ground. I dug my fingers into the loose soil and grasped the root but couldn't pull it free. With my other hand, I scrabbled in the leaf litter, searching for something else that might serve as a weapon: a stick, a rock, anything. But all I found was damp leaves and rich dirt and a few mushrooms.

One of the bugs stood right in front of my face and now I saw it wasn't a bug at all. It was only as tall as my fingernail but its form was human. Tiny wings fluttered from behind its shoulders as it pointed one hand at me and made a high-pitched noise.

More threads shot over me, pinning me to the ground at shoulder and waist and legs. Panic welled within me and my chest tightened. I was trussed like a pig about to be roasted.

The tiny winged folk swarmed over me, their footsteps so light, they felt like nothing more than stray hairs brushing against my skin. I strained against the ropes and they dug into my skin.

"What do you want?" I asked.

Once I was fastened to their satisfaction, the tiny creatures flew down to the ground and assembled in front of my face. They flitted around, seeming to spin and turn and dip.

"Release me." I glared at them. "We can talk if you untie me."

They seemed to laugh again and one in front of me shook his head.

"I could squash you," I said, raising one fist. They hadn't thought to tie my hands. "I could squash you like the bugs you are."

An indignant chatter reached my ears. Those close to my hands flitted backwards out of reach.

"If you don't let me go immediately, I am going to hunt you down and squash each and every one of you. I will stomp you into the ground."

The creatures seemed to confer but it was obvious they couldn't reach an agreement. While they talked, I strained at my bonds, but the delicate threads held me fast.

SUMERLED

The mortal woman's face is pale and her eyes large as the sprites pin her to the ground. I fancy I can almost smell her fear from where I hide beneath a hawthorn bush.

They laugh and mock her, although her feeble mortal hearing probably doesn't allow her to hear their words. I have to slap a hand over my mouth to stop myself from laughing as the sprites bring her to the ground and dance on top of her. She challenges and threatens them. Are all mortals so stupid? Or just this one that Kalen has chosen?

I am so absorbed in the spectacle before me that I don't notice Kalen until he grabs me by the shoulder and hauls me to my feet.

"Sumerled, what are you doing?" he hisses. "I told you to take her to the portal. Not to spy on her."

I glare at the ground. "I would have. Sooner or later."

"You were supposed to do it straight away. Eithne must be terrified. We are used to creatures such as these but mortals are not."

That's what makes it fun, I think, but I only kick the ground and continue to glower at it. Kalen gives me a final shake and shoves me away.

"I don't know why I waste my time with you," he says. "You're not worth it. Just go away."

I flee. He will forgive me. He always does. And I have not forgotten the promise she owes me. I will collect on that before she returns to the mortal world. I now know exactly what I want for my promise.

EITHNE

*W*ell-worn boots appeared in front of me. I craned my neck to see their wearer.

"Release her," Kalen said, his voice like thunder. "Then leave, before I make you regret coming here today."

An angry hum reached my ears and the little creatures darted around. The threads securing me suddenly disappeared. Kalen stretched out a hand to help me up but I ignored him and scrambled to my feet. Why had he come back now? He had made it clear he cared nothing for me.

A sudden wave of dizziness sent me pitching forward into his arms. He grasped my shoulders but I shook him off. I didn't want to be near him. Didn't want him to touch me. I might not be strong enough to do what I had to if he did.

I busied myself with brushing leaves and dirt from my clothes. The flying creatures circled my head making angry chattering noises. Kalen waved a hand at them.

"Go," he said, louder this time.

With a final vexed buzz, they flew away. We looked at each other. Or rather he looked at me and I glared at him.

"They meant you no harm," he said.

"No harm?" My voice was embarrassingly high.

"They were toying with you. Had they intended harm, you would have been dead before you ever saw them."

What other horrors did these woods hide? I bit down the words that rose to my tongue. I wouldn't thank him. I didn't need him to rescue me. I would have rescued myself eventually, just like in the tales I used to tell myself.

"Where is Grainne?" I asked.

Kalen looked away and swallowed before meeting my eyes again. "She is safe enough."

"What does that mean? Is she safe or not?"

"She is with someone I know."

"A fey? You left her with one of the fey?" My voice rose in both volume and pitch.

"I didn't leave her by choice. He sent me away."

"And you just left? Without her?"

"Grainne is not my responsibility." He shot me a look I couldn't read.

"She is my friend. My sister. You should have stayed with her."

"I came to find you."

"She needs you more than I do."

Kalen shrugged but said nothing.

"Why are you even here?" I was suddenly exhausted. It was all I could do to not throw myself to the ground and wail like a child.

"I hurt you." He said it as if only just realising.

I glared at him.

"I didn't mean to. I was trying to protect you."

"I don't need protecting."

"I was doing what I thought was best. Having me around put you in danger. The only way to remove the danger was to remove myself."

"You should have told me. Let me decide for myself whether the danger was worth the risk."

"Are all mortal women so stubborn?" he asked with a sigh.

"If you wanted less stubborn, you should have chosen someone else."

Kalen met my gaze steadily and my heart faltered. "But I chose you."

I swallowed. This was dangerous territory. I was too close to letting him back in. I steeled myself.

"Then why did you stop coming to visit me?"

Kalen dug the toe of his boot in the dirt. In his silence, I heard the wind moving through leaves. Birds called. Life continued all around us while I waited for his next words.

"I was trying not to draw Titania's attention. I didn't want her to know about you."

"Why?" My voice was calm and even, giving no hint of the crazy way my heart pounded.

"Because she would forbid me from fraternising with a mortal. And because I didn't want you to be in danger."

"Was I in danger? Before I came here?" I plucked a stray leaf off my ragged sleeve and watched as it fluttered down to the ground.

"Not as long as she didn't know about you. That's why I stopped coming. Somebody knew and threatened to tell Titania."

"Why?"

"Because he could."

I longed to know more but for now, it was enough that he had finally told me the truth. The reason he stopped coming to me wasn't because he didn't care. I clung to this new knowledge, letting it soften my heart just a little.

"Where is Grainne?" I asked.

"He has probably taken her to his home."

"Will he hurt her?"

Kalen looked away, shuffled his feet, cleared his throat.

"Kalen, will he hurt her?"

"I don't know."

I batted my softening feelings away. The fey never changed. "What do you mean, you don't know? How could you hand Grainne over to someone who might hurt her?"

"He wanted her. I had no choice."

"There is always a choice. You should have kept her safe."

"I know. I knew. But he... there is something he holds over me. A threat. I am protecting someone else, somebody who can't protect himself."

"Take me to Grainne. Please."

"There's nothing you can do for her. He won't hand her over until he gets bored. Anything you do will make things worse for her."

"Grainne has been by my side through this whole thing. All the months Titania forced us to work as slaves. She offered to come with me. She didn't have to. I can't just walk away and leave her in danger."

"There's nothing you can do."

"I have to try. There must be something."

An emotion I couldn't read flashed briefly across his face but eventually he sighed and nodded. "You have to do what I say. Promise me that if I say we are leaving, you will. I'll protect you as best as I can, but..."

"I'm not promising anything. If you won't take me to her, I'll find someone who can. Sumerled might be able to find her. He found you, after all."

"Leave Sumerled out of this."

"Then take me to her yourself and I won't have to ask him."

We eyed each other.

"It's a long walk from here," he said.

"It can't be any further than I've already walked."

Kalen sighed again. "Let's go then."

EITHNE

*A*s we walked, I studied Kalen out of the corner of my eye. He looked exactly the same as when I last saw him, wearing clothes that were a size too large and with raggedly cut hair. He glanced towards me and I quickly looked away.

I couldn't afford let myself feel anything for him. Once we found Grainne, he would take us to a portal and after that, I would likely never see him again. There was no point dwelling on the way my heart ached at being so close to him and the way my hands itched to reach out and touch him.

Those thoughts reminded me of my own filth and I wished he hadn't seen my tattered clothes and tangled hair. Grime covered every inch of my skin and I stank of sweat. But at least I wasn't limping. Whatever fey magic had straightened my foot continued to hold.

"Is there a stream near here?" I asked. "Could we stop somewhere I can bathe?"

"I can take you to a place where you can bathe," he said, then whistled sharply.

A moment later, a rustling noise came from behind us. I turned around in time to see Sumerled creeping out from beneath a bramble bush. Kalen glared at him.

"Were you spying again?" he asked, his voice stern.

Sumerled's face was sullen and he glowered in my direction. "Not much worth spying on around here."

Kalen inhaled deeply. "Sumerled, you try my patience."

The boy merely shrugged and looked away.

"Go find Eithne some clean clothes," Kalen said.

Sumerled opened his mouth to speak.

"Now," Kalen said.

Sumerled fled into the trees. Kalen resumed walking and I hurried to catch up.

"Why does he hate me?" I asked.

Kalen shook his head. "It's not you. He hates everyone. He's... he's not had an easy life."

"Is it true that he's half mortal? That you and he are brothers?"

Kalen's gaze flickered sideways to meet mine ever so briefly. "He told you that?"

"Yes."

"Our father is Oberon." He spoke quickly, as if to get the words out before he changed his mind.

I stumbled over a tree root but caught myself before I fell, pretending I didn't see Kalen stretching out a hand to help. "The king? You're... what, a prince?"

And I had fancied myself in love with him. Fooled myself into thinking he felt the same.

Kalen barked a laugh. "Not exactly. An outcast, more like. Titania hates me. I live here only at her sufferance and on the condition that I keep out of her sight. She would prefer to forget I exist."

"Why don't you live in the mortal world? You wouldn't be beholden to anyone."

"I am only half fey. If I were to live in your world, I would age and die. This-" He gestured at the woods that surrounded us. "This is my birthright. I should be here, amongst my own kind."

"If you are indeed half mortal, then my world also contains your own kind."

Kalen flinched.

"You despise us so?" I shouldn't let it bother me because I would never see him again after today, but still I was bitterly disappointed. "Are we that far beneath you, that you would rather live here, where you are an outcast, than live in freedom in the mortal world?"

"I am trying to live the way Titania expects. I hope... I hope that if I live the way any other fey does, she will realise I belong here."

I looked away into the trees, composing myself before I spoke further. I didn't want my voice to give away my disappointment. "She hates you?"

"She hates what I represent. Oberon's dalliance with a mortal. Titania doesn't care about his indiscretions with women of the fey. He has had plenty and she too has her own affairs. But she was gravely offended that he would choose a mortal over her, and not just once. Sumerled's mother is also mortal. Titania hates him even more than she hates me. Once, I think, she might forgive such an indiscretion, but not twice."

I concentrated on keeping my footing and pretending Kalen's revelation meant nothing to me. But it explained so much.

"And this is why you stopped coming to see me," I said eventually. "You didn't want Titania to think you were following in your father's footsteps. Fraternising with a mortal." My voice was bitter, however much I tried to suppress my feelings.

"If I had only myself to think of, I wouldn't have stopped. But I have to look after Sumerled. What would happen to him if she threw me out of her realm?"

"So what happened?"

"Sumerled found out about you. He thought this knowledge would grant him favour with somebody we both know. He told. The... person threatened to tell Titania."

"So you give me up to protect him, knowing he would betray you in a heartbeat."

"I was protecting you too."

"But mostly him."

"Both of you."

Kalen stopped walking and reached out to take my hand. He finally looked me in the eyes. "I care about you, Eithne. I don't know the words to tell you how I feel. This is not what I planned when I first started visiting you. I was merely curious."

Sumerled suddenly appeared beside me, seemingly out of nowhere. Kalen dropped my hand and took a step away from me. Sumerled thrust a bundle towards me.

"Here," he muttered.

It was heavier than I had expected and I almost dropped it.

"Thank you," I said. I couldn't bring myself to look at him. If it wasn't for him, Kalen wouldn't have stopped coming to see me. Grainne and I would never have come here. We wouldn't have spent months imprisoned as slaves. All because Kalen wanted to protect this unlikeable boy.

"Go now," Kalen said. "No spying."

Sumerled glared at each of us in turn and then disappeared into the woods.

"There's a small pool just over there," Kalen said. "Nobody will disturb you. I'll wait here."

Less than a dozen steps, past a row of thickly-leafed hawthorn bushes, took me to a rocky pool filled with clear, still water. It was surrounded by a blanket of lush moss. There was no sign of the stream that fed the pool but perhaps the water came from underground.

I placed Sumerled's bundle on the moss and untied the cord. Wrapped inside a large piece of linen cloth was a dress, underthings and boots. They were clean and in far better condition than my own. There was also a hairbrush and a bundle of soapwort leaves — unexpected luxuries. I was surprised at Sumerled's thoughtfulness.

With a quick glance around to ensure neither Kalen nor Sumerled lingered nearby, I stripped off my threadbare gown. The fabric fell apart in my hands. I slipped my aching feet from my worn boots and stepped into the pool.

The water was blissfully warm. I sank down to my knees and the warm water surrounded me to the neck. Gods, it felt good. For a while, I just kneeled there. How long had it been since I last bathed? The water soothed my sore feet but stung the many cuts and abrasions that covered my skin. I knelt there until my fingers wrinkled then I ducked beneath the surface to drench my hair.

I scrubbed myself with the soapwort, sloughing off months of grime and sweat and dirt. The water around me turned grey. I scrubbed until my skin was red and stinging. I sniffed my arm, just for the pleasure of smelling clean skin. This was the first time I had seen my naked body in months and I tried not to notice how far my ribs stuck out or how my belly curved in towards my spine. If I ever got out of this place, I would never miss a meal again.

Eventually I climbed out of the rocky pool and wrapped myself in the piece of linen. I brushed my hair as best I could but there were sections that were so tangled, they would need to be cut. The thought reminded me of how I had cut Grainne's hair after she was attacked. I still didn't know what secret she hid about that night or who her attacker was. I supposed it didn't matter much anymore. We had been here for months at least, maybe even a year or more. Caedmon was long dead. I pushed my feelings aside. Once we were out of this place, I would grieve for him.

When my hair was as tidy as I could make it, I dried myself and then put on the clothes Sumerled had provided. They fit surprisingly well. I returned to where Kalen waited. He leaned against a tree, arms crossed over his chest. My heart ached when I saw him. How different might things have been if he were mortal? Or even if he had cared less about pleasing Titania? When I got home, I would never again let myself think about him. In time, I would forget and my broken heart would heal. That was what a sensible woman would do.

"Now take me to Grainne," I said.

Kalen sighed. He opened his mouth and I knew he was going to argue again.

"She came here to help me, to protect me. I'm not leaving her behind."

"You don't understand."

I stood straight and held my head high. "I understand as much as I need to. And you're going to help me find her."

Kalen's gaze flicked to something behind me and his face paled. As I turned around, a fey man stepped out from behind an oak tree.

"It's Grainne you seek, is it, my dear? I might just be able to help you."

EITHNE

*K*alen stepped forward, one hand held out in a strangely beseeching gesture.

"Lunn-" he said, but I interrupted.

"Let him speak." I nodded toward the stranger. "How do you know Grainne?"

He had the pale skin and dark eyes typical of his race and was slightly taller than Kalen. His dark hair was cut shorter than Kalen's and more neatly, and his mouth held a hint of cruelty.

"Grainne and I are old friends," he said with something that might have been a smirk.

If Grainne hadn't mentioned him, there was a reason for it.

Kalen moved to stand in front of me. "Lunn, please, let her be."

"Friend of yours, Kalen?" Lunn asked. "How interesting that you've never mentioned her. Seems we both have secrets when it comes to mortal women."

"Eithne was just leaving."

"No I'm not," I said, stepping out from behind Kalen. "I'm not leaving without Grainne."

"Fascinating," Lunn said. "But I don't think she will be interested."

"What do you mean?"

"She's determined to find her man. She seems to believe he needs rescuing."

"Caedmon is here? He's alive?"

"Of course. Grainne came in search of him. You did know that, didn't you?" Lunn raised his eyebrows and I got the distinct impression he was enjoying himself.

What was the truth? That Caedmon was here and Grainne somehow knew? That she came, not to support me, but to find him? That she wasn't searching for me now, as I was searching for her, because she was busy looking for Caedmon? I took a deep breath. I would not cry in front of the fey. Any of them.

"Can you take me to her?" I asked Lunn.

He tipped his head to one side and looked me up and down. "I could, if you were to make me the right offer."

Kalen grabbed me by the wrist. "No, Lunn, you cannot have her."

Lunn's gaze never left me. "Mind yourself, Kalen."

"I will not let you have Eithne."

I wrenched my wrist from his grasp. "What do you mean, have me?"

Kalen met my eyes briefly. "Eithne, trust me. You do not want this. Even to find your friend."

"I don't know what you're talking about. All I want is to find Grainne and go home. And if Lunn is able to help me, I want to hear what he has to say."

"No," Kalen said. He turned back to Lunn. "Lunn, don't do this. Please. She is… special to me."

"How interesting. The mongrel has broken his leash and thinks to attack? You can't protect them both, you know. If you have to choose one, which will it be?"

"Leave Sumerled out of this."

"Oh, but you know how I feel about that lying, thieving half-breed. I've tolerated him for far longer than I would have, were it not for your interference. So now you choose. Sumerled or the girl."

"My name is Eithne," I said. "I don't appreciate being referred to as *the girl*."

"She has spark, this one," Lunn said, with a laugh. "I'm going to have fun with her."

Kalen grabbed my hand and held it a little too tightly. His fingers were warm, his palm sweaty.

"They are both under my protection," he said.

"Choose." Lunn's voice was cold now and he gave up any pretence at a smile. "One or the other. I take the one you don't choose."

"What do you want with Sumerled?" I asked. Beside me, Kalen stiffened and I glanced at him. "What is Kalen protecting him from?"

Lunn barked a laugh. "From me, my pretty. The half-breed needs to learn a lesson about keeping his sticky fingers off other people's property."

"He's just a boy," Kalen said. "He doesn't know any better."

"Then I'd be happy to teach him," Lunn said.

"We have an agreement," Kalen said.

"We *had* an agreement. You can continue to protect the little half-breed or you can keep the girl. Sorry, *Eithne*," Lunn said with a mocking glance towards me. "It's one or the other."

"I don't need your protection, Kalen," I said. "Look after Sumerled if you must. I can look after myself."

"You can't protect yourself here," Kalen said. "No mortal can."

"You're choosing the girl?" Lunn said. "I just want to be clear about your choice. Because then I'm going to find Sumerled and finish drowning him."

"What?" I asked. "You can't do that."

"He took something that belonged to me. Drowning seems a fair punishment. Unfortunately Kalen interrupted the last time but I'm willing to try again."

"You'll kill him," Kalen said. "He needs to breathe."

"That's the whole point." Lunn's voice was dry. "Get rid of the half-breed. Should have been drowned at birth."

"Don't hurt him," Kalen said. "He's a thief, but he doesn't deserve to die."

I suddenly felt very tired. If Grainne didn't need me, I no longer had any reason to stay.

"I'm going home," I said. "You two can stay here and argue all day for all I care. I found the portal once and I'll find it again. I don't need you. Either of you."

I stomped away into the trees. It didn't matter what direction I went, only that it was away from them. Behind me, Lunn laughed, loud and mocking.

"Go ahead, little girl," he called after me. "Let's see how far you get on your own. You'll come back soon enough, looking for help. And I'll be most pleased to assist you."

EITHNE

I stormed through the woods, wishing I could knock down everything that stood between me and the portal, wherever it was. Brambles grabbed at my dress and weeds tangled around my ankles but I tugged them off and kept moving. The air was hot and heavy and I was drowning in it.

Emotions swirled. Disappointment that Grainne had kept secrets from me. Anger that she had left me here, not knowing whether I was safe. Relief that Caedmon was alive. Anger at Diarmuid for that stupid tale that left us all thinking Caedmon was dead. Fury at Kalen for so many reasons.

I stomped along without caring about how much noise I made. So what if I was attracting attention? What could possibly be worse than what I had already suffered? I was going home and anyone who got in my way this time could be damned. If Titania was watching, she could come and face me and I'd tell her exactly what I thought of her and her kin.

"Damn you, Titania," I yelled, uncaring of the silence that swept through the woods at my voice. "You hear me? Damn you."

I was so focused on the maelstrom of emotions swirling through me that I almost didn't notice the *pull*. It felt exactly the same as it had so many months ago. The portal was close.

I stopped, closed my eyes, concentrated. The pull was stronger when I turned to the right. I moved cautiously now. I wanted to get through the portal and be back in the mortal world. Away from the politics and infighting of the fey. Away from a dictatorial queen whose subjects lived in fear. Away from cruel fey who solved a problem by drowning a boy. Away from a certain heartless fey who toyed with a woman's emotions and chose his half-brother over her. I didn't need any of them. I never heard Kalen's approach but suddenly he was beside me.

"Eithne." He grabbed me by the arm. "Stop. We need to talk."

I didn't even pause as I shook his hand off. "Don't touch me. You have no right."

"Please stop. I can explain."

"Who is Lunn?" Now the pull came from further off to the left. I corrected my path.

"Would you stop walking for just a moment? Let me explain."

I was tempted to keep going. Find the damn portal and get out of here. Leave Kalen behind and hope his heart hurt as much as mine did. But I stopped. I held my head high and looked him in the face. I squashed down the feelings that rose when I saw the pain in his eyes. Whatever I might have once felt for him was gone, I told myself. He had no control over me anymore.

"Has anything you ever said to me been the truth?" I asked. "Or was it all just tales, made up to amuse yourself as you toyed with a mortal woman?"

"It was all true. I promise. I've never lied to you. I mightn't have told you everything but I never lied."

"Who is Lunn and how does he know Grainne?"

"Lunn is — was — an old friend. We played together as boys, before he knew I was half mortal. I didn't know it then myself. The day he found out was the day he started hating me.

"And then Sumerled came along. I have more of Oberon's blood than my mother's and can pass for fey, but he can't. He bothered Lunn one too many times and one day I caught Lunn holding his head under the water in a pond. I talked him into letting Sumerled live on the condition that I keep the boy away from him. But Sumerled doesn't listen to anyone, including me. He does what he wants."

"How does Grainne come into all this?"

"I don't know. Lunn is not nice to women and there's only one way a mortal woman would attract his interest. You want to hope your friend hasn't experienced that."

"She wouldn't have given herself to him. She loves Caedmon."

I started to walk away but Kalen's next words stopped me in my tracks.

"I meant everything I said, Eithne. And all of the things I didn't say but probably should have. You meant — mean — a great deal to me. There were days I almost wished I was fully mortal, just so we could spend more time together and I didn't need to worry about Titania finding out about you."

"It's too late," I said. "I was a foolish girl but I've learnt a lot the last few months, about myself and about the fey. I can't be with one of your kind. I'm not willing to sit and wait and hope that one day you'll come back to me. Not willing to pray every night that you haven't lost inter-est. If I'm ever with somebody, he'll be mortal."

"I've treated you badly, I know. I can make amends though. We could start over."

He caught up to me and walked beside me. His arm brushed my sleeve and suddenly I couldn't think straight. I couldn't concentrate on finding the portal while he was so close. I stopped walking and turned to face him although I couldn't look at him for fear I would change my mind. I stared down at my boots, half buried in golden leaves, and forced myself to say the words I knew I had to.

"It's not what I want anymore."

"I never meant to hurt you."

Kalen reached out one hand and touched me on the cheek. His fingers were cool and gentle. It seemed my stupid heart, which was leaping crazily, didn't yet understand that we couldn't be together.

When I didn't berate him for touching me, Kalen took a step closer. He was barely a handspan away from me. If I leaned in just the tiniest bit, I could close the gap between us. But it would only be temporary. I could never close the gap between mortal and fey. There was a reason our two races weren't meant to mix. The fey were addictive but they were also unfeeling, calculating, unknowable. We were emotional, irrational and totally unprepared for how they could make us feel. No wonder so many of the old tales told of mortal women who gave up everything for them. I understood it now. But I hardened my heart. It didn't matter. The only thing that mattered was finding my way home.

I turned away and started walking again. Kalen followed me.

GRAINNE

*S*everal days after he had captured me, Lunn finally gave me a bucket of almost-warm water and allowed me to bathe. He refused to leave while I washed so I had no choice but to strip in front of him. He had already seen me naked anyway. When I had finished, I still didn't feel clean and there wasn't enough water to wash my hair or my clothes but at least I managed to remove some of the grime from my skin. Lunn waited until after I had finished bathing before he left.

There was no need for him to restrain me when he was gone for there was no exit other than the doorway that appeared only when Lunn wanted it to. I carried the chain attached to my collar as I explored. His chamber was clean to the point of fastidiousness. When I ran my finger over the wooden surfaces, there was not a trace of dust. Other than the clothes he dropped on the floor each night — which were always gone before I woke — everything else he owned was neatly put away. I investigated every corner of his chamber and felt no guilt at going through his meagre possessions.

Where he went, I had no idea and I preferred not to know. When he was at home, I badgered him. I demanded he take me to Caedmon. I reminded him of the sad life he himself led. I told him of everything Caedmon had to live for in the mortal world: his family, the son he wanted, his career, the home we were building, Silver Downs itself. And gradually cracks appeared in Lunn's facade. He became snappy with me and sometimes he ignored me for hours on end.

He had been gone for at least half a day this time. When he returned, I was sitting in the chair in which I slept, half dozing while I waited.

"Let me try," I said as the doorway appeared and he stepped inside. "I have the right to at least try to bring my husband back."

"You have no chance of getting through to him." He sounded exasperated. He pulled his shirt over his head and dropped it on the floor, then sprawled on one of the chairs, his legs stretched out in front of him. His torso was lean, the skin as white as his face. He leaned his head against the chair back and closed his eyes. "I have told you over and over. He will not remember you. And he will not willingly give up his life here."

"Then what does it hurt to let me try?"

"Why are you so certain you can get through to him?"

"Because I am his wife. I represent everything he has to live for."

He didn't reply although I waited for a long while.

"Lunn—"

He cut me off. "What would you give for the chance to speak with him?"

Vivid memories of my night with him flashed through my mind. I pushed them away and kept my voice steady. "I have nothing to give. You have already taken everything I have."

Lunn opened his eyes and looked at me. "I will give you one chance. One chance in which to convince your man to hear you. If you fail, you will stay here with me forever. And you will never mention him again."

"Three chances," I countered. "Three and if I fail, I stay."

Lunn considered my offer for so long that I really thought he would refuse.

"Fine," he said at last. "Three chances. And if you fail, you are mine."

I swallowed hard and reminded myself to breathe. The thought of spending the rest of my life wearing Lunn's collar was unbearable. I'd find a way to kill myself before I endured that.

Lunn rose and came to stand in front of me. I shrank back into my chair a little when he reached for me, memories of his clawed hands overwhelming me. But all he did was touch a finger to my collar. It opened and fell into my lap. At the same time, the doorway appeared in the earthen wall.

I touched the tender skin of my neck. It was raw, bruised and swollen. But at last the collar was off. I was determined to never wear it again.

"Will you take me to the place where the hunt will pass by?" I asked.

"I think I've done enough already." He returned to his chair, leaned back and closed his eyes again.

The collar still lay in my lap. I wanted to throw it away from me but was reluctant to touch it even that much.

"Please Lunn. Give me a fair chance."

"I've already given you three chances. I hope, for your sake, you don't squander them."

"I will get through to him. You'll see."

He shrugged but didn't open his eyes. "You will or you won't. Time will tell."

"Take me to him. Please."

He sighed. "Oh, what difference does it make. I may as well. I've already all but handed him to you."

I kept my mouth shut. He might well change his mind yet. When he stood and went to the doorway, I followed. The collar fell to the floor. I left it there.

I kept close behind him as he strode through the woods. He left me by an old oak tree. It might have been the same one we hid behind the last time we watched the hunt.

"They will come past here sooner or later," he said. "It may not be today though, or even tomorrow."

"I will wait."

"Keep out of the path of the horses. They will not hesitate to ride straight over you. You will be crushed to death if they do."

"Thank you for the warning."

Lunn shook his head. "You are determined, for a mortal woman. It almost makes me hope you will succeed."

"Thank you," I said. "I think."

Lunn turned and left without a backward glance. I sat in the leaves beneath the oak and leaned back against its trunk. I breathed in the earthy scent of the woods. There was nothing to do now but wait.

GRAINNE

$\mathcal{T}$ime passes slowly in the fey woods. Or perhaps it doesn't pass at all. Leaning back against the rough trunk of the oak tree, I shredded a fallen leaf, gradually reducing it to slivers. My mouth was dry and my fingers shook a little. What would Caedmon do when he saw me? Perhaps he would lean down and swoop me up so we could ride like the wind to the portal? I could see myself sitting behind him astride the horse, the scraps of my skirt trailing behind me, my arms around Caedmon's waist. But perhaps he would tell me he didn't want to leave. That he liked his life here and I should go home and forget about him.

Or if Lunn was right, he would see me but not remember his wife or that we had handfasted only a few weeks before Lunn stole him away. He might have forgotten the home we had started building at Silver Downs or the son he had hoped I would be carrying before he left for the campaign front. He might not remember his career as a soldier, the enemies he had faced, the scars he bore, the nightmares that sometimes woke him in the dead of night. I didn't let my thoughts linger long on this possibility, for I would lose all hope if I did. No, he would remember me. He would want to come home and we would leave this place together. I would make sure of it.

I dozed on and off, sometimes waking with a start, certain I had heard the hunt approaching before realising it had been just a dream. I wondered whether Caedmon had been with the fey riders who captured Eithne and me when we first passed through the portal. Could I have found him then if I had thought to look? Perhaps he had even attended the feast where I had stood behind Lunn's chair and eaten the scraps from his plate.

Eventually, the ground began to vibrate and the faint baying of the hounds reached my ears. The rough bark of the oak's trunk caught at my hair as I scrambled to my feet. I stood close to the oak as Lunn had instructed, eager for my first glimpse of Caedmon. My hands trembled and I clasped them tightly together.

At last the hounds tore by. Then the horses came into sight. I leaned back against the oak's trunk and held my breath. As the riders came into sight, I scanned them impatiently. At last I saw Caedmon. He rode right in the middle of the hunt. There were horses on each side of him, and in front, and behind. I could get no closer for fear of being trampled. I called out, but he didn't even look towards me. They were gone before I could do anything else.

I sank down to the ground. Tears trickled down my cheeks and for just a moment, I let them. Then I wiped them away and sat back against the tree to wait. One chance gone.

The time before the hunt came again was long and lonely. Even after all these months — or was it years? — I couldn't tell what time of day it was. The noon-bright light never changed. Yet there were times when the woods quieted around me, as if all of the creatures were asleep. I had come to think of this as night, even though the sun was just as strong.

I dozed and ate juicy blackberries from a nearby bramble bush and stared at my ragged nails. My palms were calloused and the skin on my fingers was peeling. A far cry from the smooth, white hands I once had. Back then these hands knew no harder work than mending or cooking or pulling weeds in the garden. Now they knew what it was like to labour day after day without respite or soothing salves. These were nothing like the smooth fingers that had once touched Caedmon. What would he think of my new hands?

When the distant sounds of the hunt came next, I was ready. The hounds ran past, sniffing and baying. When the riders appeared, I held my breath as I scanned every face and prayed Caedmon would be where he might see me.

The fey no longer looked peculiar to me, with their thin frames and pale skin, their angular faces and high cheek bones. Caedmon was dark haired and dark eyed like them but his shoulders were broad and well-muscled and he was not as tall as them.

My heart leapt when I saw him for this time he rode on the outer edge, on the side where I waited. I risked stepping out a little further. I took a deep breath. Just a little closer. A little more. Then I would jump out and call to him.

Something slammed into me from the side and I fell back into the leaves. My head smacked against the oak. Before I could recover, Caedmon was gone.

"No," I cried. "Caedmon!"

But of course he didn't hear me.

I lay in the leaves, catching my breath. At last I forced myself to rise. My head ached and bright lights sparked at the edges of my vision. My palms were grazed and my back throbbed.

What had happened? It couldn't have been one of the horses for I would have been trampled. A fey rider perhaps, leaning out to the side, to knock me away, out of Caedmon's sight? Whatever the cause, it was done and Caedmon was gone again.

Two chances gone. Only one left.

GRAINNE

J was ready for them the next night. I would risk being trampled to death if I must for this was my last chance. Death was better than forever as Lunn's plaything.

As the thundering of the horses and the hounds' baying reached my ears, I stepped out into the middle of the area through which they would pass. My stomach was tense and my heart pounded so loud that it merged with the sound of the approaching herd until I could hear nothing else.

The leaders came into sight, bearing down on me on their enormous white horses. The rest of the hunt was only moments behind. I braced myself, half expecting that they really would trample me as Lunn had said. Instead they reined in their horses and surrounded me. I could see nothing but horses and the legs of the fey riders.

"Caedmon!" I screamed. Where was he?

One of the horses whinnied and reared up. I jumped out of the way of its enormous hooves and then, in a gap between horses, I saw him. He leaned over his horse's neck, murmuring to it as it danced sideways. I pushed my way through the gap.

"Caedmon, it's me, Grainne. Your wife."

If he heard me, he gave no acknowledgment. I stepped closer and grabbed him by the leg.

"Caedmon, look at me."

He still didn't respond. Panic flashed through me. I had only moments, if that, in which to act. If the fey decided to leave now before I could get his attention, my last chance would be gone.

I grasped Caedmon's leg and pulled hard. His horse scuttled sideways again but I held fast to his leg and suddenly he came sliding off. We landed on the ground in a tangle of limbs. Something hit me hard in the chest. His elbow, or maybe a knee. I clutched his leg, gasping for breath.

A slow clapping reminded me we were not alone. Several fey riders stood in a loose circle around us.

"Well, wasn't that impressive," said one who held himself with a regal air. His voice had the tone of one accustomed to being obeyed. The leader of the hunt, I assumed.

"His name is Caedmon and he is a mortal man," I said, the words springing to my mouth before I even had time to think. "He is mine and I claim him."

I had no idea what made me say such a thing but the words felt right.

The leader laughed and that seemed to be a signal for the others to laugh also.

"Do you understand the rules?" he asked. "If you seek to claim him, you must be able to hold him."

"I can hold him," I said, still clinging tight to Caedmon's leg. He had twisted himself around and half sat up, although he made no attempt to remove his leg from my grasp. He stared at me blankly. I tried not to fear the lack of recognition in his eyes.

"He is mine."

"We'll see how long you last," the leader said.

Caedmon began to squirm in my arms and as I looked at him, his familiar features melted away. He became a black hog, wriggling and snorting in my arms. Its rank odour filled my lungs and brought bile to my throat but I clutched its bristly leg tightly. It kicked and its hoof caught me in the stomach, but I gritted my teeth and held on.

This is still Caedmon. He is mine.

Eventually the hog stopped wriggling and relief flooded through me. It was over.

The hog's features began to shift and soon my arms were wrapped around the leg of a brown bear. It swiped me with its paw, catching me in the shoulder and knocking me onto my side. I held tight to its leg.

You will not take him from me.

The bear became a horse, which became a snarling hound. The hound bit my hand and its tooth sliced through my skin, all the way down to the bone. I ignored the pain and hung on.

Mine.

I was only vaguely aware of the fey who surrounded us. They laughed and jeered, but I barely heard them.

As a raven, Caedmon cawed and pecked at my face. As a bee, he slipped right through my fingers but I made a wild snatch and caught him. He stung me twice before changing into a tom cat. Fierce and wild, the cat sank claws and teeth into my arms.

Mine.

Hour after hour, creature after creature, some I couldn't even name. I hung on with everything in me. With every new creature, I thought *Mine.*

A serpent wriggled in my grip. I wrapped both hands around its slender body as its fangs sank into my arm.

Mine.

The serpent grew bigger. Limbs appeared. Then suddenly it was Caedmon, in his own form, who lay in my arms. He didn't struggle but appeared to be sleeping. I still clutched him, afraid he would change again and slip away from me if I let go.

"Is it over?" I asked, panting.

The leader shrugged and turned away. He mounted his horse. Only once he was astride did he look at me again. "Take him if you wish. I tire of this."

"He is mine?" Was this just another of their tricks?

"You have held him all night," he said. "It is your right to claim him now if you wish."

"I claim him. Caedmon is mine."

The other fey mounted their horses and then, in a thundering of hooves, they were gone.

Caedmon lay on his side. His clothes were clean enough and someone had patched them, but his face was lined and deep shadows underscored his eyes. He was thinner than I remembered and dirt was crusted under his fingernails. He smelled different, as if the fey realm had tainted him, but I detected a faint underlying scent that I recognised as his.

Mine, I thought, fiercely.

"Caedmon." I shook him gently. "Wake up."

Eventually he stirred and opened his eyes. He stared up at me blankly for several heartbeats but slowly recognition seeped into his gaze.

"Grainne?"

"You remember me?" Tears filled my eyes and I blinked furiously to chase them away.

"Where are we?"

"You don't know?"

Caedmon shook his head and winced. "I feel like I have been in a deep sleep and just woke up. I dreamed, vividly, but it's mostly gone now. What happened?"

"You were taken by the fey but I claimed you."

"We're in the fey realm?" Caedmon slowly started to rise and I reluctantly let go of him. "Grainne, we need to leave."

He extended his hand to me and I gratefully accepted his help. Once I was on my feet, I wove my fingers through his.

"I will hold on to you until we get out of here," I said. "Just in case."

With his free hand, Caedmon touched me briefly on the cheek. "I don't know what happened but I assume I am not here by my own choice. I guess you came to find me. So thank you."

More tears and I dashed them away.

"I did what I had to, and it's my fault you were here anyway. Now let's go home."

As we started walking, I remembered Eithne. I hesitated to tell him for I didn't want to give him any reason to linger, but he would want to know.

"Your sister is here, somewhere."

Caedmon froze. "Why?"

"It's a long story."

"Is she safe?" He didn't look at me, as if not wanting to guess the truth if I lied.

"I don't know. There is one of the fey who might help her. But even if he doesn't, she is strong. You have no idea how strong she is."

"Do you know where she is?"

"No. This realm is vast and we have been separated for weeks."

Caedmon exhaled, long and slow. "Then whatever fate has befallen her is probably long past. I want to see you safely home, then I'll come back for Eithne, if I can."

Caedmon and I walked for hours, hoping to find the portal. We stopped to rest once, lying on soft moss. My back was pressed against Caedmon's chest, his arms were around me and even as we lay there, I kept my fingers threaded through his. I would not risk someone snatching him away from me.

"You should sleep for a while," he said. "I will keep guard."

"Do you promise you will stay awake? And not let go of me?"

"I promise."

I woke with a start from a dream in which Caedmon had turned into a raven and flown away as I slept.

"I'm here, Grainne," came his voice from behind me, even before I realised his arms were still tight around my waist. "You didn't sleep long."

"It was enough. You should sleep now."

He did although I sensed he wanted to argue. But he held his tongue and soon his breathing deepened. I was content to lie with his body pressed against mine, the smell of him all around me, and his fingers tangled with mine. He slept for only an hour or two and then we continued on our journey through the woods, hand in hand.

"What does the portal look like?" Caedmon asked.

"I don't know. We passed through it without realising."

"They wanted you to come then."

"Does that mean they can stop us from going home?"

"Probably."

Leaves crackled behind us. "Who would do such a thing, my dear Grainne?"

I knew who it was even without looking. A shiver of disgust crept over me. I had spent enough days listening to that voice and had hoped never to hear it again.

We turned to face Lunn. Caedmon looked puzzled as if he vaguely recognised him.

"You remember my husband," I said.

Lunn raised an eyebrow. "So. You managed to claim him. You impress me, Grainne."

"We are going home."

Lunn smiled and my blood froze. "Aren't you forgetting something?"

"What?"

"He can never go home."

Beside me, Caedmon was very still. "Explain yourself."

"The tale your bard brother told. As long as you are in this realm, its power cannot reach you. But if you return to the world of mortals, you are again subject to the magic your brother wrought."

"I claimed him," I said. "He is free now."

Lunn's lips lifted into something that resembled a smile. "You have gone to much effort to locate him, my dear, but I'm afraid it has all been for naught. For if you wish him to live, he must remain here."

"No," I said. "There must be a way around that. There has to be, or you would have said something earlier. You would have dissuaded me if you could have."

"I didn't believe you would succeed," Lunn said. "It seemed pointless to tell you."

"How do I break the enchantment? Tell me and I will do it."

"I'm afraid you can't. Your man's brother is a powerful bard. It is only a matter of time."

"But I've claimed him," I said. I wrapped my fingers tighter around

Caedmon's, fearing that even now he would be torn away from me. "The leader of the hunt agreed. He is free to leave."

"Yes, he may leave, if he wishes. But as soon as he steps foot in the mortal world, his life is forsaken."

"I don't believe there is nothing I can do. There is always a way."

If Lunn felt any pity for me, it did not show in his face. "Your man may remain here, if he wishes. Or he may leave. The choice is his."

"Then he stays," I said, and my heart shattered.

Caedmon's hand tightened around mine. "Grainne-"

"No, I know what you are going to say and I won't allow it."

"Can Grainne stay with me?" Caedmon asked.

"I'm afraid not," Lunn said. "My contract with her requires I allow you to stay in order to protect you. But I have no further obligation to her."

"I will make a new contract with you," Caedmon said. "To protect Grainne."

Lunn laughed. "Ask Grainne how she forged her contract, but wait until I leave before you do so."

"There must be something we can do," I said. "I'm not giving up now."

"It wasn't for nothing. You saved your man. If he chooses to abandon that, it's his decision. He can stay here where he is safe, but once he passes through the portal, our contract is void."

"Let me make a new contract," I said. "One that will protect him in our world. Or one that will keep me here. I don't care which."

"Aah, lovely Grainne. No, as pleasant as it was, I have no interest in repeating myself."

"So that's it?" I asked. "You're going to let Caedmon be killed?"

"I've fulfilled our contract."

"You can't just let him die."

Lunn turned and walked away, moving as silently as he had appeared. "Goodbye, Grainne."

We watched as he disappeared between ash and beech. I turned back to Caedmon.

"You can't do this," I said. "You can't just walk out of here and back into danger."

"You forget I'm a soldier." Caedmon placed his palms on my cheeks and kissed my forehead. "Walking into danger is what I do."

"Please. Anything but this."

"My one regret, my dear, will be leaving you. I chose well when I picked you. I was just trying to find a wife I thought I could tolerate waking up to each day. I didn't count on finding one I could fall in love with."

A deep sorrow entered my heart as he gently touched his lips to mine.

"I love you, Grainne. My time here has felt like a dream. I could feel my body move. I could hear what I said, feel what I ate. But I had no control over it. I kept your image fixed firmly in my mind and every day that passed, every step I took, I pretended I was moving that much closer to you. Even when I could hardly remember who you were, your image reminded me I had something to live for. Something waiting for me. I just couldn't quite remember what or where."

"Please, stay here." I didn't realise I was crying until Caedmon wiped the tears from my face with his fingertips. "I could bear being separated from you for the rest of my life if I knew you were safe. I promise I won't come looking for you again."

"This is no life here. It might seem like every man's dream, doing as you want all day, with no consequences, no cares. But it's a shallow life, half-lived. I would rather come home with you, even if I can't stay long. Now dry your tears, sweet Grainne. Don't leave me with the memory of you crying. I want to be able to picture you smiling as I die."

"I won't be smiling."

"Are you ready?"

"No."

He held my hand firmly. "Together, Grainne."

We stepped forward and suddenly we were at the edge of the woods. And somehow I knew the road in front of us and the far-off mountains shrouded in clouds were in the mortal world. We had already passed through the portal.

GRAINNE

his was not the same portal Eithne and I originally passed
through, for instead of gazing across the lower end of Silver
Downs, we faced an unfamiliar road. A smudge of smoke near the
horizon indicated a lodge. Somewhere nearby, but out of sight, cows
lowed. The air was fresh and clean after so long breathing the moistness
and decay of the woods.

"That way." Caedmon indicated with a nod of his head. "We are less
than a day's walk from home."

"Maybe we should go back, try to find the other portal. The one that
leads directly to Silver Downs."

"I can't avoid my fate, Grainne." Caedmon's voice was gentle and his
dark eyes full of sorrow. "I know you mean well and you've done more
than any man could ask. I'm sorry I won't be returning home with you
but I'll go as far as I can. You'll make someone else a fine wife one day."

Tears sprang to my eyes and I blinked them away. "I can't bear to
start for home just yet. Can we rest for a while?"

"Of course."

He led me back a little ways into the ash and oak and birch. I
watched carefully for any unseasonal lushness but saw no sign that we

had returned to the fey realm. Caedmon made us a bed of leaves between two stout hazel shrubs. I tried to help but he shooed me away.

"Let me do this, Grainne. You've already saved my life, twice over. Let me provide somewhere for you to rest."

So I stood back and watched as he heaped up the leaves, adding more and more until the pile was almost as high as my waist. Then he held out his hand and helped me into it.

I sank straight down and leaves drifted in to cover me with a soft blanket. Caedmon climbed in beside me, burrowing in until his body was pressed against mine. I turned to face him.

"I've missed you, Grainne." His breath was warm on my face.

"I missed you too. I wish-"

"I know, but we don't have enough time for regrets."

He kissed me then and soon I forgot we were in a pile of leaves in the woods. I forgot too my grimy skin and greasy hair and the stench of my body. His touch was gentle and my body responded as if it had been only yesterday that he last touched me. Memories of Lunn's hands on me wormed into my brain and I pushed them away. If this was to be my last time with Caedmon, I would not let it be tainted with thoughts of Lunn.

Some time later, we tumbled out of the pile of leaves. Caedmon wrapped his arms around me and rested his chin on the top of my head. I pressed my forehead to his chest and breathed in his scent.

"Ready to go home?" he asked.

"You can still change your mind."

"You know I won't."

"I know."

He took my hand and we started walking back towards the road. I stumbled over a tree root shrouded in leaves but Caedmon grabbed me around the waist before I could fall. I clung to him for a moment longer than necessary.

"Caedmon, I need to tell you something."

"Anything."

I took a deep breath and peeled myself off him. We kept walking.

Somehow I had never imagined saying this to him. It had seemed too big. Too needy. But I didn't want to live with regrets.

"I've loved you since I was seven summers old."

He took another few paces before darting a glance at me. "Really?"

I nodded, shy now that the words were said.

"I never knew."

"I'm surprised you didn't. My sisters did their best to tell you every time they saw you."

He tipped his head back and laughed. "They were always prattling on about one thing or another. I mostly didn't listen. I must have missed whatever hints they dropped."

"And here I was, mortified every time you were within calling distance."

"I wish I had known."

"Would it have made any difference?"

He considered my question, his face serious and thoughtful. "Yes, it might have. It's a serious matter to ask a woman to handfast with you. You never know if you'll be rejected. I had been toying with the idea for some time but didn't know whether anyone would want a soldier who is away from home most of the year. Had I known you would respond favourably, I might have asked earlier."

We reached the road and turned towards the setting sun. The golden orb joined the horizon in a riot of gold and lavender and scarlet.

"How beautiful," I murmured.

"Indeed." But Caedmon was looking at me, not at the sun.

I blushed and ran my fingers through my knotted hair. "I must look like a fright."

"You look like the most wonderful thing I've ever seen."

He took my hand and we continued to walk. In the distance, far ahead of us, a shadow appeared against the flaming sun. It was too far away to see clearly but my heart froze. I knew what it was. Already Caedmon's fate came for him.

From the corner of my eye, Caedmon looked as calm as ever. He walked in his usual straight-backed way, a result of his soldier training, I assumed. His fingers around mine were no tighter than they had been, although his palm now sweated just a little.

We walked for many minutes before they were close enough to make out. My father and my two brothers. They looked no older than when I had last seen them. Perhaps time had passed no faster here than in the fey world. Finally they were right in front of us. We stopped and now Caedmon's grip on my hand was a little tighter.

"Father," I said. "Piran. Wynne. Don't do this, please."

But their eyes were glazed and if they even saw me standing beside Caedmon, they didn't acknowledge me.

Caedmon turned to me. He raised our joined hands and kissed my fingers. His lips were warm against my skin. "Farewell, Grainne."

Then he pushed me so that I stumbled away and was not caught in the middle as they came for him.

GRAINNE

I sat in the ditch on the side of the road with Caedmon's head in my lap as the sun went down. His blood soaked into my skirt and the fabric stiffened as it dried. I stroked his hair and kissed his forehead and cried bitter tears.

As the sun sank behind distant hills, I dragged his body off the road. It was a difficult chore for he was much larger than I, and solid muscle, even after months of living with the fey, but I couldn't leave him where he had fallen.

I finally managed to haul him over to the grassy edge. I had no way of starting a fire for a pyre, nor any digging implements to bury him. I searched for rocks, thinking to build a cairn over his body, but in the dark I could find nothing but a handful of pebbles. I hated to leave him lying by the side of the road but there was nothing else I could do. So I kissed him one last time and walked away.

The moon was high in the sky, providing plentiful light as I walked. All around me was still and silent, the birds and dogs and cows all bedded down for the night. I prayed I travelled in the right direction, that this road would lead me back to Silver Downs, but I recognised nothing here, especially in the darkness. The air was warm but grew cool as the night wore on. Late summer, perhaps. Had Eithne and I been gone for as little as two seasons?

I encountered nobody during that long night of walking. I paused to rest only twice and then only briefly. It was as if I was the last person alive in the world. Perhaps I would walk through the quiet dark forever.

As the sun rose, I reached a crossroads and finally knew where I was. I took the road that would lead to Silver Downs. It was only a few hours walk from here. My stomach grumbled and my mouth was dry.

When I finally reached the edge of Silver Downs, the tears I had been restraining all night broke free and for some time all I could do was stand there and cry. At length I dried my tears and set off again.

The lodge loomed over me, large and imposing as I approached. My footsteps slowed. All night I had kept walking with this one aim, to reach Caedmon's family and tell them of his fate, tell them I had tried to save him but that it wasn't enough. But now that I was here, I was afraid.

I forced my feet to keep moving and finally I stood at the front door. I was gathering my courage and wondering whether I should knock, when the door opened. Diarmuid slunk out. He met my eyes with a startled gasp.

"You," I spat. I wanted to call him every vile name but none came to mind. I wanted to scratch his eyes and kick him and spit on him. But I just stood there and glared at him.

"Grainne," Diarmuid said. His face was pale and haunted. "You're back. Is Eithne with you?"

"Eithne is somewhere in the realm of the fey," I said. I could hear the bitterness in my tone but didn't care enough to restrain it. "And Caedmon is lying dead by the side of the road, although I doubt you were going to ask about him."

Diarmuid leaned heavily against the door and sucked in a breath. "I'm sorry. I'm so sorry. You have no idea-"

"I have no idea?" My voice was high and loud. "*You* are the one with no idea. I did everything I could to save him. I spent months as a slave. I escaped and was captured by another fey. He kept me as a prisoner, shut up with him in a hole in the ground. I finally escaped and found Caedmon.

I found him and I claimed him, even though they were so sure I couldn't. He knew he would be subject to your vile magic as soon as he left the fey realm but he did it anyway. And now he's dead and it's all your fault."

I was screaming by the time I finished. Diarmuid huddled against the door and said nothing. Agata had appeared behind him while I spoke. She covered her mouth with her hand and her eyes filled with tears. Then Fiachra was by my side. He wrapped his arm around me and suddenly there was no fight left in me. I sobbed as I let him lead me away.

He took me around the corner of the lodge where there was nobody other than a sheep which must have escaped its paddock. It nibbled at some long grass and considered me with serious eyes. It was some time before I could compose myself. Fiachra simply stood beside me and looked out over the fields.

"It's not fair," I said. "Caedmon should have been safe."

Fiachra said nothing.

"It should have been him. Diarmuid. I sent Caedmon away so he would be safe. The magic should have come for Diarmuid instead."

"Does the death of one brother ever compensate for the life of another?" Fiachra asked.

"But I loved him."

"You have suffered much for your love, and he knew the truth, in the end."

"What truth?"

"Of your love and of his own for you. It might not have been what he expected in handfasting but it found him anyway. He was at peace with himself when he died."

"He should have fought them. He could have killed them before they killed him."

"Would you have your husband kill your father and brothers, even to save himself?"

I couldn't reply.

"He did what he thought was right. We grieve him, yes, but we must also respect his decision."

I wiped the tears from my cheeks with my palms. "Has Eithne come home?"

If I hadn't been looking at Fiachra in that moment, I would have missed the brief flash of sorrow on his face. "No, Eithne yet has a long journey to travel."

"Is she safe?"

"As safe as she can be in that place and with one of them."

"Did she find Kalen again?"

He gave me a sad smile. "Aah, Grainne, there's much I can't say of Eithne's tale. She will tell us of it when she can."

EITHNE

*K*alen and I walked in silence. I tried to ignore his presence and instead concentrated on the pull of the portal. I didn't trust myself not to blurt out what I really felt if I spoke to him. The time of our final separation was close now and I was starting to doubt my decision.

To distract myself, I focused instead on the sorrow that welled within me when I thought of Grainne. Why had she left me here alone? And why had she concealed the true purpose of her journey from me? I had thought we were friends, sisters even, but now it seemed I never knew her at all.

Kalen cleared his throat as he stopped walking. "The portal is here. Another few steps and you will be back in your own world."

The woods around us looked no different. A mix of ash and oak and beech. Hawthorn and bramble bushes. Mushrooms grew in the shelter of a rock. Birds called and unseen creatures rustled through the leaf litter. The portal still tugged at something inside me but I could see no sign of it. No wonder Grainne and I never even knew when we passed through it.

I studied Kalen, with his ill-cut hair and his pale skin. The clothes that were too big, the high cheekbones, the dark lips. It had all been for him. Was he worth it? He waited silently while I thought. He had never been inclined to ask me to speak before I was ready.

What was it about him that drew me in? It was more than just mortal fascination with the fey with their long lives and indifferent hearts. We had a connection I had never experienced with any mortal. I could walk away now and leave him. I could do it; my heart was hard enough right now to let me leave.

But if we parted now, I would regret it until the end of my days although they would pass like the blink of an eye to Kalen. Hundreds of years would pass before he grew old. Would he still remember me? Or would there be many mortal women after me — too many to count? Eithne, he would say, which one was Eithne? Should I take one last chance before I walked away with a lifetime of regrets? I took a deep breath and spoke before I could change my mind again.

"Come with me," I said. "Back to my world."

Kalen tipped his head to the side, considering. "I would have to leave Sumerled. He wouldn't survive there. He knows nothing of mortal ways."

My breath caught. I couldn't show him how much this meant to me. Even if he came with me, it would probably only be for a while. Years, months, maybe only weeks. But I was too far gone. I would take whatever he offered, even if it wasn't enough.

"It would do him good to look after himself for a change. Father could find work for you at Silver Downs. And we'll find you somewhere to live. We have some tenants who might like to take in a boarder."

He studied me for a long moment. I couldn't tell what direction his thoughts went in but at length he nodded slowly. He stretched out his hand and I took it. His fingers were cool and steady. Before he could speak, a voice came from behind us.

"You owe me a promise, Eithne."

Sumerled waited there, as small and bedraggled as when I last saw him.

"What sort of promise?" Kalen's tone was suspicious and his fingers tightened around mine. "Eithne, what did you agree to?"

Sumerled danced a little jig. "She made me a promise. I can choose what I want and she has to give it before she leaves here."

"What exactly did you offer in exchange for this promise, Sumerled?"

"To take her to you."

"You should not have agreed to that."

"But she wanted to find you. I was helping her. You always say I should be more helpful."

"Not by extracting promises from mortals who don't understand what they are agreeing to."

"I knew exactly what I was agreeing to," I said somewhat indignantly, wrenching my hand from his grasp. "And it was my own choice to do so. Sumerled had something I wanted and I had something he wanted. He was the only one who offered us aid. What else could I do?"

"What else? You should never make a promise to the fey. No matter what the reason. The cost is always too high."

His words stung, although I tried to hide it. "But I never would have found you."

"I would have realised you were here, eventually. And I would have come for you."

"I couldn't wait any longer. I had to find you before Titania found us again. She would have made sure we didn't escape again."

Kalen shook his head and looked back at the boy. "Sumerled, what do you intend to request for your promise?"

Sumerled continued to dance, his feet stepping lightly in the leaf litter, and his face bore an enormous grin. "You, of course."

"What?" I asked. My heart thudded sharply against my rib cage.

"No, Sumerled, you can't," Kalen said.

"I can and I will. It's my promise," Sumerled said. He stuck out his lower lip and crossed his arms. "I can do whatever I want with my promise."

"You knew I only came here to find Kalen," I said. "It's not fair to take away the one thing I want from this realm."

"You didn't say the promise had to be fair," Sumerled countered. "I can ask for whatever I want."

"No," I said. "I refuse. I take it back. I won't give you a promise."

"You have to," he said. "Kalen, tell her she has to."

We both looked at Kalen. His face was filled with regret but also something that looked strangely like relief.

"I'm sorry, Eithne. If you made Sumerled a promise, it must be fulfilled. There is no other option."

"He can't force me to keep it."

"A promise is the ultimate commitment. Nothing is worth more. I won't help you break a promise."

My stomach sank and when I spoke my voice wobbled. "But that means it was all for nothing. All those months of slavery and being starved and living in a horrid, dark hole. I endured it only to find you."

"That's how promises work. They are dangerous things. You shouldn't have promised Sumerled anything."

"I was desperate. I had no other choice."

I might have thought he would argue with Sumerled, somehow fight to come with me, but Kalen merely released my hand and stepped back, towards the boy.

"Goodbye, Eithne."

"Kalen, don't do this."

He and Sumerled turned and started walking back into the woods. I tried to follow, but tangly weeds wrapped around my boots and rooted them to the ground. As long as I tried to follow Kalen, I was stuck fast.

"Kalen, please."

He and Sumerled melted away into the trees and were gone.

EITHNE

*W*ithin a couple of steps, I was suddenly standing at the edge of the woods on the far end of Silver Downs' lower pastures. Time enough had passed for the last of the snow to melt and the grass to grow tall.

It turned out I was no different to any other mortal woman who went chasing after some fey, only to find she had already been forgotten. I glanced back at the woods once, twice, hoping Kalen had changed his mind. That he might have been merely pretending to leave with Sumerled. But he didn't return.

The sun was warm on my shoulders as I made my way across the fields. I felt strong, eager to be home at last. I would not look back again. The chapter of my life that contained Kalen was over. Yet I couldn't help but steal a glance over my shoulder from time to time, pretending I was checking whether a bee had landed on my shoulder or some such other nonsense.

I had walked for only a few minutes before I noticed I was limping. It had been so long since my twisted foot had bothered me that I barely remembered what it felt like. Already the familiar shortness of breath and light-headedness crept over me.

I pushed on, striding only slightly slower through the thick grass.

The months I had spent as a slave had taught me that what I used to think were my limits were a construct of my own imagination. But soon the ground began tilting from side to side and I sank down into the grass to rest. It seemed my limits were not artificial constructs after all, at least not in the mortal world.

The grass where I rested was verdant and stood almost to my knees. This would make fine grazing ground. We rarely grazed the livestock down here in the lower fields, only in the upper pastures where the soil had better drainage and more sun. But it seemed these fields were much improved. I had better remember to tell Father or Eremon.

I set off again, more slowly this time. Everything looked bigger, wilder, more colourful than I remembered. The sky was bluer, the sun brighter, the grass an emerald shade.

I walked and rested, walked and rested. The sun was starting its journey down toward the horizon before I reached the stand of beech trees where Kalen and I had secretly met so many months ago. I paused to rest on my rock. It was more weathered than I remembered, and blackened with mould, but it still held the sun's warmth, just as it always had. The beeches were taller and their branches spread further than I remembered. I didn't dare wonder just how many months had passed. I would find out soon enough.

I slid off the rock and started the last part of my journey home. The lodge was only just out of sight. I would see it as soon as I crested the small rise in front of me. Some of my brothers might even still be out working in the fields. The rise was only gentle but my fatigued legs resisted even so small a hill. My calf ached from the effort of walking with my deformed foot. I trudged on and at last I came to the top. I could hardly believe what I saw.

The house was still recognisable but only barely. The bones of what I once knew were there but one wing was entirely gone, replaced with another of different materials and a different structure. The barn which Father had always kept watertight and snug so that the animals would be warm on winter nights was gone. A new, larger barn stood some distance away. New fencing ringed a paddock, new vegetable gardens. Day's eye bushes were planted in front of the house, a new path laid. It was wrong, all wrong. Men worked in the fields and even a couple of women, but nobody I knew by silhouette, at least not from this distance. Nobody who was recognisable as Papa or Eremon or Marrec or Conn.

I ran the last of the way home with my heart pounding and my breath catching in my lungs. How long had I been gone?

"Papa," I shouted, although I knew I was too far away for him to hear me if he wasn't out in the fields. "Papa, where are you?"

The workers turned to stare at me. They weren't close enough to see clearly but I was sure none were my brothers.

"Papa," I called again.

The front door opened and an old man hobbled out. His back was stooped and his slender shoulders hunched. He walked slowly, leaning heavily on a cane. He had the look of our family about him but I could not place his face. He peered at me carefully then took a few steps closer.

"Eithne?" he asked, and his voice was full of wonder. "Is it really you?"

"Where is my father?" I asked. I tried to swallow my fear.

"Eithne." Tears began to trace their way down his wrinkled cheeks. "Eithne, it's me. Diarmuid. Your brother."

I opened my mouth to call him a liar but the words died on my lips as I looked harder. Traces of the Diarmuid I once knew were still there, in the slant of his forehead and the colour of his eyes. His hair was mostly grey now and his face bore wrinkles that were testament to the passing of years.

"Diarmuid?"

"It's been sixty years, Eithne," he said and his voice wobbled. "Everyone else is gone. It's just me left, and Fiachra, although he doesn't come here often."

"I don't understand." My legs shook and for a moment I thought I might faint.

Diarmuid called into the house, "Boy, bring a chair. Quickly now."

A boy of about ten summers ran out with a wooden chair that looked almost as heavy as he. He placed it beside me and bowed with a small flourish then skipped away.

"One of Eremon's great-grandsons," Diarmuid said. "He keeps me company. He has aspirations of being a bard and he thinks I might teach him something if he stays long enough."

"Do you still tell tales?" It wasn't what I wanted to ask but there were so many questions, I didn't know where to start. How could I ever ask them all?

"Not anymore. I did, for a while. Enough to learn how the magic worked but then never again. I have regretted that last tale you heard for sixty years. I killed Caedmon with it. Better that you know. We buried him near the house he had built for himself and Grainne."

"I've only been gone a few months," I said.

"And you look little older than the last time I saw you. They always hoped you might return home some day."

"Papa?"

"He died about thirty years ago and Mother followed him only a year or two later. Our brothers died one by one over the last few years. Eremon was the last, just a few months ago. He wanted to be here when you came home. Papa made him promise he would be."

"Who runs the estate now?"

"His eldest son. The younger is a druid."

An elderly woman appeared in the doorway behind Diarmuid. Time had been kinder to her than to him although the wisps of hair that escaped her bun were solid grey. She stared at me keenly with eyes that were still as sharp as a hawk's.

"Diarmuid?" she said. "Why don't you bring your visitor inside."

"My wife," he said, tipping his head towards her. "Brigit, although I call her Bramble. Dear, it's Eithne."

"Your sister?" She covered the ground between us swiftly to hug me with the strength of a much younger woman. "Welcome, my dear. One of the boys sleeps in the bedchamber that used to be yours but I'll have it cleaned out and ready for you by night."

If she thought anything strange in my appearance, she gave no indication of it.

"That's very kind of you," I said, suddenly feeling like a stranger.

"You must have a curious tale to tell," Brigit said, her steady gaze giving nothing away.

Tears sprang to my eyes and I brushed them away. I nodded, not trusting my voice.

"There will be time enough to tell it. Come inside. You look like you need some rest, and some good food. Annick, Eremon's youngest daughter, does most of the cooking these days. She'll fatten you up in no time." Brigit leaned closer and rested a hand against my cheek. "The fevers, they still come?"

"They haven't, for a while. But maybe now..."

She nodded. "I'll make up a potion for you. I can help keep the illness at bay."

We went into the house, Diarmuid hobbling ahead of us, calling directions to boys who seemed to spring out of nowhere. The children scattered, each sent off on his own task.

Brigit led me into the family room and pulled a chair close to the fireplace. The furniture in this room was all different. One or two chairs I thought I recognised, although they had been restored and maybe they were different chairs entirely.

"This is where you used to sit, is it not?" she asked.

"How do you know?"

She smiled at me and there was both wisdom and acceptance in her smile. "I see things that others don't. I too once travelled a long way in search of something I thought I wanted, only to discover that what I wanted most in the world was already right in front of me."

I sank down into the chair. A boy already crouched in front of the fireplace and soon a small fire blazed merrily. Its warmth bathed my skin and I sighed with relief, closing my eyes as I leaned back. Home.

"You can come in now," Brigit said, and something in her voice made me open my eyes.

There in the doorway stood Kalen.

I tried to say something but my mouth wouldn't work. I didn't know whether to fling myself at him or to pretend I didn't care why he was here. I supposed it didn't matter though as I didn't have the strength to rise.

"Kalen," I said and although I tried to sound disinterested, my voice broke. "Aren't you breaking my promise?"

"You're the only one who can break your promise."

I was tired and feeling all too easily confused. "Why are you here?"

"Because I don't want to be there without you."

"Where's Sumerled?"

"Safe."

"I don't understand."

"You made a promise. You had to keep it. The only way you could was if you left with no intention of coming back again. You had to leave me there."

"So you intended to follow me all along?"

"Of course I did. Did you really think I would let you walk away, after everything you went through to find me?"

"Why didn't you tell me? I thought you didn't care."

He came closer and crouched down in front of my chair so that we were at eye level. "Eithne, of course I care. But if you didn't truly believe you were leaving me behind, you would be breaking your promise."

"People break promises all the time."

"The fey don't. A broken promise is a very serious thing. There are consequences."

"What sort of consequences?"

"It doesn't matter now. You kept your promise."

"Does Sumerled know you are here?"

"He knows. He's not happy about it. He was only trying to protect me."

"Will he come after you?"

"He promised he wouldn't."

"I'm not the same here as I am there. It won't be long before the fevers return."

"I know all about your illness. Remember?"

I suddenly felt terribly tired. "Would you ask Brigit whether my bedchamber is ready?"

"Go ahead, Eithne," came Brigit's voice from the doorway. "The boy has moved his things and the bed has been made up fresh for you."

"Thank you." My voice was much weaker than I wanted it to be. I tried to stand but my legs wobbled violently and my vision dimmed. I sat back down abruptly. Kalen scooped me up in his arms.

"Tell me which way to go," he said. "You're too exhausted to walk."

I directed him through the house in which I had grown up, a house that seemed at once familiar and strange. The door was open when we reached my bedchamber. Kalen set me down just outside the doorway and waited in the hallway. I entered my old bedchamber alone on unsteady legs, both hands grasping the doorframe for support.

The slope of the ceiling was the same, and the knots in the walls. But everything else was changed. Gone were the thick, dark green drapes that had kept the winter chill out. In their place hung lightweight yellow curtains. My bed had been replaced with a newer, larger frame with intricately carved knobs. The dresser too was new, and the cupboard. The ewer and basin on the dresser were made of delicate white pottery and were much finer than my own. It might be my old room but the spirit was new.

"Everything is different," I said. "It's all... wrong."

"This has been someone else's bedchamber for a long time." Kalen closed the door, then came to place his hands at my waist, supporting me as my legs trembled. "Probably several someone elses."

"I didn't know so much time had passed. I knew things might be different but I thought perhaps a year for every month I stayed, at most. Or perhaps no time at all and I would come back to the same day I left. I never expected to find almost everyone I ever knew is dead." My voice broke and tears welled in my eyes.

"You never quite know how much time will pass, and it isn't always the same. If you went back to the fey realm now and returned in six months, you might find only six days had passed."

"My mother died without ever knowing what happened to me. She must have thought... I don't know what she thought."

"Ssh." Kalen turned me around to face him. "Nothing about the realm of the fey is fair or right. It just is what it is. The time has passed. There's nothing you can do about that now, only live for each new day. And I'll be here with you, if you'll have me."

"You'll age here. You'll get old, like Diarmuid. You'll die if you stay here."

"So will you. But you can't return to the fey realm, so I must stay here with you. We will grow old together."

"I just wish I had told Mother where I was going. She would have understood. She would have known I had no other choice."

A tear spilled down my cheek and Kalen wiped it away with his thumb.

"My kind aren't very good at loving, Eithne. You will have to teach me. And you will have to be patient when I don't understand or I get it wrong. All I know about love I have learned from you. And I know there is more to learn, if you will have me."

He kissed me then, gently and carefully, as if he had never before kissed a woman. He lifted me onto the big bed that wasn't mine. His hands were soft and gentle as he showed me things I had never expected to experience for myself. For who would want one such as me, damaged, ill, likely unable to bear children? But Kalen wanted me. It wouldn't last, but I would take whatever he offered.

EITHNE

*W*e were woken by a gentle tapping on the door.

"Aunt Eithne, Uncle Diarmuid says you should come downstairs," someone said. The voice was young and male, presumably one of Eremon's many descendants. "He says there is someone you will want to see."

I opened my eyes to sunlight streaming through the summery curtains. My old, thick curtains had shielded me from both light and cold, a useful thing when one is often in bed in the middle of the day.

"Who?" I asked.

"I'm not supposed to tell you."

"I'll be down there shortly."

The boy scampered away down the hallway. Kalen already stood and was pulling on his clothes. I paused to admire his lanky form which I suddenly knew more intimately than I had ever expected.

"I will need some more clothes," he said. "Two or three sets will suffice."

"I'm sure Diarmuid will sort it out. Or Ronan, for he is the master of Silver Downs now." It pained me to think of the estate in the hands of someone other than Papa or Eremon.

I pulled on the dress Sumerled had provided and tried to ignore the small twinge of guilt that he was now without Kalen's protection. I looked around the bedchamber of a stranger. What had happened to my old clothes and the small things I had possessed? My hairbrush, my hand mirror. My wash basin. My favourite plate and mug. Had they been broken in the intervening years? Or were they discarded, unwanted, the remnants of a forgotten inhabitant? I might never know, for Diarmuid would likely not remember such detail and Eremon's descendants wouldn't know. They would care little for the personal items of some long-lost ancestor.

As I was leaving the room, I noticed a wooden box by the door. It was knee-high to me and bore no decoration or label. I must have walked straight past it last night. I knelt beside it and lifted the lid.

Inside were my most treasured possessions. The hairbrush and mirror I had been so fond of. My favourite mug. My two good dresses. A pair of shoes. A wooden ring carved by one of my brothers and accidentally left behind the day I departed, for I had always worn it until then.

Tears dripped from my cheeks as I unpacked memory after memory. I hadn't been discarded after all. Someone had put away my favourite things, perhaps against my possible return, perhaps just wanting to keep something I had loved. Mother probably, for I couldn't imagine any of my brothers doing such a thing.

I swiftly removed my gown and pulled on my old favourite grey dress. It smelled a little musty, and the fabric felt more fragile than I remembered. I slid my feet into my old shoes. They were tighter than they used to be. Perhaps my feet were swollen after my journey.

"Ready?" Kalen asked, wrapping his arms around me from behind.

I leaned back into his embrace. "I'm ready."

We went downstairs hand in hand. My deformed foot was uncomfortable to walk on and my thigh muscles were already tired by the time we reached the bottom level. I had no idea who might be here that Diarmuid thought I would want to see. There was nobody left who I cared about except... I ran the last few steps as I realised who was waiting.

But instead of Grainne, an old woman stood at the fireplace with her back to me. Her shoulders were hunched and she shivered, her arms wrapped around herself despite the summer morning. Her grey hair lay loose against her shoulders.

"Hello?" I said.

She turned to me and my heart dropped. It was Grainne after all, but not the Grainne I remembered. Her face was lined with deep wrinkles and her frame had the thinness of an old woman. When she stretched out her arms to me, her hands shook.

"Eithne," she said. "Oh, Eithne, I am so happy you have finally returned."

"Grainne? What happened to you?"

"I got old, Eithne. Only a few months had passed when I returned. I've lived all the years since then wondering whether you were safe. Fiachra said you were, but you never know with a druid."

"I was safe," I said. "For me, it's only been a day or two since we were separated."

She stared at me for a long moment. Her eyes were rheumy and the skin under her chin sagged. I saw only shadows of the Grainne I knew in her but the warmth with which she looked at me was the same.

"I've always regretted that I left you behind," she said. "Fiachra said your journey wasn't finished but I knew I still shouldn't have done it. I was only there to find Caedmon. I lied to you about why I went."

I had believed he was dead before we even left home. It hurt a little to know that she had kept such a secret, after all those long, dark months together, but I pushed the pain aside. It didn't matter anymore.

She embraced me and her body was far too delicate in my arms. When we pulled apart, she looked at Kalen for a long moment. "So, you brought him with you."

"Not exactly. He followed me."

"I am glad it was not for naught."

Kalen dragged a chair up behind me and gently pushed me down into it. It was only then I noticed how my legs trembled, although whether it was fatigue or merely the shock of seeing Grainne so aged, I didn't know. A boy bustled in with a tray bearing delicate cups filled with steaming liquid. I accepted one and found it contained a sweet tea. I felt much restored after a few sips.

Kalen had disappeared to the back of the room, leaving Grainne and me with a measure of privacy. I sipped my tea and listened to her tale.

I cried as she told me how bravely Caedmon had died and of her long, lonely journey back to Silver Downs. My brothers had retrieved Caedmon's body and buried him near the house he had been building for Grainne. She still lived there with one of Eremon's granddaughters.

When Grainne finished her tale, I told her what she didn't know of mine.

"I am glad you found him," Grainne said. "Truly."

It was only then I noticed Diarmuid standing in the doorway. His shoulders were hunched, his posture defeated. I didn't know what to say to him. I didn't even want to look at him.

"I know you must hate me," he said, his voice slow with age and choked with tears. "Both of you. And you are right to. But when I told that tale, I didn't believe it would come true. Caedmon was always my favourite brother. I never meant to kill him."

"He was everyone's favourite," I said, perhaps cruelly. "And he is dead because you were young and foolish."

"I won't be here much longer," he said, abruptly. "My time is close to its end and something eats at my insides. You will only have to share this house with me for a while."

Brigit bustled into the room. "I think that's enough for now," she said. "Diarmuid has already talked longer than he should have. He needs to rest."

"I'm glad you have someone who cares for you, Diarmuid," Grainne said, her voice bitter. "Would that I had the same."

She left then. I started to follow her but Brigit stopped me, her wrinkled hand gentle on my arm. "Let her be, child. She knows you are here for her and she will come to you when she is ready."

"Has she never forgiven him?"

"She has, I think, but your return has stirred up old feelings."

I looked into her eyes which were sympathetic and still clear, despite her age. "How can you stand to be with him, knowing what he has done?"

"We've been together for a long time. I knew what he was when I fell in love with him. He has been a better man than he would have if not for this. You don't know him, child. He is not the man he was when you left. He has atoned for what he did, in ways you couldn't even begin to imagine. So let him be. Let him die in peace. He has been holding on, hoping you might return one day, but now he can let go."

Her eyes were dry but her voice was filled with anguish.

"I'm glad he found you," I said.

She smiled. "Me too, Eithne. Me too."

EITHNE

$\mathcal{M}$onths passed, and then a year. Brigit's potions helped hold the fevers at bay. There were still days where I didn't have enough strength to get out of bed, but they were few and not as harsh as they once were.

With time, my body began to change. My belly became swollen with Kalen's child, and my breasts, which had never been much larger than hazelnuts, became plump and round. I feared the babe's birth but Brigit promised to aid me through it. She became something like a mix of grandmother and sister to me.

Diarmuid didn't live to see my child's birth. We buried him under the great oak where so many of our family had handfasted. My parents were buried there too, and my brothers, except for Caedmon.

Brigit mourned Diarmuid's loss and buried herself in her work. She was well respected as a wise woman, apparently, and folk travelled a good distance to consult her. One of Sitric's granddaughters was apprenticed to her and a long line of our women had already been trained by Brigit, starting with a daughter each of Eremon and Marrec, and Conn's twin girls.

I found it hard to comprehend that my brothers had left so many descendants, some of whom had died before I came home. Silver Downs was filled with the shouts and laughter of children and the thundering of feet. Most lived nearby but Eremon's granddaughter Annick, who had never married, and his grandson Rogan lived in the main lodge, along with Rogan's wife and his seven sons.

Nobody complained about me claiming my old bedchamber and several days after I arrived home, I discovered a new bed had been moved in there, large enough for two. Kalen and I never formally hand-fasted. After all I had been through to find him, it didn't seem necessary, and indeed without my parents there to witness it, I couldn't bear the thought.

One day, just a few weeks before the babe's birth, we went to the beech trees where we used to meet. It was a long, slow walk, for the child sat low in my belly and carrying her was exhausting. I was puffing long before we reached my rock and I sank down onto it gratefully.

The air was warm today and heavy with the scent of honeysuckle. It pleased me that our babe would be born during the summer months. Kalen and I sat together on the rock and talked quietly. We had already agreed the babe's name would be Agata, for my mother. He wanted to choose a boy's name also but I was adamant the child would be a girl.

Absorbed in our conversation, it was some time before I noticed Titania. She stood beside a grey-trunked beech, her lips lifted into a sneer. Kalen's words died as he saw her.

"What a lovely setting," Titania said. "Look at the two of you, laughing and carefree."

"Why wouldn't we be?" I asked. I wished I could get to my feet but my legs still trembled from the walk.

"You choose this?" Titania directed her words at Kalen. "You choose this frail mortal and this world over your own?"

"It was never my world," he said. "You made that perfectly clear. With everything you did and everything you said, you reminded me that I lived there only at your indulgence."

"Do you not wonder about the boy? Who protects him without you there to do it?"

"It was time for him to learn to look after himself," Kalen said. "He is no longer my responsibility."

"What do you want, Titania?" I asked, suddenly feeling impatient. "You've already taken almost everything I ever loved. What is left for you to take?"

Her gaze went straight to my belly. I immediately clasped my hands over it.

"No," I said. "You will not take my child."

"She's bred of a fey. She's mine to claim if I will."

"No, she's bred of two mortals. You never recognised Kalen as fey before and you can't now."

"The child is an abomination. Half mortal, half fey. It should not be allowed to live."

Now I did climb to my feet, slowly and shakily. My voice was low and calm.

"If you harm her, if you touch one hair of her head, I will find you. I will make you pay for it, you and all the rest of your kind. Now go away. Leave the children of Silver Downs in peace. We don't intend you any harm unless you harm us first."

"I could rip the child from your belly as you stand there," Titania said, looking me up and down with the same scornful expression she had used the very first time we met. "Who do you think you are to threaten me?"

I lifted my head and held myself proudly. "I am a daughter of Silver Downs. You know there's magic in our blood. We could be dangerous to the fey, if we chose."

Titania spluttered and a faint blush tinged her cheeks. "You impudent wretch."

My legs trembled more violently now, but then Kalen was beside me with an arm around my waist. I leaned against him thankfully.

"The children of Silver Downs are strong, Titania," I said. "We're only just discovering how strong we are. You don't want to cross us again."

Titania glared at me for a few moments longer and then suddenly she was gone. I sank back down onto the rock. My legs trembled even after I sat.

"I think you scared her," Kalen said with something like a laugh.

"Somebody told me once that I have my own power. I think it's time I figured out what it is."

"Brigit can probably help you with that."

"I'm sure she can," I said. "I will speak to her as soon as we get home. My child will not live in fear of Titania. I'll find a way to protect her, and a way for her to protect herself. We must sit here a little longer though. I don't think I can manage the walk home just yet."

Kalen sat back beside me on the rock. He draped an arm around my shoulder. "Take as long you need, my love," he said. "We have all the time in the world."

The story continues in
Book 3: *Druid*

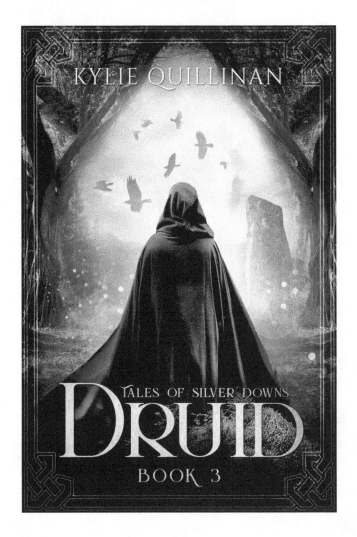

ACKNOWLEDGEMENTS

Thank you to my beta readers, Megan and Hannah.

Thank you to Deranged Doctor Design for once again producing a beautiful cover. I love this one even more than the last.

Thank you to Meghan for assisting with editing.

Thank you to those who read *Muse* and, even more, to those who enjoyed it. *Muse* was a story about a boy who didn't want to be a hero. *Fey* is about strong women who readily step up to be heroes. It was also an attempt to keep Caedmon alive. I spent the entire story trying to find a way around the magic of Diarmuid's tale but regrettably it just wasn't possible. Caedmon accepted his fate with more grace than I did. The story in *Druid* takes place a little later than *Muse* and *Fey* and continues the theme of heroes.

And, finally, thank you to my family for tolerating my continued absence while I write.

ALSO BY KYLIE QUILLINAN

The Amarna Age Series

Book One: *Queen of Egypt*

Book Two: *Son of the Hittites*

Book Three: *Eye of Horus*

Book Four: *Gates of Anubis*

Book Five: *Lady of the Two Lands*

Book Six: *Guardian of the Underworld*

Tales of Silver Downs series

Prequel: *Bard*

Book One: *Muse*

Book Two: *Fey*

Book Three: *Druid*

Epilogue: *Swan* (A mailing list exclusive)

See kyliequillinan.com for more details

or to subscribe to my mailing list.

ABOUT THE AUTHOR

Kylie writes about women who defy society's expectations. Her novels are for readers who like fantasy with a basis in history or mythology. Her interests include Dr Who, jellyfish and cocktails. She needs to get fit before the zombies come.

Her other interests include canine nutrition, jellyfish and zombies. She blames the disheveled state of her house on her dogs, but she really just hates to clean.

Swan – the epilogue to the Tales of Silver Downs series – is available exclusively to her mailing list subscribers. Sign up at kyliequillinan.com.